Pierre de Nolhac

Marie Antoinette

the queen

Pierre de Nolhac

Marie Antoinette
the queen

ISBN/EAN: 9783337322212

Printed in Europe, USA, Canada, Australia, Japan

Cover: Foto ©Andreas Hilbeck / pixelio.de

More available books at **www.hansebooks.com**

MARIE ANTOINETTE

THE QUEEN.

FROM THE FRENCH OF

PIERRE DE NOLHAC.

PARIS:
GOUPIL & CO.,
JEAN BOUSSOD, MANZI, JOYANT & CO., SUCCESSORS.
LONDON:
SIMPKIN, MARSHALL, HAMILTON, KENT & CO., LTD

DEDICATION.

The Translator is permitted by M. de Nolhac to dedicate the English version of **LA REINE MARIE ANTOINETTE** to the memory of

EDMUND BURKE,

and also to quote, as fore-word, that immortal passage from the illustrious statesman's "Reflections on the Revolution in France," which renders to the unfortunate Queen a tribute unrivalled for eloquence, beauty, and passionate earnestness.

"It is now sixteen or seventeen years," writes Mr. Burke, "since I saw the Queen of France, then the Dauphiness, at Versailles; and surely never lighted on this orb, which she hardly seemed to touch, a more delightful vision. I saw her just above the horizon, decorating and cheering the elevated sphere she just began to move in—glittering like the morning-star, full of life and splendour, and joy. Oh! what a revolution! and what a heart must I have to contemplate without emotion that elevation and that fall! Little did I dream when she added titles of veneration to those of enthusiastic, distant, respectful love, that she should ever be obliged to carry the sharp antidote against disgrace concealed in that bosom; little did I dream that I should have lived to see such disasters fallen upon her in a nation of gallant men, in a nation of men of honour, and of cavaliers. I thought ten thousand swords must have leaped from their scabbards to avenge even a look that threatened her with insult. But the age of chivalry is gone. That of sophisters, economists and calculators, has succeeded; and the glory of Europe is extinguished for ever. Never, never more shall we behold that generous loyalty to rank and sex, that proud submission, that dignified obedience, that subordination of the heart, which kept alive, even in servitude itself, the spirit of an exalted freedom. The unbought grace of light, the cheap defence of nations, the nurse of manly sentiment and heroic enterprise is gone! It is gone! that sensibility of principle, that chastity of honour, which felt a stain like a wound, which inspired courage whilst it mitigated ferocity, which ennobled whatever it touched, and under which vice itself lost half its evil, by losing all its grossness."

[illegible] CHAPTER.

[illegible] [illegible]IGN.

On the tenth [illegible] people. [illegible] first time in [illegible] heart. [illegible] the reign of [illegible] [illegible] Saint- [illegible] was uninteresting in appearance; [illegible] well- [illegible] trifling in com[illegible] reign was over. And [illegible] seemed born to [illegible] lively, witty, fond of [illegible] and a special [illegible] indeed, but [illegible]

THE FIRST CHAPTER.

THE REIGN.

On the tenth day of May, 1774, the French were a happy people. For the first time in many years the nation had a king and a queen after that nation's own heart. Louis XVI., although he had played but an insignificant part in the reign of his grandfather, had already displayed valuable and truly royal qualities. He was well known to be absolutely upright, to be profoundly imbued with a sense of the onerous obligations attached to the crown he wore, with the love of justice, and a dread of favourites; to be in short the exact opposite of that contemptible king who had been borne to Saint-Denis amid the hisses of the people. He was uninteresting in appearance; his manners were awkward; his blood was sluggish; his just and well-balanced mind was slow. But even such defects as these were trifling in comparison with those of the too attractive prince whose reign was over. And then, the Queen had all that the King lacked; she seemed born to please the national taste. Marie Antoinette, brilliant, lively, witty, fond of pleasure and festivity, with all her husband's goodness and a special grace of her own, less on her guard against favourites indeed, but having made no ill choice as yet, won all hearts even as she charmed every eye. Four years of Versailles had transformed the little German princess who was received at Strasburg in 1770, into a finished French woman.

To those who studied the political aspect of the accession of the young sovereigns,* the name of the fair Queen signified peace and prosperity. The marriage of the Dauphin, one of the great achievements of the Choiseul ministry, had put an end to the rivalry between the Houses of France and Austria—in appearance at least—and secured the country against the recurrence of lamentable warfare. The "French Party" in the Court, holding by former traditions, found it hard to tolerate the presence of "this Austrian Archduchess;" but public opinion, which was already controlling affairs, although indirectly, was much less accessible to prejudice, and suspended its judgment until certain results of the new system should be before it. It was so great a relief that an end to the reign of scandal and "mistresses" had really come; that decent people might now hail a truly good and amiable woman as Queen of France, the consort-occupant of that throne of the Bourbons where there had been so little room for lawful wives for so long a period. Was not this throne all the more brilliant and all the more secure because she shared it? The young King and the young Queen were greeted with a spontaneous and unanimous cry of admiration and affection, so many and so fond were the hopes that were founded on them, and so bright was the aureole that shone around those youthful heads.

How was it that so fair a dream vanished, how was it that the welcome of the accession changed into mutterings of disapproval, and then into the clamour of hatred; how was it that a queen, whom a whole people had adored, became to them a monstrous portent first, and later on their victim; how was it that the woman who possessed qualities which ought to have restored the prestige of the monarchy helped to hasten its fall? Ah! here we have one of the saddest problems of history, but one which it only requires impartiality and veracity to solve.

* See Appendix, Note 1.

We are separated by the lapse of a century from that frightful crash, that lurid epoch of history which attracts us strongly at each stage of its evolution, and holds us appalled at its awful close: it is no longer impossible to speak dispassionately of the years that preceded the French Revolution without being subjected to the influence of either enthusiasm or anger. We may relate the story of the far-off past with the respect absolutely due to the remembrance of a great soul and a prolonged martyrdom, and yet bring to our solemn task that serenity of mind which is essential to a clear and impartial comprehension of events. Every troubled epoch in the history of peoples and rulers admits of the abridgment of its history without detriment to its purport, if the narrator desires it; we find no exception in this instance. Here we have the reign of a woman: it began with acclamation, it ended in malediction: it has all the simplicity of an antique drama. Like the Greek poet of old, the narrator has to deal only with details which plainly demonstrate the blindness of the mortals who hold the stage and their unconscious fatalistic march towards ruin, and, amid the infinite complication of human facts, to make manifest the silent rôle of the chief actor, whom the ancients in affright call Destiny, and we know as Providence.

The reign of Marie Antoinette opens with festivity and the union of hearts. The Queen and the Nation have come together and each is charmed with the other. Louis XVI., being at La Muette, has caused the Bois de Boulogne to be opened to the public, who were always excluded from it whenever Louis XV. was in residence, and Marie Antoinette may be seen there, not attended by any guard, roaming in the side avenues on foot or on horseback, talking to everybody, taking the papers containing their requests from the hands of her petitioners herself. A procession of carriages fills the broad avenues; the Parisians have come to salute their young sovereign and to learn to love her. When the royal family drive along the boulevards in Paris the warmest greeting is given to the Queen. They are pleased with her for having renounced the *droit de ceinture* * levied for queens on

* See Appendix, Note 2.

each accession, and for having declared herself against the renewal of the monopoly of grain, which was so cruel to the poor, and had just been abolished. They thank her for having caused the Du Barry and all who bear that detested name to be banished from her Court. They attribute to the Queen a share in the dismissal of Chancellor Maupeou, rightly interpreting that dismissal and the fall of the Comptroller-General of Finance, the unpopular Abbé Terray, as a promise of the recall of the Parliaments. When Paris burns the effigies of the two ministers (in straw), it is done with shouts of *Vive la Reine!* The opening of a series of performances at the Opera is at hand, and there the public will rapturously greet the Queen who shares their pleasures. When the *Iphigénie en Aulide* of Gluck is performed, the whole "house" will rise to repeat the chorus of the second act : *Chantons, célébrons notre Reine,* and the frantic cheers of the wildly-excited crowd, not to be silenced for fully ten minutes, will draw tears of emotion from the eyes of Marie Antoinette.

During the ceremonial days of the "Sacre"—consecration and crowning included in the word—when Marie Antoinette will be regarded as the symbol of royalty grown young again, the enthusiasm of those first days will be redoubled. The provinces, like Paris, will resound with the echo of the fêtes at Reims; rejoicings in honour of Louis XVI. and his consort will be universal in their realm, and the inscription which the Basque people put on the façade of the Hôtel de Ville at Pau, in the picturesque language of Henri IV. will be imitated everywhere. "Our Henry has come back, this time better married : Long live the King! Long live the Queen!"

The Court seems no less pleased. During their first summer, the sovereigns visit all their residences, Marly, Compiègne, Choisy, Fontainebleau. At Choisy, ladies from Paris are invited every day, and Marie Antoinette receives in charming fashion; the King, who takes pains to please, talks freely, and is not too "shy." The Queen gets the credit of this desirable alteration in her husband's habits. At Fontainebleau the Court is more splendidly lodged, and the apartments are thronged. For many years no Court so numerous, well selected, and assiduous has been seen. The Queen's reception of all who visit her there makes them wish to return, and Marie Antoinette decides that she will visit the palace of the Valois, which is to be vastly improved and beautified, each recurrent autumn. And she will indeed come back to Fontainebleau, to find external things the same; the courtiers, the hunting parties, the forest fêtes; but she will not return in the same mood or with similar hopes.

There was one flaw in the splendid and touching situation of the royal couple whose virtues the gazettes lauded lavishly: the King was twenty years old, the Queen was eighteen. Neither one nor the other understood the peril of succession to Louis XV., or realised what a responsibility the century then nearing its close had laid upon their innocent heads. Marie Antoinette became Queen of France without misgiving or presentiment. She had been brought up for a throne, she knew or believed she knew its duties, and her impatient youth gave her a foretaste of its delights. Four days after her accession she sent her impressions of royalty to Maria Theresa. Here they are: "Although God caused me to be born in the rank which I occupy to-day, I cannot refrain from wondering at the arrangement of Providence which has chosen me, the last of your children, for the fairest kingdom in Europe. I feel more than ever what I owe to the tenderness of my august mother who has procured this great position for me with so much pains and exertion. Never have I so longed to be able to place myself at her feet, to embrace her, to show her my whole soul and make her see how full it is of affection and gratitude." * To this outpouring of ingenuous joy, the Empress, who knew life, responded in a sentence: "You are both very young, my dear children; the burthen is great; I am anxious and very anxious."

Marie Antoinette had her first difficulties to encounter in the royal family itself. We now know every detail of those difficulties from the private correspondence of the Comte de Mercy-Argenteau with Maria Theresa. The Ambassador of the Empire, who was at the same time the Mentor of the young Queen, notes everything from day to day that can enlighten the

* See Appendix, Note 3.

mother respecting the conduct of the daughter and the dangers that surround her. His reports form the most accurate and curious picture in existence of that Court of France, where every word hid a betrayal, and every smile was a snare.

It is quite true that one day, the King, coming in from a walk, found the Queen and the princesses, like a group by Greuze, seated on a garden-bench and eating strawberries and cream, and that, to use a phrase of the period, "his sensibility" was aroused by the spectacle. But all this familiarity failed to put sympathy into the hearts of the women. The Comte and Comtesse de Provence and the Comte and Comtesse d'Artois had already refused to go in the morning, to "make their Court" to the King and to the Queen as they had done in the late King's time "at the hours of representation." The new sovereign, irritated by this, marked her rank in public by the haughty carriage of her head and her attitudes. Her two sisters-in-law, who had narrow minds and jealous tempers, repaid her slights in kind. The Comte d'Artois ostentatiously treated his elder brother as formerly, passing in front of him twenty times at an evening reception, pushing him, almost treading on his feet, and interrupting him when he spoke by contradicting what he said. The methods of the Comte de Provence were less "bad form," but they were also less frank. Louis XVI. found certain letters among his grandfather's papers which clearly proved the double-dealing of Monsieur, and the Queen mistrusted the man whom she knew to be "of a very weak character, addicted to underhand and sometimes very base ways."

The King's brothers had no influence with him sufficient to counterbalance that of a young and charming wife. Mesdames, on the contrary, had the claim of an affection dating from his infancy upon the heart of Louis XVI., and over his mind they exerted the prestige of age and experience. The four daughters of Louis XV. were ill-disposed towards Marie Antoinette, from Madame Adélaïde, tenacious, and proud of her long spell of authority in her father's time, to Madame Louise, the Carmelite nun, who still kept a look-out on Versailles from her cell at Saint-Denis. Mesdames, then, associated themselves, more or less openly, with the claims of their younger nephews. Madame Adélaïde made it plain from the beginning that she intended to "direct" the King and to designate his counsellors.

Marie Antoinette had similar intentions. She had a minister to propose to whom she was bound by ties of gratitude and friendship. Unfortunately, M. de Choiseul was the one man whom Louis XVI. would not have at any price. Maria Theresa too, lacked confidence in the character of the brilliant minister, and was not desirous of his reinstatement at the head of affairs. Austria no longer had anything to gain from Choiseul. But the Queen would listen to nothing except the prompting of her own heart and her simple woman-like motives. She tried at first to effect a reconciliation between her husband and the diplomatist who had "made" their marriage. The King, she said prettily, "could not give her a more agreeable proof that he was glad he had married her." But she only succeeded in inducing Louis XVI. to receive Choiseul at Versailles, thus indicating that his "exile" was ended; and the interview was short and embarrassed. The wife abounded in gracious and kindly speeches, but the husband made only one remark : "You have aged, M. de Choiseul, you are growing bald."

The duke returned to Chanteloup, and Marie Antoinette had to content herself with recalling his sister, the Duchesse de Gramont, who had been banished from Court by Madame Du Barry. This first check taught her the limit of her power; this prompt disenchantment proved to her that to be a queen was not necessarily to be obeyed, and that she must secure her hour of influence by a sustained line of conduct. To this she did apply herself at a later period, notwithstanding her distaste for the serious side of government and its "affairs," but when she made up her mind to do so the reign had already taken its own course.

The selection of the principal minister, on whom so much would depend, was a lottery. Madame Adélaïde had proposed Cardinal de Bernis : "I won't have him," was the King's reply, "he is a poet." Nevertheless he took a poetaster for his minister : it is true his verses were only bad satirical songs, samples of a literature of slander which does not lead to the Academy.

The Comte de Maurepas did not come to Versailles as a candidate for the ministry; he was accidentally introduced. The King was puzzled about the very first questions of etiquette which arose on his accession, and about the ceremonies for the funeral of his predecessor; M. de Maurepas, a former minister of Louis XV., had the traditions, he brought them to the young King, and made himself *persona grata*. It happened too that M. de Maurepas was one of those whom the Dauphin, when dying, had commended to his son for fidelity to the old French policy which Choiseul had betrayed. He had a reputation as a wit, and he justified it; might he not also justify his reputation as a statesman? The way being thus prepared, Maurepas made himself agreeable, made himself necessary; he remained, he was "Minister." M. de Choiseul would have to finish his "age-ing" at Chanteloup.

Marie Antoinette, having failed to accomplish the restoration to the ministry of the only man in whom she had confidence, wanted at least to succeed in securing the dismissal of the man whom she most detested, that Duc d'Aiguillon, the "creature" of Madame Du Barry, who had so bitterly opposed the Dauphine as the pledge and symbol of the Austrian policy. The Minister of Foreign Affairs, however, was not a personage to be attacked incautiously. It was of some importance that the man who was in possession of the recent State secrets should remain in office. Mercy himself besought the Queen to lay aside her resentment, or at least to keep it in abeyance, for the sake of the interests of the country; but the Queen preferred to listen to the interested promptings of the Choiseul party. Day after day she attacked the Minister on the subject of d'Aiguillon, when with the King. Madame de Maurepas, who was his aunt, defended him to her husband, but the latter was no more true to his friends than he was to his principles, and he surrendered to the Queen. By this action he did a grave dis-service to Marie Antoinette (and probably knew that very well) by setting an adversary free who would have been far less formidable in the Ministry.

Maria Theresa was displeased by the dismissal of M. d'Aiguillon, and all the more displeased because Marie Antoinette evinced complete indifference

THE EMPRESS-QUEEN TO HER DAUGHTER.

From the drawing by Louise Massard.

[illegible] candidate for the [illegible] puzzled about the [illegible] about [illegible] former [illegible] to the young [illegible]

[illegible]

[illegible] agreeable [illegible]

M. de Choiseul would have to finish his [illegible]

Marie Antoinette, having failed to accomplish the restoration to the ministry of the only man in whom she had confidence, wanted at least to succeed in securing the dismissal of the one whom she most detested, the Duc d'Aiguillon, the "creature" of Madame Du Barry, who had so bitterly opposed the Dauphine as the pledge and symbol of the Austrian policy. The Minister of Foreign Affairs, however, was not a personage to be attacked incautiously. It was of some importance to the man who was in possession of the secret [illegible]

[illegible]

[illegible] formidable [illegible]

[illegible] d'Aiguillon, and all the [illegible]

A Madame la Duchesse de Chartres

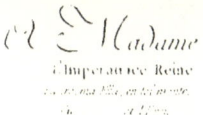

L'Imperatrice Reine a sa Fille

with regard to his successor. It was enough for her that her enemy was defeated; she did not see that her own interest was deeply concerned in his being replaced by a man who would be on her side because his good fortune had been due to her. She gave no serious support to either Bernis or Breteuil; she allowed the post of Minister of Foreign Affairs to be given to Vergennes with hardly an enquiry into the matter. Very soon, however, she had an opportunity of repairing that serious blunder. The obscure birth of the Comtesse de Vergennes, whom her husband had met during his embassy at Constantinople, apparently forbade her appearance at Court; but the Queen, acting under her mother's advice, obtained the King's consent to the presentation of the countess, and announced this favour herself to the lady's husband. Vergennes, who was affected to tears, vowed eternal fidelity and devotion to Marie Antoinette.

Vergennes was not hostile to the Queen, though he is said to have been so. The Ministry was chosen, it is true, without reference to her, but was not formed against her. She found among its members M. de Sartines, Minister of Marine, who was a *protégé* of hers; M. du Muy, Minister of War, one of the worthy persons who had held aloof from the preceding Court and whose prejudices were disarmed by the flattering reception given to his wife; and lastly, M. Turgot, the Comptroller-General, who was a close friend of the Abbé de Vermond, the former tutor of the Archduchess at Vienna, and was still the confidant and most trusted adviser of the Dauphine at Versailles. Turgot made haste to display his zeal: although he was instituting financial reform and economy, he did not hesitate to raise the insufficient "cassette" of the Queen from ninety-six thousand livres to two hundred thousand.

Marie Antoinette failed to profit by the favorable disposition of the ministers. The sole desire of these men was to please her, but she did not try to bind them fast to her. Being bent wholly on getting Choiseul back into power she allowed herself to be turned against Turgot, and showed Maurepas and Vergennes that she barely endured them. The two ministers, who were reasonably uneasy respecting their own future, and invariably found the Queen among their adversaries, had to make up their minds to fight her. Without declaring open war, and even while abetting her minor wishes, they secretly destroyed her authority, and left the field free to more daring enemies. It was upon Louis XVI. especially that they acted. M. de Maurepas was domiciled at Versailles very near the King, and could reach his apartment at any hour by a private staircase. Many a time was the Queen surprised to find that the effect of an interview with her husband in the morning had gone off before the evening, she knew not how. The staircase of M. de Maurepas played its part in history; not in vain had Louis XVI. lodged his Minister where Louis XV. had housed his mistresses.

The Queen's tastes did her harm with the King. His wife was too lively, too gay, too fond of fashionable amusements and late hours for that quiet, methodical man who liked a regular life on the "early to bed and early to rise" system. Would the Queen be likely to combine good sense with such tastes as hers, and to prove herself "of good counsel?" This skilfully-insinuated doubt made some impression upon Louis XVI., but love dispelled it quickly : the public, however, entertained it still. The censures of Mesdames de France upon the Queen's pleasures were echoed from the first by folk of the severe and rigid sort; this chorus of complaint was destined to go on swelling throughout the reign, and an event at Court had already made a "party" of the malcontents.

The Queen's brother, the Archduke Maximilian, had come on a visit to her ; but her joy in the fulfilment of this long-indulged anticipation was soon turned to bitter vexation. The Princes of the Blood, that is to say the Houses of Orléans, Condé, and Conti, refused to call on the Archduke, and insisted that the first visit was due by him, as he was travelling incognito. The Queen warmly supported her brother, and made him resist the demands of the princes. "The King," she observed to one of them, "has treated the Archduke as a brother, for he has made him sup with us in the privacy of the royal family, an honour to which I suppose you never have pretended. However, though my brother will be sorry not to know the princes, as he has only a short time in Paris, and many things to see, he will do without that." This sally did not settle the affair, and the Archduke received due honour at Versailles from the King's brothers only. An "interlude" by the Italian Opera company was given, also a ball in the Salon d'Hercule, and a brilliant fête at the Manège; on another day a fair was set up in seven improvised streets with all the customary games and shows, and companies of actors were brought down from Paris.

The cost of that festival gave offence; it amounted to more than a hundred thousand francs; the public immediately made it six hundred thousand. The Archduke was not thought worthy of such profuse expenditure. He was pronounced to be stiff, stupid, and devoid of taste for the arts. The Princes of the Blood were highly applauded for keeping away from Versailles. The Duc d'Orléans was at Sainte-Assise, the Prince de Condé at Chantilly, the Prince de Conti at l'Isle-Adam. The young Duc de Chartres made himself conspicuous in Paris during the Versailles fêtes, and the Comte de La Marche, son of the Prince de Conti, did the same. They too were highly applauded. All these Bourbons secured popular favour by resisting the claims of an Archduke of Austria, and the national "amour-propre" resented the Queen's being less French than the nation.

The Queen involuntarily and unintentionally gave offence by her first acts of kindness to her suite. Was not the Duc de Fitz-James made a Marshal of France without any other title to the bâton than his being the father of the Princesse de Chimay, who was the Queen's Lady of the Palace? And had not Louis XVI., to salve his conscience, been obliged to make Marshals of France of six other general officers who had better rights than the duke, thereby exposing the highest dignity of the army to ridicule and contempt?

The "affair" of M. de Guines was more serious. He was one of the Queen's familiar friends, and the representative of France in England. He was accused of smuggling, under cover of his Embassy, and of gambling in the funds by availing himself of State secrets. The facts were proved; M. de Guines threw the onus of them on his secretary; the latter declared that he had acted in connivance with his chief. The Parliament of Paris was charged with a very complicated inquiry which kept public opinion on the alert for years. From the first, Marie Antoinette, who believed in the innocence of the Ambassador, worked for him, and, notwithstanding the opposition of the Ministers, she succeeded in getting permission for him to use the official documents, and his own diplomatic correspondence. The result of these concessions was that the final acquittal of M. de Guines was regarded as an act of weakness on the part of the judges, and the public believed that the Queen's patronage might be used to shield men of doubtful reputation.

This trial stirred up all the political passions of the moment. Guines was on the side of Choiseul, and the entire party of the Duc d'Aiguillon, all the members of the Du Barry faction, strove to ruin him as zealously as the Queen strove to save him. This attitude towards M. de Guines was represented to Marie Antoinette as a result of the Minister's enmity towards herself. Schemers, entirely devoted to Choiseul, such as the Comtesse de Brionne and Baron de Besenval, fanned the flame of her anger. She was actually led to say, alluding to d'Aiguillon: "My hair stands on end every time I see that man." At the review of the King's "Maison Rouge," on the plain of Marly, when the duke's company of light-horse passed her carriage the Queen pulled down the blinds. This public affront had been preceded by an angry scene in the Queen's cabinet. The Duc d'Aiguillon having presented himself "to take the orders of Her Majesty for the review," Marie Antoinette said: "Why don't you go to Saint-Vrain instead, Monsieur, to take the orders of Madame Du Barry!"

At last the storm broke. When the duke was preparing to accompany the Court to Reims for the coronation, he was exiled to Varetz, his estate in Touraine, and as he made some delay in leaving Paris, Marie Antoinette persuaded the King to increase his exile. "His departure is entirely my doing," she wrote, subsequently. "The measure was full: that bad man kept up every sort of spying and evil-speaking; he tried to brave me more than once in the affair of M. de Guines; immediately after the judgment I demanded his removal from the King. It is true that I did not require a 'lettre de cachet;' but nothing is lost by that, for instead of remaining in Touraine as he wished, he has been requested to continue his journey so far as Aiguillon, which is in Gascony."

The Queen boasted too soon of an act of severity which recoiled upon herself. The numerous friends of M. d'Aiguillon extolled him as a martyr in the salons of Madame de Maurepas, and those who were merely indifferent now took a side. That side was the duke's, for they could not understand why, if M. d'Aiguillon was culpable, the King had retained him as Minister in the beginning of the reign, why at least he had not exiled him on his leaving the Ministry. The friends of Choiseul themselves were ready to swell the clamour; almost all of them had been exiled at some period of the late reign, and it made them uneasy to find these methods of government reappearing under the present. Women were foremost in the discussion; they talked of nothing but the "violation of the rights of the citizen," employing phrases which would shortly be all the fashion and were already a force. The Duc d'Aiguillon bore this belated and severe treatment, which was palpably unjust, with grave dignity. At Vienna there was great displeasure. Prince Kaunitz began to be seriously anxious about "imprudences which only grow and increase on the part of our lovely little Queen." Marie Antoinette, scolded in her mother's letters, blamed by Mercy, feeling herself in the wrong, faltered presently in her vengeance, and talked of letting the exile come back. Her kindness did her as much harm as her wrath, by making it evident to all that the Queen's resentment was not a lasting evil, and that against her anything might be done with impunity.

The Queen's intervention in the trial of M. de Guines and the exile of the Duc d'Aiguillon were due to what Mercy calls her "surroundings" (*alentours*). He apprized Maria Theresa of the schemes of these persons, so that, in the full confidence of the maternal letters she might put Marie Antoinette on her guard. At that time he regarded the Princesse de Lamballe as the most dangerous of those to whom the Queen could not refuse anything, and indeed the princess, if not actuated by interested motives was at least wanting in discretion. The Queen conceived the idea of offering her friend the post of Superintendent of her Household, an office which would have to be re-established, or rather, created, for no precise knowledge of the emoluments of such a Superintendence, or the kind and degree of authority in the Queen's Household attaching to that position existed. Mercy and Vermond advised that the expense and the prerogatives of a function which would inevitably encumber and embarrass the household service should as far as possible be diminished. A "Rule" was drawn-up in this sense and approved at the Council; but, at the last moment, the Duc de Penthièvre, holding that the office had been shorn of its proper importance by the provisions of the Rule, refused to accept it for his daughter-in-law. The princess went to the Queen in tears, and the Rule was torn up. Marie Antoinette saw but one thing, had but one thought: "I will make my own dear friend happy," she said, "and I shall enjoy it more than she."

Such a sentiment was not likely to appease anybody at Court. It created much discontent. The Princesse de Chimay and the Comtesse de Mailly, each considering herself slighted, hesitated to accept the posts which the Queen had reserved for them, for the princess that of Lady of Honour, for the countess that of Lady-in-Waiting. The most serious point was the expense; a hundred and fifty thousand livres was considered too big a salary for a useless function which could only create rivalry and disputes.

At this period, a young woman of merely provincial and undistinguished nobility, who had come to Versailles by chance to see one of her relations, came also into the life of Marie Antoinette, to supplant Madame de Lamballe, as well as all the ordinary female friends of the Queen, to take the first place in her heart, and to play the leading part at Court. At the date of the 19th of August, 1775, a writer in one of the gazettes remarks, in the tone of respect which was to last only a little longer: "The favour that the Comtesse de Dillon enjoyed with the Queen seems to have passed to the Comtesse Jules de Polignac; she is pretty, amiable and virtuous, and she deserves the kindness with which Her Majesty is pleased to honour her." Mercy announced the same thing to Maria Theresa at almost the same moment.

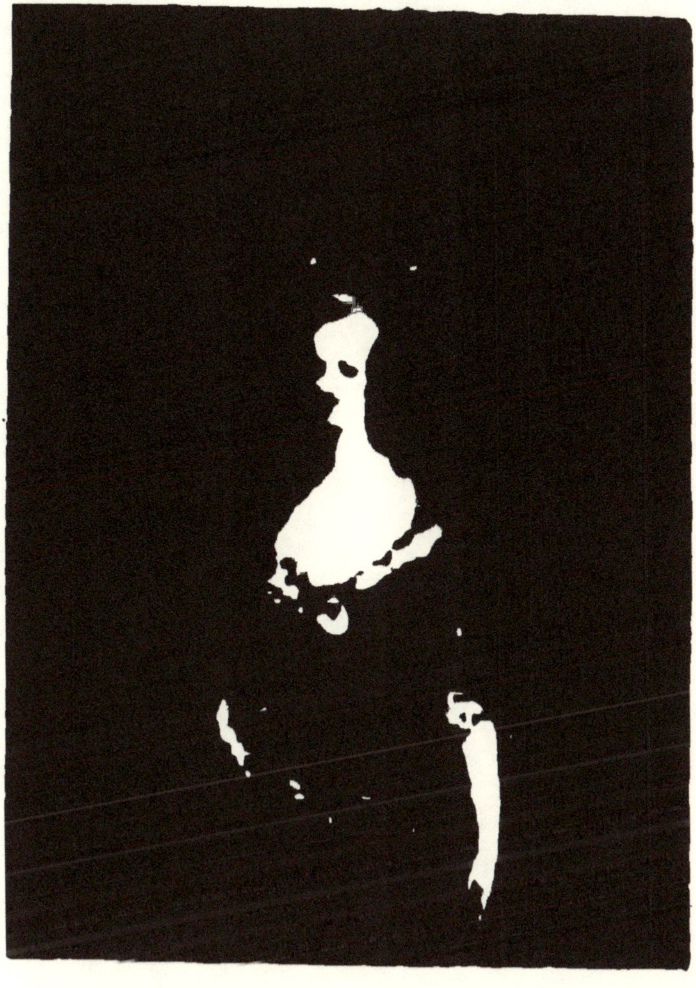

MARIE THÉRÈSE LOUISE DE SAVOIE-CARIGNAN, PRINCESSE DE LAMBALLE.

From a contemporary portrait (Musée de Versailles).

[illegible] and the Rule [illegible] one thing, had but one thought [illegible] happy, she said [illegible] I shall enjoy it [illegible]

Such a sentiment was not likely to appea[illegible] much discontent. The Princesse de Chim[illegible] each considering herself slighted, hesitated [illegible] Queen had reserved for them, for the princ[illegible] the countess that of Lady-in-Waiting. [illegible] expense; a hundred and fifty thousand [illegible] for a [illegible] function which [illegible]

With his usual keenness of observation he already perceived that the Queen's latest attachment would be more serious than the others. A few weeks afterwards, he was obliged to dispute with her, in order to prevent her from giving one of the two posts of honour in her Household to the new-comer. Thenceforth in every despatch Mercy wrote about Madame de Polignac, and the latter grew in the Queen's favour with incredible rapidity

Fully to estimate the injury this friendship did to the Queen, we must trace its progress in the letters of that wise and devoted servant; we must note every mention of the fair countess; and make similar research in the private correspondence, and in the private memoirs of annalists of the period. Such a study throws a singular light upon the history of the reign. We assist, as it were, at the formation of the coterie which afterwards had Madame de Polignac for its centre. As the Queen's affection grew and strengthened, an interested and ambitious party in the Court speculated on that sentiment more and more boldly. Marie Antoinette was hemmed in by their solicitations and intrigues; she was the prisoner of her friendship! All the State appointments were given to the Polignacs and their friends, the Treasury was at their disposal. One family was known to be rising in honours and in fortune in proportion as the ruin of the nation progressed and the public poverty increased; the spectacle alienated the best people and isolated the throne. The remonstrances which Mercy had made, speaking from the conscience of a faithful servant, low and softly, but ever more and more anxiously, year after year, were repeated by the Court coteries in tones of jealousy and enmity. From the Court the discontent reached the city, then the country; it penetrated into the bourgeois class and down into the ranks of "the People." Soon the name of Polignac was on every tongue, in ribald songs and hearty curses; linked, alas! with another name.

At first, Madame de Polignac had not a private salon. She was lodged at the Château quite close to the Queen, but in some small rooms, and she and her friends met at the apartment of the Princesse de Guémené, Governess of the Children of France, whose post was for the time being a sinecure, and left her complete leisure for intrigue. The salon of the princess competed with that of the Princesse de Lamballe, which was frequented by the Comte d'Artois, the Duc de Chartres, and the budding "party" of the Palais Royal. The Queen divided herself between these two circles, both professedly devoted to her, and certainly devoted to promoting her pleasures. She passed the evening now with one, again with the other of the two princesses, and in both cases, was overwhelmed with more recommendations and requests than her young head could carry. Each camp hoped to capture her in its turn, and nominations and affairs of State were discussed at the dances, "between two minuets."

The Rohans reckoned on Madame de Guémené to procure exorbitant favours for them; they demanded that the Ribbon of the Saint-Esprit (the Blue Ribbon), should be given to the members of their house at twenty-five years of age, as it was given to the French princes of the House of Lorraine. The Queen, however, would not comply with this demand; the slander which had been set going at Vienna by a Rohan—the Cardinal,—when he was Ambassador there, rankled in her heart. The powerful Rohan family resented her good memory. She was thenceforth a mark for the open or underhand attacks of the noble tribe: Soubise, Guémené, Rohan, were led to the attack by Madame de Marsan, a very clever woman, and presently reinforced. The husband of the Queen's friend wanted a post, but not one was vacant. Marie Antoinette caused one to be created and M. de Polignac became "reversioner" to M. de Tessé, her First Equerry: he regarded this creation, which was made without his knowledge, as an injury. M. de Tessé who was much esteemed at Court and highly connected—he was son-in-law to the Maréchal de Noailles—sent in his resignation at once. The Queen rejected it; but she had alienated an entire family, and that family one of the most influential among the nobility of France. The Noailles after the Rohans! Presently the Civrac, and then the Montmorency family, will be turned into malcontents by her blunders, and thrown into the enemy's camp.

The "little Queen" had against her also several of the women of the former Court, the vicious women of the time of Louis XV., who had not forgiven her for her virtue. They resented her frank innocence; its example condemned them, and her youthful satire, which was too open, while it wounded, also made them ridiculous. Those women whom Marie Antoinette refused to receive, who were struck out of her ball-lists, who were sent back to their lackeys at the palace gate, were embodiments of pitiless and unscrupulous rancour. One of the number was the Comtesse de Balbi, who was "protected" by Monsieur, but in spite of that fact had been made lady-in-waiting to Madame. Marie Antoinette could not refrain from reproaching her sister-in-law with this strange selection. Thenceforth the cabal was complete, the army of calumny was ready to take the field, and, as the Court was aware of the baselessness of many of its grievances, the Town was selected as the field of operations. Paris was deluged with satires and songs in which royalty was degraded without fear or scruple, for the more effectual undoing of a woman. Choice is difficult amid the mass of this drawing-room literature redolent of the sewer. Here is an epigram (inspired by an unfortunate speech made by Marie Antoinette in a moment of vexation); it is one of the most innocent, nevertheless it marks the double line of attack :

> La Reine dit imprudemment
> A Besenval son confident :
> "Mon mari est un pauvre sire."
> L'autre répond d'un ton léger :
> "Chacun le pense sans le dire,
> Vous le dites sans y penser."

In those early pamphlets which made the tour of Europe, which were printed in London and applauded at Berlin, animosity was displayed with growing audacity. The enemies of Austria, whom the marriage of 1770 had so keenly disappointed, and who existed everywhere, were both delighted and surprised to hear the following lines hummed by French lips :

> Petite reine de vingt ans,
> Qui traitez mal ici les gens,
> Vous repasserez la Bavière...

The cruel enmity of the words surpassed their hopes. Marie Antoinette's unconsciousness that she invited these attacks was very singular; she failed entirely to perceive that it was she herself who furnished the newsmongers with the canvas on which they might so easily embroider their own impure imaginings. She admitted women to her private circle whose conduct was indeed decent, but not always correct. She was surrounded by young men whose mode of life outside the Court was a scandal. Her counsellor, her friend, was not the King, whom she too readily set aside, but the Comte d'Artois, whom the most indulgent describe as a "big boy," and who passed all the time he had to spare from debauchery in frivolity. He was the Queen's friend, but the hostility of Monsieur was not more injurious to her.

It was the Comte d'Artois who accompanied Marie Antoinette to the Opera balls, one evening in riding-dress, another in the common domino which dispenses with respect and encourages familiarity; it was he who took her to Paris, driving himself "en diable" with her by his side. The King's youngest brother was the promoter of racing after the English fashion and he inspired the Queen with a taste for the sport. She appeared at Sablons among the general crowd in the midst of the loud betting and the loose talk of the sporting youth of the period; it was he who induced her to join the deer-hunt in the Bois de Boulogne without the King, and, when he remained to dine at one of the *petites maisons* of the Bois, in questionable company, it was not difficult for her foes to have the public persuaded that the Queen had stayed there also.

Reasonable people blamed Marie Antoinette for overtaxing her strength in the pursuit of pleasure; for instance, dancing at the Opera until five o'clock in the morning, getting back to Versailles at half-past six, and starting again for the races at ten. Others were particularly displeased by her adopting the most extravagant and costly fashions in dress, enormous "poufs" and plumed head-dresses from Bertin, at a time when the price of every article of food was rising, and bread riots had already occurred. Everybody said that better things, greater consideration for the public good had been hoped for from the Queen of France. Alas, the Queen of France knew nothing of "affairs," and nobody seemed to remember that she was just twenty years old.

Madame and the Comtesse d'Artois took their part in this well organized campaign. The latter was wanting in intelligence, but she gave princes to the House of Bourbon; this sufficed to ensure her exaltation at the cost of the Queen who was making France wait so long for a Dauphin. The rôle of Madame was less passive and less innocent. She adopted the tactics of her husband, who expected to be king some day, as his brother had no children, and was making himself popular beforehand. She took the exact opposite of the Queen's line; she lived simply, had no favourite friends, no superfluous expenses, appeared at fêtes only when etiquette required her presence, but attended charity entertainments and the crowning of "Rosières." Cunning and calculation, unperceived by the frank nature of Marie Antoinette, actuated her in all that she did. If the Queen arranged a party of pleasure which was to include her sister-in-law, on the morning appointed Madame would say that she was not well and could not go to it; the party would take place without her; the Comte d'Artois would perpetrate all sorts of follies, and the public would contrast the dissipation of the Queen with the reserve and moderation of Madame. Nor were there wanting people to contrast the wise influence of Monsieur over his wife with the King's weakness towards Marie Antoinette. Comparisons of this kind lessened respect for her little by little, it was leaking out of the public mind through many a rent, and the Comtesse de la Marck, in describing the Court of France to Gustavus III. dismissed the subject of the Queen in the following sentence : "The Queen goes incessantly to the Opera and the play, incurs debts, invites censure, loads herself with feathers and ribbons and laughs at everything!"

These were a young woman's follies, without real importance, inevitable and innocent, imprudent only on account of the public who took them up with an evil intention. But now came a more serious act : Marie Antoinette interfered in the government and changed the Ministers Two were displeasing to her : M. de Malesherbes, against whom Choiseul had turned her by his jests about lawyers; M. Turgot whose reforms and economy cramped her liberality and restrained her fancies. Probably she had a more serious grievance against them: she had not been pleased with their attitude in the affair of M. de Guines, Malesherbes forestalled her and retired. Turgot intended to imitate him, but he wished first to finish the financial scheme that he was to present to the King. He was not given time. Marie Antoinette even refined upon her vengeance. "The Queen's plan," says Mercy, "was that the *sieur* Turgot (mark the term!) should be dismissed, and sent to the Bastille as well, the same day that the Comte de Guines was to be declared duke. It required the very strongest and most pressing representations to check the effects of her anger."

Turgot was attacked, not only by the Queen, but by all those privileged persons who profited by the abuses which he desired to prevent, and finally he succumbed. Mercy writes, immediately after the dismissal of the Minister: "The public is aware that all this is brought about by the will of the Queen, and that she does a sort of violence to the King by it. The Comptroller-General enjoyed a great reputation for honesty and worth, and, as he is liked by the people, it will prove unfortunate that his retirement has been partly the Queen's doing. Such effects of her influence may one day bring down just reproaches upon her from the King her husband, and even from the nation." These words indicate the full gravity of the far-reaching action of Marie Antoinette, the most serious perhaps of her royal career, her part in the fall of the Ministry of reform which might have moderated the Revolution and saved the Monarchy.

Maria Theresa had been anxious for a long time. She warned her daughter concerning the dismissal of Turgot. "The public no longer speaks of you with so much praise, and attributes to you all sorts of little underhand doings, which are not becoming in your position." The Empress was well informed: she knew, for instance, that when Marie Antoinette came to Paris to be present at the first representation of Gluck's *Alceste*, the audience at the Opera, who had formerly saluted her with acclamations, received her very coldly, and left her to applaud the work of her favourite musician almost singly. A lesson of this kind ought to have struck home to the Queen. She was too sensitive not to suffer from it, but she was too proud to

A. R. J. TURGOT. Comptroller-General of the Finances.
From the portrait in pastels by J. N. Ducreux, in the possession of M. le Marquis Turgot.

grievance against them [illegible] pleased with their attitude in the affair of M. de Guines [illegible] recalled him and retired. Turgot intended [illegible] to finish the financial scheme that he was to [illegible] Marie Antoinette [illegible] "The Queen's [illegible]" says Mercy, [illegible] and sent to [illegible] to be [illegible]

[illegible] by the Queen [illegible] by the [illegible] which he [illegible] Mercy writes, immediately after the dismissal of the [illegible]: "The public is aware that all this is brought about by the will of the Queen and [illegible] to the King by [illegible]. The Comptroller-General enjoyed a great reputation for honesty and worth, and as he is liked by the people, it will prove unfortunate that his retirement has been partly the Queen's doing. Such effects of her influence may one day bring down just reproaches upon her from the King her husband, and even from the nation." These words indicate the full gravity of the [illegible] of Marie Antoinette, the most [illegible], her part in the fall of the Ministry of reform which [illegible] the Revolution and saved the Monarchy.

Maria Theresa had been anxious [illegible]. She warned her [illegible] the dismissal of [illegible]. "The public no longer speaks [illegible] and [illegible] of little underhand [illegible]. The [illegible] was well [illegible] to Paris [illegible] the [illegible] of [illegible] very [illegible] almost [illegible] the Queen. She was [illegible] but she was too proud to

appear to yield to it. She was also surrounded by favourites, who flattered and smiled on her, but her true friend, the Abbé de Vermond, weary and sick of the Court, had withdrawn by degrees, thus relieving the young Queen from counsels which she always received kindly, but never followed; a word from Madame de Polignac could make her laugh at them.

The expenditure of Marie Antoinette was severely criticized. She was blamed for her habitual card-playing, her purchases of diamonds, the augmentation of her stables, the costly alterations of her Trianon, the pensions procured for her friends, even for the ladies' suppers in the King's "cabinets" after the hunting-parties, which she instituted. Mercy, who knew the details of these expenses, perceived at a glance that the consequences of them were coming. He writes: "Among the rumours that are arising there is one which appears more dangerous and more vexatious than any of the others; it is dangerous, because it must from its nature make an impression on all the orders of the State, and particularly upon the people; it is vexatious, because, when the lies and exaggeration inseparable from public rumour are deducted from it, there still remains a number of authentic facts to which it would be well that the Queen had never lent herself; the public complain that the Queen personally incurs and also occasions considerable expense. The outcry can only grow louder unless she very soon adopts some principles of moderation in this respect." Let us briefly mention here that, at the beginning of the year 1777, the personal debts of Marie Antoinette amounted to four hundred and eighty-seven thousand livres. The King paid them out of his privy purse in a few months, without having recourse to M. Necker, who had shortly before assumed the direction of the Finances. But it had not been possible to hide the debts from everybody, and more than one apocryphal anecdote shows how largely they contributed to the unpopularity of the Queen. Even at Court, according to the Prince de Ligne, her prodigality was discussed and freely exaggerated by "the little women who had not been so much admired as the Queen at the winter balls, and were vexed in consequence." In a notorious trial, that of a woman named Cahuet de Villers, the name of Marie Antoinette was brought in; the accused had embezzled immense sums on pretence of borrowing them on behalf of the Queen, and had furnished false receipts. Would the woman have been able to impose upon the bankers had not the excessive expenditure of Marie Antoinette been notorious? This incident disturbed the public mind, gave rise to much calumny, and foreshadowed the affair of the necklace.

Marie Antoinette found an unprejudiced censor in her brother Joseph II., who came to Paris, not as the Emperor of Germany visiting the King of France in state, but as a brother desirous to make himself acquainted with his sister's new life, to see for himself whether she was happy, and if necessary to give her advice and support. He availed himself of his excursion to acquire information on French manners, interests, and ways; he visited arsenals, manufactories, academies, and theatres, he went through the official Paris programme for princely visitors; but the Queen was his chief object and concern, he passed whole days with her, in her private rooms at the Château or in the Trianon grounds. He had come to France, unfortunately, after a very dissipated winter. The Court had not been brilliant, the excessive favour shown to some families had kept others away; but costly and undignified amusements had profusely prevailed. The Queen had set the example; the King's weakness and his love had hindered him from restraining her.

Joseph II. observed everything, the habits of the royal family, the defects of its head, the dangerous surroundings of Marie Antoinette. He was particularly impressed by certain incidents, among others the following, which Mercy relates: "The Emperor informs me that, having accompanied the Queen, in order to please her, to the apartment of the Princesse de Guémené, he was shocked by the " mauvais ton" and unbecoming familiarity prevailing among that lady's company. His Majesty saw them playing at faro, and actually heard Madame de Guémené reproached with her suspicious play in the presence of the Queen. The Emperor was indignant at this impropriety; he told the Queen plainly that the place was a "hell" (tripot). The Queen endeavoured to palliate the facts; she even returned after midnight to the said princess, on the pretext that she had promised to do so. The Emperor was vexed at this, and imputed it to disheartening obstinacy." The elder brother interfered without hesitation. At the outset he had regained the affection of the "little sister" so long unseen, and her former confidence; of these he availed himself to save her. He induced her to acknowledge her frivolity and love of amusement, he made her see that she was neglecting her duties as wife and queen, and received a promise from her that she would change her mode of life. He even left with her a long "instruction" in writing, in order to fix the remembrance of his visit in her mind.

The young Queen, hitherto intoxicated by flattery, was told the truth for the first time by stern lips speaking with the authority and unreserve of blood-relationship; she was now forced to interrogate her conscience, and the sincerity of her nature replied. From a mistaken "point of honour," she would not appear to yield to advice; but was anxious to have it believed that the reform came from herself and from her own will. This, however, did not matter, the effect was produced. The Queen went less frequently to the Paris plays, she accompanied the King on his hunting-parties, passed some hours every day in her private rooms and read regularly; hardly ever played except at home, and, although she still retained her affection for Madame de Polignac, she gradually detached herself from Madame de Guéméné; she behaved more graciously to persons who had the claims of age and rank, and took greater heed of "susceptibilities." The sojourn of the Court at Choisy, which had always done harm because of the exclusive favouritism in which the Queen indulged there, did not give rise to any discontent that year. All were treated according to the rank and merit of the individual.

Marie Antoinette must be given credit for the attempt at reform that marks the summer of 1777. The absence of the Comte d'Artois made her task less difficult. Monsieur and his brother were touring in France as Joseph II. had just done; the comparison, however, was not to the advantage of the French princes. "They are travelling," says the Comtesse de la Marck, "as these people do travel, at frightful expense, and causing devastation of the posts and the provinces."

But, if the Comte d'Artois was of service to the Queen by taking himself out of Paris, on the other hand he still contrived to injure her at a distance. He was unconsciously sowing the Revolution in his track, and creating unpopularity for the Queen, by letting the people see what manner of man he was whom they knew to be her friend and the sharer of her pleasures.

On his return the Comte d'Artois resumed his rôle of evil genius. He was now very intimate with Madame de Polignac, and the two together ruled the Queen. The evil that Joseph II. had but checked broke out more strongly than ever. Play became the chief occupation of Marie Antoinette, at home and abroad. Formerly the "jeu" of the Court took place on the great occasions of representation and etiquette solely, and only cavagnol and lansquenet were played; now the tables were set three times a week in public and faro was the dangerous game. Anybody might approach the Queen's table and play, either sitting or standing, without being specially presented: if he brought money and was prepared to lose it—for certain ladies cheated with calm effrontery—that was enough. The stakes were so high that persons of quality took fright and gave place to the first comers. It was regarded as scandalous that games of chance, which were prosecuted by the government in Paris, should be encouraged by the Queen. English people at Vienna said that the "tables" of Versailles and Fontainebleau competed with those of Spa, and the word (tripot) which the Emperor had applied to a certain salon, was applied by the people to the whole Court of France. The news-sheets made it known to all Europe that the Duc de Chartres had lost thirty thousand louis for the amusement of the Queen. Marie Antoinette cared nothing about the English and the newsmongers. She laughed at her brother's advice and jested while reading his letters. She did not even hearken to the cry of her mother's heart: "Your future makes me tremble!"

Europe did not know, but we know at this later day, the secret of that terrible dissipation for which the Queen had to pay so dearly. She strove to justify it by replying to the reproaches of the Comte de Mercy: "What would you have? I dread ennui." Neither play, nor the racecourse, neither theatres, balls, nor change of place could conquer that "inexorable ennui" which takes possession of the hearts of queens, who, as women, have not attained the natural aim of their lives. Marie Antoinette lived in a whirl to escape the remembrance that she was not a mother. There came a moment, however, when she might hope for a child! On the 3rd of October, 1777, Maria Theresa wrote to her daughter, not without emotion and joy: "I tenderly embrace my dear little woman whom I dearly love." A little later, the Queen received the compliments of the Court upon her expected maternity, which was officially announced, and the people of Paris rejoiced at the good news. Alas! clouds were gathering on the political horizon, and the joy of Marie Antoinette's precious and cherished hope was overcast.

The question of the Bavarian succession arose, and imperilled the very principle of the Austrian alliance. The Cabinet of Versailles would not associate itself with the claims of Joseph II., who had laid hands on Lower Bavaria at the death of the Elector; it refused to defend a too-ambitious ally against the reprisals of Frederick II., whose army had invaded Bohemia. This was a question to be settled between chancelleries. The French were indifferent in the matter, for they were completely occupied by the American War of Independence and Franklin's embassy to Europe; besides, public feeling, never well-disposed towards Austria, was not unfriendly to the King of Prussia, Voltaire's friend. Maria Theresa herself understood that it would not do to bring Marie Antoinette into the negotiations, at the risk of rendering her, if she were asked to take a direct part, "troublesome to the King and odious to the nation."

She did this very thing, nevertheless, being driven to do it by the critical position of the Empire. Letter followed letter entreating her daughter to apply to Louis XVI. and to the Ministers so as, at least, to get diplomatic pressure put upon Frederick II. Marie Antoinette soon came to regard herself as the only hope of her family. Mercy persuaded her that to comply was to serve her two countries at the same time, and besides, her sole idea of politics was that the "alliance" was to be sustained and Prussia to be detested. She intervened energetically.

Thenceforth, her whole mind was given to the war in Bohemia, from whence ill tidings came in quick succession: when the posts came in from Vienna her eyes were red; the public learned that she had countermanded a fête at Trianon, as a mark of her grief; her interviews with the Ministers, whom she frequently summoned to her cabinet, were much discussed. It was known that she argued with them, in the King's presence, repeating the lesson which she had learnt from the Ambassador of the Empire. To Louis XVI. she had but to speak of their then unborn child, and she might use the irresistible argument of tears at her pleasure.

This was more than was needed to make the cabal protest that the Queen wanted to hand France over to Austria. The Empress, the Emperor and M. de Mercy, all three "of good counsel," were nevertheless dangerous advisers for Marie Antoinette on this occasion; they crowned the decisive years of her reign by a grave error. She was fated never to be forgiven for having entered so warmly into questions which she had mistaken for family affairs. Many there were already who called the Queen of France by that fatal name which was to abide by her to the end: "l'Autrichienne!"

"I do not flatter myself with (the hope of) a Dauphin," wrote Maria Theresa, "I am not accustomed to have complete consolations." The French, on the contrary, expected an heir for the throne, that male first-born child of the Bourbon Kings whom the nation regarded as its property, and whose traditional name still held its high prestige. If he had come at that moment, the early years of the reign might have been forgotten, and the popularity of the Queen revived. The child was born on the 19th of December, 1778, and was a girl, Madame Royale.

In vain did the young mother employ the hundred thousand livres given her by the King in good works and in gifts; in vain did the Curés of Paris distribute alms in the Queen's name and empty the debtors' prisons; in vain were a hundred young couples dowered by her: on the day when she came to the capital to make her thanksgiving at the churches, no enthusiastic greeting attended her passage through the streets. The immense crowd was indeed curious, but the cries of "Vive la Reine!" were few and far-between. The people, who lacked bread, attributed a share in the ills of the nation to the Queen, and regarded the birth of a princess as a poor compensation for their sufferings.

With the birth of her child, Marie Antoinette entered upon a new life. She had already said to Mercy that from the day on which God should give her the grace of maternity she would renounce frivolity and live entirely for her duties. She kept her word. No more recklessly high play, no more costly whims; the Queen even gave up the Fontainebleau and Compiègne "voyages" which entailed too great an expenditure, and substituted brief visits by the Court to Choisy and Marly. She curtailed her amusements and her late hours; she had her daughter with her several times a day and gave the King more of her companionship. The royal family adopted the custom of meeting at Trianon every week to sup with the Queen in private. "My health is entirely re-established," she writes to Maria Theresa. "I am about to resume my ordinary life, and consequently I hope soon to be able to announce fresh hopes to my dear Mamma. She may be quite without anxiety as to my conduct, and I feel the necessity of having children too strongly to neglect anything concerning that. If I did wrong formerly it was from childishness and levity; but at this time of day my head is much more steady, and she may rely upon it that I feel all my duties deeply. Besides, I owe it to the King for his affection, and I may venture to say, his confidence in me; for this I have more and more reason to be thankful." What a change from the flippant tone of her letters of the former time! How quickly the futile pursuits and tastes of the Queen fled away at the sight of her transformed future, before the duties of her new life with a baby's cradle for their centre!

The reform was real and durable. If Marie Antoinette did not keep all her promises to the letter, at least she did not allow the follies of former years to tempt her. Unhappily, it was too late. The French nation had formed and fixed its opinion of the consort of their King. They believed her to be incapable of the dignified seriousness befitting a queen, and even doubted her virtue as a wife. Foul calumny, together with malicious gossip, too often, it must be admitted, not quite groundless, had done its work, noiseless, slow, implacable and final, just as Beaumarchais had described it at that very moment in *Le Barbier de Séville*, with its slight sound just ruffling the surface of the ground, *piano*, *piano*, then circulating in the crowd, *rinforzando* from mouth to mouth, until it swells into the general cry, into the public *crescendo*, into the universal *chorus* of hatred and proscription.

The most innocent actions of Marie Antoinette were distorted by this unsparing and indefatigable calumny. She went in disguise to the Opera, to the Shrove Tuesday ball, with the Princesse d'Hénin, the King only being in the secret of this little escapade. Her carriage broke down in Paris; in order to get to the theatre the Queen had to wait in a shop and take the first hackney-coach that passed. Nobody would have known it, had not Marie Antoinette hastened to relate the adventure to the friends whom she met at the ball. "I, coming in a hackney-coach to the Opera! isn't it funny?" The newsmongers got hold of the story, and made I know not what scandalous adventure out of the Queen's drive in a public vehicle on that Carnival night.

In summer, during the hot evenings, the royal family usually went out after supper and walked on the terraces at Versailles, where a band played and the public had free entry: the crowd might elbow the princesses. This diversion was rather unseemly, and the Comte d'Artois, whose idea it was, might have been blamed for it justly enough; but it was the Queen who was attacked. The English newspapers, with an utter disregard of truth or probability, travestied the accounts of the royal evenings, adding preposterous details, and transformed these informal promenades into indecent revels. Even in Paris the falsehood gained credence; reasonable people, who were sincerely attached to the throne, talked indignantly of the "nocturnales" of Versailles. Every action of the Queen was perverted, all her intentions were misrepresented in a similar manner, and amid this irruption of slander

YOLANDE GABRIELLE MARTINE DE POLASTRON, DUCHESSE DE POLIGNAC.

From the portrait by Madame Vigée-Lebrun, in the possession of His Royal Highness the Grand-Duke of Saxe-Weimar.

[illegible] com-

[illegible],

[illegible] mark

[illegible]

[illegible] just

[illegible] in the

[illegible] greatest

[illegible] and

were [illegible] and

[illegible]

[illegible] the [illegible] only being

[illegible]

[illegible] and take the

[illegible] Marie

[illegible] at -

[illegible] funny!" The

[illegible]

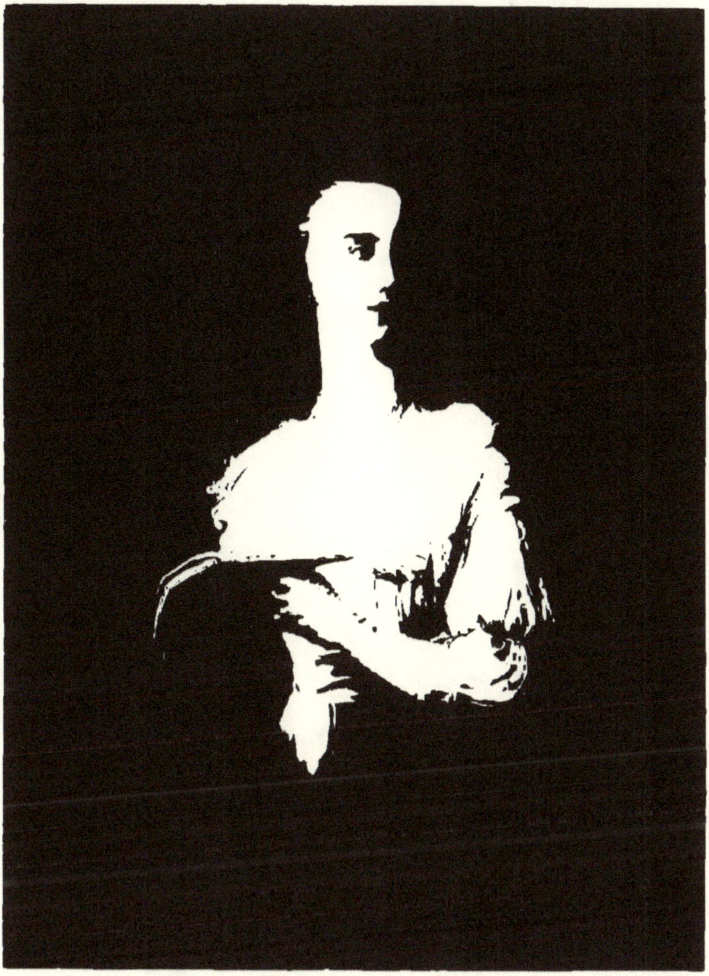

in her life, no one noticed the change that had taken place in herself, or surmised the resolutions she had formed.

There was one point on which reform had not been effected; this was the reserved corner of the Queen's conscience; her brother had failed to extract any admission concerning it. She had the same weakness for her favourites still, and she placed complete abandonment to her friendships on the list of her duties. Were the objects of her regard worthy of it? One of Madame Elisabeth's ladies will answer. "This famous society is composed of very mischievous persons and it is incredibly conceited and censorious in its tone. They think themselves fit to judge all the rest of the world. They are so afraid lest any one may creep into favour, that they never praise, but they revile and defame freely." If Madame de Bombelles, who was kindness itself, and had not to suffer from these people, gives them such a character as this what must the rest of the Court have said? Her ill-chosen associates aroused unappeasable animosity against the Queen.

In reality one person only was dear to her; but if she refused no favour to Madame de Polignac, Madame de Polignac refused no service to her friends. Thenceforth the best places and the largest pensions were for them. This one got an embassy, that one a regiment, another a bishopric, and they all got money. "It is pillage," said Mercy; "they are a gang of thieves," added Kaunitz, who was a plain speaker.*

Diane de Polignac, the sister-in-law of the countess, who was merely a lady-in-waiting to the Comtesse d'Artois, obtained the chief post in the household of Madame Elisabeth; M. de Vaudreuil, whose relations with the countess were not those of kindred, was made Grand Falconer, and Marie Antoinette procured a pension of thirty thousand livres for him on the pretext that the war with England prevented him from receiving his revenues from the colonies. She made a brilliant match for the daughter of her friend, and the son-in-law, the young Duc de Guiche, was given the reversion of a company in the Body-Guards regardless of the rights that had been acquired by others. "Within four years," writes Mercy, in

* See Appendix, Note 4.

great indignation, "it is calculated that the Polignac family have procured for themselves, in great posts and other benefits, without deserving anything of the State and by pure favour, close on five hundred thousand livres of annual income! All the most deserving families protest against the wrong that is done to them by such a bestowal of favours, and if one more, and that unexampled, is to be added, the outcry and disgust will be carried to the highest point."

The favour which Mercy dreaded was the gift of the estate of Bitche, in Lorraine. This estate formed part of the royal domain, and represented one hundred thousand livres of annual revenue. The resentment created by their demand induced the Polignacs to desist for the time being, but they exacted an extravagant compensation; eight hundred thousand livres for the dowry of their daughter, whilst the dowries hitherto given by the King never had exceeded six thousand livres annually. At a later period they got the coveted slice of the royal domain, and, with the money, the honours. In order that the favourite should have nothing left to desire, her husband was created hereditary duke and the new duchess had her "tabouret" at Court.

The Queen's friendship blinded her to the insatiable rapacity of "the Polignac set;" she was indignant at the public malignity; she said that they "reckoned more louis d'or than there were crowns in the sum of her gifts;" she scorned the popular tavern-talk against "the Polignac," which was more coarse and violent than it had been in former days when the Du Barry was its theme; she treated the displeasure of the nobility and many faithful servants of the King who openly protested against such scandalous favouritism as mere jealousy. She even disregarded the observations of Maria Theresa, and replied that she had been misinformed by public rumour. With this trouble, the anxieties of the Empress came to an end. Maria Theresa died, never having seen her daughter since she bade adieu with tears to the "little Dauphine." Marie Antoinette was never more to hear the voice that had so long appealed from the heart of a mother at once loving and severe, constantly exhorting her child to reasonableness, and betimes resembling the voice of that child's own conscience.

The Queen's judgment was, however, maturing. She began to take interest in politics. It cannot be said that she displayed the serenity and impartiality of a sage in internal affairs, or, indeed that she put the jealous patriotism of a French woman into the delicate negotiations of diplomacy: the latter fact became too evident afterwards when she espoused the cause of the Queen of Naples (her sister) and showed that she was more deeply concerned for the interests of an Austrian princess than for the "family compact" of the House of Bourbon. But, when she escaped from her female coterie at Versailles, or from the influence of Vienna, were her views as an intelligent and right-minded woman of much less value than the views of a Maurepas? The French unfortunately recognized only the faults of their Queen. They blamed her, for instance, for her ardent interest in the American cause, which was passionately defended by the whole of the youthful nobility of France, and regarded the favour she extended to the Marquis de la Fayette as merely meant for the graceful dancer at her balls. The only thing which was reckoned to her credit was the support she gave M. Necker in his first term of office as Finance Minister.

At first, when the Genevese banker spoke of reform, order, and economy, Marie Antoinette demurred: these were the ideas of M. Turgot served up to her again; but when at length, and for the first time, she clearly understood the necessities of the kingdom, she no longer offered any opposition. Necker's conversations with her, backed by the patient perseverance of Mercy, even convinced her of the exactions of her friends, and the impropriety of the gifts of money which Madame de Polignac had obtained from her. She was thankful to the Director-General of Finance for his courageous attitude; she defended him against the cabal; she even helped him to get rid of M. de Sartines, that too belligerent administrator of the Navy, who threw so many millions into the Atlantic. But she was not strong enough to protect the reforming Minister against Maurepas. Necker fell in his turn, and his fanatical followers reproached Marie Antoinette with not having saved him, while she incurred unbounded blame by having lent him her support.

Battle was waged between the Queen and Maurepas. In spite of him she had Castries and Ségur taken into the Ministry; the former for the Navy, the latter for the Army. These appointments were suggested by her "set;" they were, however, excellent, and two departments were satisfactorily filled. The old Maréchal de Ségur was integrity itself, and the army rejoiced at his nomination to a post very ill-occupied by the Prince de Montbarey, who was a "creature" of M. de Maurepas. The Minister meant to respond to this two-fold defiance; he still had the King's staircase at his disposal and in the Council two men on whom he might implicitly rely, M. Amelot and M. de Vergennes. Death took him by surprise towards the end of 1781, in the midst of his preparations for revenge. The heirs of his policy still strove to fight Marie Antoinette, but the Queen was now armed for her own defence; she had begun to learn the handling of affairs and men, and she had acquired fresh rights over the King. She had given him the son so long and ardently desired. On the 22nd of October, 1781, the succession to the throne was secured. The Court rejoiced with the sovereigns, and Monsieur and Madame put on smiles to hide the discomfiture which the birth of a Dauphin brought to them. The City of Paris gave great fêtes (these are to be described later in this narrative), in honour of the Queen; she was received with grateful acclamations which may have seemed to her like an echo, only a little feebler, of the greetings of the past. This enthusiasm was however but ephemeral, it was intended for the mother only, and it vanished away under the influence of the prejudice that had become rooted in the public mind, and the fresh attacks upon the Queen; these were redoubled in virulence, and multiplied in proportion to the additional importance and security of her position. A grave event, which touched her nearly, came like a thunderclap from a clear sky, and revived the public hostility: this was the bankruptcy of the Prince de Guéméné. At first the amount of his debts was stated at fifteen millions; but, all told, it came to thirty-three millions. The affair made much more noise in Paris than the exploits of the Comte d'Artois at the siege of Gibraltar. Hundreds of families suffered by it; and a great outcry was raised among all the tradespeople whom the Prince paid in life annuities, and the small creditors who had put their trust in the word of a great nobleman. The prince was ordered to resign his post as Grand Chamberlain and forbidden to appear at Court. Although separated from her husband for some years, the princess, who had indeed had her full share in the fêtes and the follies, was obliged to resign her post as Governess of the Children of France.

At this point we begin to see plainly that the Queen was becoming disenchanted with her friendships. She did not, in the first instance, desire to entrust the bringing-up of her children to the Duchesse de Polignac. The charge was too important for her to confide it to a woman whose character was not blameless, and who was the instrument of a dangerous clique, as the Emperor Joseph II.—he had recently made her a second visit at Versailles—had pointed out to her. Already—we know it on the best authority—the Queen "no longer loved" Madame de Polignac. She wished, as did the King, to give the post to the Duchesse de Duras, a woman whose character commanded universal respect and who set the Court an example of all the virtues. But the public was ignorant of the changes which had taken place in the Queen; no external action had revealed them; the appointment of Madame de Polignac, though not desired, was expected. "It is easy," says a contemporary letter, "to guess on whom the choice will fall; at all times that great post has been given to the favourites and intimate friends of the Queen; it is just that the mother should choose the care-taker *(bonne)* of her children." Then, during a sojourn of the Court at La Muette, Baron de Besenval contrived to persuade the Queen that any other nomination would astonish everybody. It would make people believe, he said, that the Queen had no longer sufficient influence to get the post given to her best friend. This touched Marie Antoinette on a sensitive point; she fancied herself obliged to speak to the King, and Madame de Polignac was appointed Governess of the Children of France.

The Queen took no pleasure in this selection, yet it was more disastrous to her than all the others. Not only was there much grumbling about the sums which were once more showered upon the Polignacs—although there was a justification, this time, in the expenses which so great a post must necessarily involve—but, henceforth, whenever the eyes of France were turned upon the Dauphin, the royal child in whom her future was incarnate, they must also rest upon the Governess whom his mother had given him, filling a post of honour and confidence which was perhaps the first at Court, and the growing unpopularity of the favourite would increase that of the Queen.

One little fact illustrates the evil disposition of the public towards Marie Antoinette. In 1783, her portrait by Madame Lebrun was exhibited at the Salon. She was represented "en gaulle," that is to say, wearing a long white garment, quite plain, which she had adopted from the Creoles, who were fashionable just then. The Parisians, who had inveighed so bitterly against her jewels and costly attire, were no better pleased with the Queen's new tastes, nor with a toilette entirely composed of muslin and batiste. They crowded round the portrait in order to mock at the original. "She dresses like a femme de chambre," said some. "She wants to ruin the Lyons trade," said others. They invented a title for the picture: *La France, sous les traits de l'Autriche, réduite à se couvrir d'une panne.* So coarse and unseemly were the comments on the portrait that it was removed from the Salon.

Other indications made it evident that France was falling away from her masters and losing the habit of respect. That same year a play by Beaumarchais, of which Louis XVI. himself had said that if it were acted the Bastille would have to be pulled down first, was produced in Paris with immense success. He had begun by refusing the artists of the Comédie Française the necessary authorisation for its performance; but M. de Vaudreuil, a very well-known personage at Versailles, was infatuated with the piece, had it performed at his abode, at his own expense, and cleverly stirred up public curiosity respecting the prohibited work. He got round the Queen, deceived her about the corrections which the author pretended to have made; and it was Marie Antoinette herself who induced the King to withdraw his prohibition and sanction the performance of *Le*

Mariage de Figaro, which contained a rôle intended as an insult to herself.

It needed this piece of audacity and the scandal which resulted from it, to enlighten the Queen as to the character of some of the friends of Madame de Polignac. But M. de Vaudreuil had had time, before he forfeited her favour, to render one more terrible service to the Monarchy: he had procured the appointment of Finance Minister for M. de Calonne.

To the "Salon Polignac" M. de Calonne meant the key of the royal coffers. Since the Queen had for some time past been less ready to dip into them for her friends, they arranged so as to do without her. With M. de Calonne as Minister, the public money flew about briskly. Loans and lotteries supplied him with it, and by boldly spending what the State did not possess, he created the false idea that prosperity had returned to France. Besenval, Vaudreuil, and their like, who profited by the delusion, easily fabricated the reputation of a great minister for him, at the expense of Necker. The Queen was deceived like the rest of the Court. Expenditure, checked for a time, was resumed with greater lavishness. The fête given at Trianon, in 1784, in honour of Gustavus III. of Sweden, surpassed all preceding entertainments in magnificence. To enable Marie Antoinette to go to Fontainebleau by water, ascending the Seine, a yacht with a complete "apartment" was built at a cost of sixty thousand livres. The Queen was enchanted with this costly compliment; but it was made a subject of severe reproach to her when all eyes were opened to the faults of the Minister. Calonne, the Polignac, and the Queen were bracketed together in scurrilous street songs, as, for instance, in the following verse, put into the mouth of Marie Antoinette:

"Calonne n'est pas ce que j'aime,
Mais c'est l'or qu'il n'épargne pas.
Quand je suis dans quelque embarras,
Alors je m'adresse à lui-même;
Ma favorite fait de même,
Et puis nous en rions tout bas,
Tout bas, tout bas, tout bas, tout bas."

Such literature was as dangerous as it was dull, and a few palpable mistakes sufficed to persuade people that the Queen had "created" Calonne and was responsible for his follies. As a matter of fact she had neither got him into the Ministry, nor supported him there. Calonne detested her, and, at a later period, intrigued incessantly against her from his retreat in London. But did public opinion ever reason, and was it not always ready to condemn anything that the Queen did, whatsoever it might be?

For instance, there was the purchase of Saint-Cloud. Louis XVI. gave the Queen a château near Paris at the same time that he added the fine lands of Rambouillet to the estates of the Crown. A residence of that kind might become necessary should repairs at Versailles render the removal of the Court obligatory. From the first it was beneficial to the royal children, who had not sufficient room in the Château de la Muette, and especially to the poor little Dauphin, who was beginning to die slowly of an obscure disease. The doctors recommended that he should be kept in country air. This purchase of Saint-Cloud, which was quite justified, and made for the mother rather than for the Queen, the public would not pardon. It was regarded as a source of fresh expense, and the people believed the rumour that a palace as large as Versailles was to be built; that the missioners who served the Chapel were dismissed in order that the former might be replaced by actors and the latter by a theatre; they took part with the Archbishop who opposed the Queen and wanted to keep the missioners, and they joined the inhabitants of Saint-Cloud in protesting against their being compelled to lodge the attendants of the Court for whom there was not room in the Château. Finally, the regulations for the internal ordering of the Château were headed, as at Trianon, with the words *De par la Reine*, whereupon, the most violent of the parliamentarians, M. d'Eprémesnil, declared that it was "impolitic and immoral that palaces should belong to a Queen of France." Marie Antoinette was deeply wounded by these words. "Is my name out of place," she asked, "in the gardens that belong to me? Can I not give orders there without injury to the rights of the State?"

A greater grief was in store for her at Saint-Cloud. She had hoped to

sees and the ... theatre; they
opposed the Queen ...
... court for whom
... for the ...
... with the ...

regain the affection of the capital by coming to Paris as a neighbour, to re-establish the current of love between the people and royalty, and once more to receive such tokens of sympathy as had been lavished upon her at the outset of the reign. But it was in vain that she attended the popular fêtes and went among the groups of people holding the Dauphin by the hand; they all turned to ice upon her path, and the "vivats" for the Dauphin or for the King emphasized the dead silence for the Queen. Year by year she *felt* the public more hostile, and more than once as she drove along the Route de Paris offensive expressions reached her from the midst of the jeering crowd, who would shout: "We are going to Saint-Cloud to see the fountains and the Austrian woman!" She bore herself calmly, coldly, haughtily, hiding her pain under the stateliness that was an additional grievance against her, and when the ordeal was over and she came in from that hateful drive, she would shut herself up in her cabinet and ask, amid her sobs: "What have I done to them?" On the 27th of March, 1785, a second prince was born, the Duc de Normandie, he who was to be Louis XVII., and the Muses of slander greeted his birth with their most monstrous strains. The Queen, who knew that these infamous songs existed, and knew that her people sang them, dreaded the solemn journey for her churching, her first visit to Paris, which she had to make without the King. She wanted to have the Dauphin with her, but etiquette was opposed to this, and besides, Madame asserted her right to sit at the back of the coach by the side of the Queen: if the Dauphin was to come with them, Madame would have to give him that place, and she would absent herself from the ceremony rather than forego her prerogative. Etiquette and Madame had their way. The Queen went to Paris without her son.

After the thanksgiving at Notre Dame, being fatigued by the heat, she thought she might abridge the ceremonial at Sainte-Geneviève and begged her ladies not to get out of the coach. The lower classes, who had greater devotion to the Patroness of Paris than to the Blessed Virgin herself, murmured against the impiety of Marie Antoinette. As the cortège passed through the streets no cheer was raised, no acclamation responded to the guns of the Grève, the Bastille, and the little ship *Le Dauphin*, moored on the Seine. The cold solemnity of an official fête pervaded the whole city. On re-entering the Tuileries, Marie Antoinette, being greatly agitated, avoided the assembled Court and the infliction of the customary compliments; she went up to her apartment by the "little staircase," sent Madame away, and shut herself up with Madame Elisabeth.

In the afternoon the two princesses went to the Opera, and were received with acclamation : the Queen was much affected and pleased by this small tribute, and graciously recognized it by repeated curtseys. A small supper-party at the residence of the Comte d'Artois followed ; the only non-royal guests were M. de Besenval, M. de Crussol and the Duc de Coigny, the Princesse de Chimay and the two Polignacs. This supper-party took place at the Temple, where the child in honour of whose birth it was given was to die ! What a sad festival day for the mother ! Neither the warm reception at the Opera, nor the graceful compliments of her own friends, nor the fire-works given by the Comte d'Aranda on the Place Louis Quinze, could make Marie Antoinette forget the strange attitude of the population of the streets, the sullen ill-will she had seen in so many faces. She always will remember the day when she came to the capital seeking her old Paris of the past, and Paris replied by silence.

There was a great stir in the capital in the afternoon of the 15th of August, 1785, the Feast of the Assumption. Cardinal de Rohan had been arrested at Versailles, in presence of the whole Court, on leaving the King's cabinet ; the Grand Almoner of France was in the Bastille ! As an individual, Rohan was little liked and still less respected; but his former attacks upon Marie Antoinette were known, and his disgrace was regarded as an act of feminine vengeance; everybody took the prelate's part immediately. And when, a few days later, the public learned that there was to be a great trial, and that it was the Queen who had procured the arrest of the Cardinal, the accused was absolved and the Queen was convicted in his place; the verdict of the public, blind and terrible, had been pronounced, without discussion and without appeal.

Nevertheless, this "Affair of the Necklace," which completed the ruin of Marie Antoinette, was, if not simple at least perfectly clear. We know all about it at the present day, and here is the story in a few words.

Cardinal de Rohan was a fool, notwithstanding his age and his title, and his intimacy with Cagliostro made him still more foolish. He fell into the hands of the Comtesse de Lamotte-Valois, a designing and unscrupulous woman of superior intellect. This woman, who wanted wealth at any price, was descended from a natural son of the Valois King Henri II.; Chérin, the impeccable genealogist, acknowledged her claims; the Duc de Penthièvre received her. But she had not her "entrées" at Court; she lived by her wits, and naturally bethought her of practising on the passions of Rohan. His sole desire, however, was to regain the favour of the Queen, who had frowned upon him since his return from Vienna, and no longer spoke to him; for his was not a courtier's ambition solely; a romantic and culpable sentiment pervaded it also. Madame de Lamotte was aware of the existence of a superb necklace made by Boehmer, the Court jeweller, of extraordinarily fine diamonds collected by himself, and valued at sixteen hundred thousand livres. The purchase of this splendid ornament had been proposed twice over to the Queen, but she had refused, saying that she did not want any more diamonds and that the King would do better to add a ship to the navy with the money. Boehmer, who had sunk his whole fortune in the necklace, and could not dispose of it, was greatly embarrassed, but he persisted in believing that the Queen would surely change her mind.

This conviction of the jeweller's no doubt induced the credulity on his part, which made it possible to effect the fraud. Such were the personages and the situation; the following was Madame de Lamotte's plan of action.

She began by persuading the Cardinal that she was in high favour with the Queen, inventing a series of private audiences of Her Majesty at Versailles and at Trianon. She then organised a daring scheme, in order to make the discomfited courtier believe that she would be the means of obtaining his restoration to favour. One night, having been taken by Madame de Lamotte into a "bosquet" in the gardens at Versailles, the Cardinal saw coming towards him a woman dressed in white, who had the figure, the features, and the carriage of Marie Antoinette. She gave him a letter, a rose, murmured a word that had been arranged, and passed on out of his sight. This bit of acting fired the imagination of the poor man. Shortly after, Madame de Lamotte informed him that the Queen wished for Boehmer's necklace, and that she had chosen him, her former enemy, to negotiate the purchase in secret. His public pardon, perhaps more still, would be the reward of that service. A formal document setting forth the terms of purchase, and bearing the approval and signature of Marie Antoinette was conveyed to him in Paris. Rohan, entirely convinced, and wrapped up in his delusive dream, bought the necklace, secretly indeed, but in the name of the Queen. He carried it himself to Versailles, to an appointed place; there Madame de Lamotte handed it, in his presence, to an accomplice whom he believed to be one of the Queen's servants. The adventuress kept the necklace, sold the diamonds by degrees, paid her debts and lived on a grand scale.

Months passed. The Cardinal, who had been travelling, suspected nothing; he was only surprised that he had not received any other thanks from the Queen than those transmitted by Madame de Lamotte. The jeweller, on his side, began to feel anxious; he had not received the first promised payment at the date fixed, and he applied directly to Marie Antoinette. At first she refused to listen to him and forbade him ever to mention the necklace to her again; but when the unhappy jeweller protested that he should be ruined if she did not pay for the costly piece of his goods which the Cardinal de Rohan had bought for her, she imagined that she understood the matter: the Cardinal had made infamous use of her name to cheat the jeweller out of the necklace? This was theft, and the crime of lèse-majesté. She flew to demand justice from the King. Louis XVI., an honest man above all things, was shocked, and without hesitation proceeded to prompt and signal punishment. The Cardinal was summoned to the King's presence; he perceived by the Queen's words that he had been deceived; but in his confusion he could give no explanation, he stammered, he seemed to admit his guilt. The Queen hesitated no longer; she insisted that there must be a public trial before the Parliament, so that the impostor might be confounded, and the fact proclaimed that there was nothing in common between her and the wretch who degraded the Roman purple and the name of Rohan by theft.

We learn from Marie Antoinette herself what her first feeling was: "Everything had been concerted between the King and me," she writes to Joseph II.; "the Ministers knew nothing until the moment when the King had the Cardinal summoned, and questioned him in the presence of the Keeper of the Seals and Baron de Breteuil. I was there also, and I was really touched by the justice and firmness which the King showed at that terrible meeting. When the Cardinal entreated that he might not be arrested, the King replied on the moment that he could not consent to this, either as king, or as husband. I hope the affair will soon be ended, but I do not yet know whether it will be sent before the Parliament, or whether the culprit and his family will not contest it, but leave it to the clemency of the King. In any case I desire that this horror and all its details should be made thoroughly clear in the sight of all."

Alas! the affair was not destined to prove so simple as the Queen supposed it to be. The Cardinal accepted trial before the Parliament. Madame de Lamotte, her husband, and her accomplices appeared presently upon the stage, and were arrested, to the very natural astonishment of Marie Antoinette. "The Cardinal," she says, "has taken my name like a vile and clumsy forger.... Cagliostro, a mountebank, Lamotte, his wife, and one Oliva, a street-walker, are summoned with him; he will have to be confronted with them, and to reply to their objections. What an association for a Grand Almoner and a Rohan Cardinal!"

Very soon it became evident to everybody, except to the Queen, that the Cardinal had not been a cheat, but a dupe. The lengthy trial proceeded; its progress was marked by many puzzling and surprising disclosures. The name of Cagliostro, introduced by Madame de Lamotte, powerfully excited the popular feeling. Ostensibly, the Cardinal and Madame de Lamotte were the only persons under trial, and the sole defence of the former was that he had been deceived. But the name of Marie Antoinette was constantly brought forward: it was in reality she who was being tried, and many there were who would gladly have seen her at the bar with the others. There was one notable omission in the proceedings, the principal witness did not appear. Her absence deepened the obscurity of the case, irritated the public, and gave rise to the most insulting suppositions. The far-resounding trial which the Queen had demanded rejoiced the hearts of her enemies. A dreadful doubt arose in people's minds: the forger, the thief, was she the Queen of France? That doubt has troubled history even in our time, and we find Michelet, who has conjured up the past with unrivalled power, and who carries the prejudices and the infatuation of her contemporaries into his judgment of the Queen, still struggling with the inextricable difficulties of the Affair of the Necklace. His narrative reflects with terrible sincerity the alarm, suspicion and anger that filled the public mind.

The trial comes to an end. The guilt of Madame de Lamotte is clear; she is convicted and sentenced. Will Cardinal de Rohan be convicted? The Queen believes him guilty, but even supposing that he has been deceived, was it not because he thought Marie Antoinette capable of employing him as a go-between, nay, what am I saying? capable of selling herself for a necklace? This also was a crime against the royal majesty; the honour of the Queen was concerned in the matter of his conviction or acquittal. But who cared for the honour of the Queen at that moment? All the enmity against Marie Antoinette that had been accumulating throughout so many years manifested itself then, and her foes brought an unexampled pressure to bear on the tribunal: the women of the Rohan family besieged the judges with flattery, with bribery, and with threats. At last, on the 31st of May, 1786, the Parliament, the Grande Chambre being assembled, acquitted the Cardinal. The people of Paris, gathered in a vast concourse about the Palais de Justice, hailed with enthusiasm the triumph of the Rohans and the dishonouring of the once-adored Queen.

Marie Antoinette was not at the end of her humiliations. All she understood of the trial was that her ruin was desired; yet it haunted her like the remembrance of a bad dream, and its work was not yet done. While the Queen wept at Trianon, and the Cardinal was in banishment at the Abbaye de la Chaise-Dieu, Madame de Lamotte escaped from La Salpêtrière and fled to London. There she took her revenge for the rods with which she had been whipped and for the hot iron that had branded her on the shoulder, by publishing those odious Memoirs, of hate and lying "all compact," in which the Crown of France is pulled down into the depths of calumny and disgrace. Between the word of the Queen and the word of this hussy, France hesitated; before long she made her choice, and Madame de Lamotte's pamphlets caused the legend of the vices of Marie Antoinette to be definitively accepted. It was from them that Fouquier-Tinville took his arguments; by them he justified his award.

At this point we ought to get a clear view of the various responsibilities involved in the events that were approaching. Contemporary testimony makes known the people who authorized and propagated the calumnies against the Queen. The Comte de la Marck, who saw them at work, does not hesitate to designate them. "The pretexts for the accusations of the revolutionary tribunal against Marie Antoinette, in 1793," he writes, "must be sought for in the slanders and the lies spread *by the Court* from 1785 to 1788." These accusations were already to be found in obscene pamphlets which were circulated in the clubs, and passed on from the boudoir to the antechamber; they were also to be found in manuscript collections which were stamped, shameful to relate, with the arms of nobles, and bore women's book-plates. The allusions to Messalina and to Frédégonde, that filth which the Revolution was to stir up, were daintily conveyed in piquant verses most elegantly rhymed, and you sang them, fair ladies, sang them to fashionable airs at the choice supper-parties of your own particular "sets." But your windows were open, the passers-by in the street listened and repeated, and so your songs went down from the salon to the tavern. This "People," whom you teach to despise queens, wives and mothers, will bear in mind your lessons: the songs which they learned from you shall accompany you to the guillotine.

From the date of the "Affair of the Necklace," France hurried on towards the Revolution. Royalty had lost its last scrap of prestige. Marie Antoinette was discrowned already. In a fitful way she busied herself with the education of her children, thus seeking forgetfulness of the foul pamphlets and songs which assailed her. Again, she would rush madly into amusement, as though peradventure she might find oblivion there. The sojourn at Fontainebleau after the trial of the Cardinal was no less "dissipated" than on former occasions. Although she was now thirty years old, Mercy still continued to regard the Queen as "ignorant of, and having a distaste for serious affairs." It was then to be hoped, at least, that she would abstain for the future from interference in affairs of State? Unhappily she continued, on the contrary, to interfere in them, failing to perceive that her only chance of safety lay in letting herself be forgotten.

She was fatally imprudent in foreign affairs, and even her true friends made use of her. She blindly pursued the unfortunate Austrian policy which had already done her so much harm. Queen Caroline of Naples, her second son's godmother, took complete control of her. Marie Antoinette threw over the diplomatic agents at Naples, three good servants of the King, simply because they had spoken freely of the public scandals of her sister's Court at Naples. That Queen, also the wife of a Bourbon, who boldly delivered up her husband's kingdom to Austria, was a dangerous confidant for the Queen of France. The example of Marie Caroline must have been very alarming, when Cardinal de Bernis, the French Minister at Rome, ventured to say in writing to M. de Vergennes, or in other words to the King, "Beware lest it be suspected in Europe that Austrian influence can rule at Versailles as it rules at Naples!"

The Queen's infatuation is still more evident in the Dutch affair. Marie Antoinette ardently backed the claims of Joseph II. upon Maestricht and the opening of the Scheldt. All the traditions of French policy required that the Cabinet of Versailles should lend its support to the Dutch. The Ministers of Louis XVI. were fully agreed, and endeavoured to reconcile the national interest with the "susceptibilities" of the Austrian alliance.

THE QUEEN MARIE ANTOINETTE, MADAME ROYALE, AND THE DAUPHIN IN THE GARDENS OF TRIANON.

From the portrait by A. U. Wertmüller (Royal Gallery of Stockholm).

[illegible] over

[illegible] simply

[illegible] Court

[illegible] delivered

[illegible] the

[illegible] very

Rouse [illegible]

to the King.

[illegible]

[illegible]air. Marie

[illegible] and

[illegible]quired

But the Queen was in the hands of the Emperor, who was now flattering her in order to make use of her, and directed her through Mercy. She contended, single-handed, against her husband's Ministry, besieged and intimidated the King and wrung pledges from him which he could not keep. She browbeat Breteuil, finessed with Vergennes, and kept back his despatches, sending on those of Mercy beforehand, so as to advise the Emperor of the intentions of France in advance. On one occasion, she opposed the Minister so vehemently in the King's cabinet, that the former presented his resignation then and there to Their Majesties.

This state of things continued for eighteen months; it was a repetition of the Bavarian affair already narrated, which ought to have conveyed a serious warning to the Queen, and it was aggravated by the lapse of time which involved consequences of greater import. Marie Antoinette cheerfully compromised herself in this grave matter, for a brother who did not thank her in the least, and for the interests of a House which should no longer have been hers. Her interference became more widely known than was suspected at Court, and, once divulged, to misrepresent its motive and to magnify its results was an easy matter. In reality, mediation and diplomacy only had been employed, but a story was circulated that immense subsidies had been given to Austria, boxes packed with gold having passed the frontier. The most absurd inventions gained credence, in a short time people asserted unhesitatingly that Marie Antoinette had sent two hundred millions (livres) to Joseph II. to keep up the war against the Turks! These were ridiculous rumours, but such as might lead the popular imagination far, for it was dangerous that there should be an atom of truth in them.

So much for foreign policy. Was the Queen's action in home policy, in which she sincerely desired the welfare of the State, more fortunate? M. Loménie de Brienne, Archbishop of Toulouse, had been for a long time hoping to get into the Ministry through the influence of the Abbé de Vermond. Joseph II. had seen him formerly in his diocese, believed him to be a capable administrator and recommended him to the Queen. He owed nothing to the Polignacs, and when their "creature" fell from power, Marie Antoinette, who was beginning to shake off their yoke, immediately proposed him to replace Calonne. M. de Vergennes was quite recently dead, and the King, left to himself, could no longer refuse anything to his wife. The archbishop evinced his gratitude by taking her into all the counsels of the government, and affecting to give her the preponderating voice in every decision. "The Queen governs!" became the public cry. In reality, it was Brienne who governed; but the prelate-philosopher was not a sufficiently strong man to take the management of a disturbed kingdom, to resist the Parliaments in coalition, to carry out the reforms demanded by the Assemblies of Notables, and to remedy the financial situation which was becoming worse and worse. The public held this ephemeral Minister responsible for the accumulated errors of the past, and Marie Antoinette paid heavily for the archbishop's lack of genius.

Never had the enemies of the Queen such advantages against her as the situation then afforded. Her long-past extravagance was denounced as the gulf in which the public finances were swallowed up; it was currently discussed in pamphlets; those who had not been able to profit by it and those who profited by it no longer, agreed together to exaggerate and condemn it. The public allowed itself to be duped by this virtuous indignation. Sincere adherents of the Monarchy separated the cause of the King from that of the Queen. Epigram was the prelude of insult: the portrait of Marie Antoinette in the Salon of 1787, being removed temporarily from its frame, was significantly called *Madame Déficit*. (This malicious *bon mot* is ascribed by several of the Memoir writers to the Queen's brother-in-law, the Comte de Provence).

"Manifestations" in the streets, in August and September, 1788, testified to the growing ferment. One evening, at the Italian Opera, when the lamps were lighted, the spectators perceived a placard pasted on the front of the Queen's box, and read the following in large letters: "Tremble, tyrants, your reign is near its end!"

Marie Antoinette had to abandon Brienne and personally ask him to resign. Lamoignon, the Keeper of the Seals, followed him in his fall. The populace lighted bonfires on the Place de Grève and Place Dauphine, and burned the two Ministers in effigy, as they had previously burned Maupeou and Terray; but times were changed, and the cry: "Vermond's turn to-morrow!" was meant for the Queen. M. Necker had returned; his reinstatement as Minister of Finance was inevitable; it was peremptorily demanded by the will of the nation, and the urgent necessity for bold and thorough reform. Marie Antoinette, who had proposed this measure to the King, writes the following sad note on the morning of Necker's return: "There is no hesitating any longer; if he can set to work to-morrow, so much the better. It is urgent. I tremble—forgive me this weakness,—because it is I who bring him back. My lot is to cause misfortune." "If he does not succeed," she adds, "they will detest me all the more."

In the meantime, she set the example of diminishing the Court expenses; she allowed her gifts to her servants and to her friends to be withdrawn. Posts in the Queen's Household amounting to more than twelve hundred thousand livres were suppressed, and reimbursement was required. What sacrifices could have cost her so dear? She went farther still, as though the foreseen danger inspired her with the prudence she had lacked so long. She supported the Minister in his project for the double representation of the Tiers État at the approaching Assembly of the States-General. In this she did not hesitate to oppose the Comte d'Artois, who took offence and publicly manifested the decline of his affection for the Queen. This was the beginning of a disagreement which lasted during the emigration, and baulked the efforts of the royalists. But it availed the Queen nothing that she separated herself from her friends, backed the plans of the popular Minister, and urged the King, at least at the outset, along the path of liberal measures. It was the interest of too many people to widen the breach between her and France; the country was deceived with regard to every act of the Queen, and the voice of its sovereign reached it not.

One party especially, an entire party, had made it its business to prevent that reconciliation at the decisive hour; this was the Orléans clique. What were the causes that acted upon the Duc d'Orléans to make him the most inveterate enemy of the Queen? How was the youthful friendship of the Duc de Chartres changed into hatred fierce and mortal? We can guess how a campaign of disunion was carried on, through those ten eventful years, by certain associates of the duke, a band who lived at his expense and wrought upon his weak mind. The King's personal dislike to him was represented as the direct doing of Marie Antoinette; thoughtless sayings were envenomed, offensive sayings imputed to the persons about the Queen were invented. The rest was wrought by the vengeance of certain women at Court. In 1789, the rupture had long been complete.

The banishment of the Duc d'Orléans to Villers-Cotterets, for having defended the Parliament, merely accentuated a situation which was entirely to his advantage. The Palais Royal had become the centre of opposition to the Court, and the Prince of the Blood had allowed himself to be put at the head of the malcontents.

His numerous and daring friends kept a hold on public opinion by means of the press, the salons, and the cafés. They made popularity for their master at the expense of that of the royal family, by distributing money, pamphlets, and newspapers. There was something in this beyond the mean strife of personal enmity; there was the action of a political party, without precise views, but skilfully organized, which tended to nothing less than the overthrow of the Constitution. This party had not yet ventured to attack the King, every blow it struck was aimed at the Queen, always the Queen.

Such an attack is homage. The woman who deserved that homage was no longer the frivolous girl of past years, incapable of serious purpose. She was the mother of a Dauphin, the wife of a King. Her faults, even the gravest of them, were now to be explained by her maternal love, and by her profound belief in the Divine right of Monarchy. New qualities, unsuspected virtues, were revealed in Marie Antoinette, as the incapacity of Louis XVI. became more and more apparent. Those qualities came too late to save her, but came in time to exalt the part she played and to leave us her ennobled image. The years she still had to live placed an aureole around her doomed head, for she truly proved herself "every inch a queen" during the last agony of the kingdom.

That last agony was the Queen's also, and the whole reign had led up to it. Why should we be astonished that the Paris revolutionist hated Marie Antoinette most of all, that from the first day she was the exacted victim, she was the hunted prey? For fifteen years one woman had been pointed out to him as the national danger and the author of all his ills. In proportion as poverty, massacre, and war maddened him more and more, that idea became increasingly tenacious, and all his wrath was concentrated upon it. Criminal recollections, accusations all the more dangerous that they were vague, haunted the brain of the populace: Trianon, the favourites, male and female, the orgies of the Park of Versailles, the theft of the necklace, above all, the sale of France to Austria by the foreign woman who governed the King!

The legend that led the Queen to the scaffold was made up of many elements. In its composition we can trace the grumbling of Mesdames Tantes and the slander of Madame de Lamotte, the jests of Maurepas and the infamy of the satirical street-songs, the hostility of Monsieur to the mother of the Dauphin and the vindictiveness of Frederic II. against the daughter of Maria Theresa, the spite of the women of quality, the poverty and the rapacity of pamphleteers. Everybody lent a hand to the construction of that fateful legend; the Court and the Capital, Versailles and Europe, Rohan, Vergennes, Calonne, Philippe d'Orléans and Lauzun, princes and valets. Joseph II. aided the work without intending to do so, and the Comte d'Artois did the same without knowing what he was about. Marie Antoinette herself built it up, by her innocent levity, her diamonds, her Polignac, her long-lasting and thoughtless youth.

A day is destined to dawn upon the Queen of France when she will be forced to take account of the whole of that past life of hers. Not indeed as she had believed it to be; not as its hours had gone by to her consciousness; not as they will then be flitting in a vague, vaporous confusion about the mist-filled chambers of her memory; but as the people of the land hold it to have been, and as it shall be chronicled for the near and recorded to the distant epochs of that land's history. In that day she will not be allowed to retain any merciful ignorance of the things that have been laid to her charge. All will be revealed to her; the accusations founded on her trivial acts, heavy structures built upon the slight foundation of her youthful errors, in the craving for sympathy of a friendless girl at first, the credulity of a flattered woman at a later period. Many unexplained puzzles will solve themselves in the brief flash of terrifying light that will be shed upon her past; the origin of the merciless spite that had lurked under the tutored smiles and hypocritical homage of her family foes; the hatred that her artless and disproportioned generosity to the worthless few had inspired in the many who were eager to prey upon it, and would have proved themselves equally ungrateful. All these and more will the Queen apprehend and comprehend, when the daughter of the Cæsars, bereft of her mother and her husband, torn from her children, unable to conjecture the fate of her son, the most forlorn figure in all France, or perhaps in all the world, shall grow suddenly to the full stature of her soul. The purpose of the pamphlets will be made plain in that day. How and by whom?

A strange man, seemingly a magistrate after a fashion, will rise up before her, and explain all her life to her at full length, and the Queen will listen to the summing-up of her history in amazement, as one looking into a distorting mud-splashed mirror sees, but does not recognise, one's own face. This is what the strange man will say:

"Examination made of all the evidence... it ensues that after the manner of the Messalinas, Brunchilds, Frédégondes and Médicis, who were formerly called Queens of France, and whose names, for ever hateful, will never be effaced from the annals of history, Marie Antoinette has been, since her sojourn in France, the scourge and blood-sucker of all the French; that even before the happy revolution which has restored its sovereignty to the French people, she had political relations with the man who is called King of Bohemia and Hungary; that those relations were contrary to the interests of France; that, not content, in concert with the brothers of Louis Capet and the infamous and execrable Calonne, their Minister of Finance, with having dilapidated in a frightful manner the finances of France (fruit of the sweat of the people) for the satisfaction of her disorderly pleasures and the payment of the agents of these criminal intrigues, it is notorious that on several occasions she has had millions conveyed to the Emperor which have served him and still serve him to sustain the war against the Republic, and that it is by these excessive dilapidations that she has exhausted the national treasury...."

What is this extraordinary harangue? It is the acte d'accusation of Marie Antoinette, Veuve Capet.

the mist-filled chambers of his ... it to have been, and as it shall be ... the distant epochs of that land's ... to retain any ... charge ... ects, ... to the ... will ...

... ungrateful ...

... when the daughter ... husband, torn from her ... the most forlorn figure in ... grow suddenly to the full ... will be made plain in that day ... complete

A strange man, seemin... up before ..., and explain all ... will listen ... into a dis... ...'s own fate.

... the ... were formerly ... will ... her ... French, that ...ignty to the ... people, ... called King ... Bohemia and ... the interests of France: that, not content, in concert with the brothers of Louis Capet and the infamous and execrable Calonne, their Minister of Finance, with having dilapidated in a frightful manner the finances of France (fruit of the sweat of the people) for the satisfaction of her dissolute pleasures and the payment of the agents of these criminal intrigues, it is notorious that on several occasions she has had millions conveyed to the Emperor which have served him and still serve him to sustain the war against the Republic, and that it is by these excessive dilapidations that she has exhausted the national treasury...."

What is this extaordinary harangue? It is the "acte d'accusation" of Marie Antoinette, "veuve Capet."

LUDOVICUS DECIMUS SEXTUS FRANCORUM REX.

From the portrait by Duplessis.

Ludovicus Decimus
Rex

The [illegible]
nette was [illegible]
the an[illegible]
the Com[illegible]
respect [illegible]
reckon[illegible]
and nev[illegible]
the Com[illegible]
fund[illegible]
enforc[illegible]
at the [illegible]
edifi[illegible]
[illegible]
[illegible]
yield[illegible]
[illegible] would be [illegible]

THE SECOND CHAPTER.

THE COURT AND THE FÊTES.

The friends of the Monarchy have frequently reproached Marie Antoinette with a miscomprehension of her queenly functions, with having treated the ancient customs of Versailles too lightly, and sacrificed the duties of the Crown to her love of pleasure and to her private friendships. In some respects this censure is just. Her contemporaries have not erred in reckoning the familiar friendships of the Queen, and her love of pleasure and novelty at any price, as the first causes of the "disorganization" of the Court of France. Etiquette, which seemed to be inseparable from the fundamental principles of royalty, and had been invariably confirmed and enforced by the imperious will of Louis XIV., was set aside and destroyed at the caprice of a woman. A stone, it is true, was detached from the edifice by this means, but we may refuse to believe that the ruin of the entire structure was effected thus: the harm really done was the nation's learning by a dangerous example that certain ancient institutions had yielded to the first onslaught. While we must admit that she erred in this respect, it would be unjust to make Marie Antoinette solely responsible for the abrogation of etiquette, and, for a graver grievance, the decline of the royal prestige. Some of the Princes of the Blood, beginning with the Comte d'Artois, were more culpable than the Queen; and if she is to be censured for her rustic amusements, her sheep-folds, dairy, and theatre, what is to be said of the King, his plebeian habits, and the mornings devoted to his locksmith's forge? Besides, Marie Antoinette really strove to her very utmost to play a part which was too much for her. Notwithstanding the fleeting hours of freedom which she passed at Trianon or in her private rooms at Versailles, she did not always fail to remember that she was Queen of France; and she never attempted to evade the obligation of public representation imposed by national tradition upon the consort of the King.

The remembrance of the Queen retains its association with years of gladness and festivity which have not been blotted out by the tragic days that came after. Court balls and plays, sumptuous receptions of illustrious guests, great popular rejoicings on the occurrence of many public events, made that reign with which the old régime came to its end one of the most brilliant that France had ever seen, notwithstanding the prevalent poverty and the disquiet of men's minds. Marie Antoinette regulated and presided over the fêtes of her time with supreme tact and ability; if, indeed, by a singular fatality, she contributed to the fall of the Monarchy, it is only just to acknowledge that the Court of Versailles owed its final graces and its farewell smiles to her.

"What a day was that of the coronation!" exclaimed Marie Antoinette, "never in my life shall I forget it." Let us look back upon that day, or rather upon that week of popular and liturgical fêtes, and picture to our fancy the inauguration of the reign, with sound of drums and trumpets amid the loud rejoicing of the people.

Only the King, the heir of Charlemagne and of Louis XIV., the exceptional being whom the unction of Reims was to send back to Versailles consecrated by God Himself, as ruler of the nation and worthy to govern it, was personally concerned on this great occasion. The King only appeared in the cavalcades and ceremonies. This was regulated by an antique custom, which was restored for the occasion by the enemies of the Queen; but she did not care about it; she had come to Reims to see and to be seen, to afford a provincial populace the opportunity of knowing their sovereign, the pure young woman whose fair and gracious image was to efface the memory of the Pompadours and Du Barrys. In vain had she been left out of the official programme, not even allowed her public entry like Madame Clotilde and Madame Elisabeth; she was everywhere the first object of eager enquiry and interest. She arrived in the city at night and without escort, according to the instructions of the Grand Master of the Ceremonies; but crowds of peasants assembled along the roadside in the moonlight, greeted her with acclamation, and the next day an unparalleled spectacle was beheld at the archbishop's palace. The salons were thronged with such a concourse as had never before been seen: all the nobility of Champagne, Picardy and Lorraine, ladies and gentlemen, gathered around Marie Antoinette, and left her presence under the spell of her gracious welcome.

Great preparation had been made for the entry of the King and for the sacred ceremony. M. de la Ferté, the Intendant of the Menus-Plaisirs had been in the city for several days, with his army of workmen, in constant communication with the Chapter and the municipal officers, giving orders, distributing the articles of Crown furniture which had been brought from Paris, regulating the adornment of the Church with rich hangings, the putting-up of galleries, and the housing of the Court. The very smallest details of the solemnity were carefully arranged beforehand, and it promised to be very grand. Those among the inhabitants who remembered the famous coronation of Louis XV., wondered, and asserted that it would be surpassed by that of Louis XVI. M. de la Ferté was of the same opinion, but he was not free from uneasiness about the bill that he was running up, for the grant of the Menus had been far exceeded. Let us not dwell on such a trifle as this, however, but give ourselves up entirely to the splendour of the scene, as we take our places at a window in the Rue de Nesle, close to the balcony where the Queen sits, on Friday, the 9th of June, 1775, at one o'clock in the afternoon.

The French Guards, who keep back the crowd, line the way from the

Cathedral to the gate of the city, where the first triumphal arch is erected; beyond the gate, all along the faubourg and the high road, the City Militia and the company of Arquebusiers line the way. A picket of Archers of the Guard passes with the city trumpeters, preceding a group of gentlemen in black cloaks and white bands. These are the representatives of the city who are going to receive the King, a fleur-de-lys is embroidered on each man's coat. In about an hour a deep rolling volume of sound comes from the direction of the country, reaches the faubourg, the streets, and pervades the entire city : "Vive le Roi! Vive le Roi!" The gentlemen of the City Corps have met the royal coach half a league beyond the walls ; bent the knee before its doors, and been presented to His Majesty by the Intendant-General and the Lieutenant-General of the province. Then the coach resumes its way, and enters the city; the salutes by salvos of artillery from the ramparts begin, and all the bells ring out their welcome. Here comes the cortège! It is headed by a detachment of Musketeers, the Gendarmes of the Guard, the pages of the Master of the Horse, the carriages of the princes and the Court, then the King, escorted by his Household troops, followed by Body-Guards and Light Horse. The procession is closed by the Municipality and the Militia.

Throughout their whole length the streets are decorated with garlands, green arches, and symbolic statues. Inscriptions in French or Latin, laudatory of the virtues of Louis and anticipatory of the blessings of his reign, are placed at equal distances. The King salutes the Queen and the princesses as he passes, and the applause is redoubled. The people think he looks kind and well-pleased, and rush to the metropolitan church to get a better view of him.

Louis XVI. is received under the portico by the Cathedral clergy, wearing their most splendid vestments, and by the bishops of the province, who are grouped around the Cardinal de la Roche-Aymon, Grand Almoner of France and Archbishop-Duke of Reims. He kneels down at the threshold, is sprinkled by the cardinal with holy water, kisses the book of the Gospels, and enters the church processionally. The King of France, "l'évêque du dehors" comes last, behind all the prelates. He hears the *Te Deum*, receives the Benediction, and retires to the Archbishop's palace, which is to be his abode during his stay. The Queen is expecting him there, but she has hardly time to embrace him hurriedly: the official deputations are assembled and impatient to be admitted to the presence of the sovereign.

Each of these groups passes in its order before the King and is then received by the Queen in an adjoining salon. She listens to the several addresses of the Chapter, the Civic corps, the University, the Presidial and the officers of the Election.* "The virtues that characterize Your Majesty," say some of the speakers, "are inseparable from those graces which attend upon them." "When the happy destiny of France," say some others, "united the life of Your Majesty with that of our august monarch, an inexpressible feeling of joy was conveyed to all hearts; never had a more touching light, a day more pure, shone upon our heads." She has to reply to all these interminable and monotonous compliments. What a tiresome task for a young Queen! but what a pleasure also to do this so well as she does it, saying exactly the right thing to each and all of these good people, and using the very gesture of kindness and good-will that goes to their hearts!

The next day but one, Sunday, the feast of the Holy Trinity, is the day of consecration and crowning. At six in the morning prayers have begun in the Cathedral which is superbly decorated. A lofty structure in carved wood-work of the Corinthian order has been erected all round the choir, the reliefs and the flutings are gilded. Graduated rows of benches in amphitheatre form are divided at regular intervals by groups of statues and elegant stands for lights, and from the roof lustres are suspended. Behind the altar an orchestra, consisting of one hundred musicians, is stationed. Between the choir and the nave, a jubé has been erected, and there stands the throne under a cupola-shaped dais draped in violet velvet adorned with fleurs-de-lys. The pillars of the Cathedral are hidden by a profusion of drapery. Everything has been done to hide the hideous gothic, the architecture of barbarous times, which an enlightened age could not

* See Appendix, Note 5.

endure. When we do not look up to the vaulted roof we may easily believe ourselves to be in a fashionable church, one even more sumptuous than the Opera House. The officials of the Menus have done things very well indeed, and praise of their work is finding unanimous expression, when the Queen and the princesses come in and take their appointed places, facing those of the ambassadors. The Chapter already occupy their stalls. It is now seven o'clock. A march is played outside by trumpets, drums and hautboys. The cortège arrives from the Archbishop's palace preceded by a band. The King, in his long robe of cloth of silver, walks between the two bishops who have "awakened him" in his chamber of state. The ensuing ceremonial dates from the ancient times of the Monarchy, and the twelve peers of Charlemagne re-appear in it. The Constable of France, represented by the Maréchal de Clermont-Tonnerre, precedes them, holding the royal sword point upwards. Each of the representatives wears a costume specially designed for the occasion. What rich and splendid attire! What gold and silver stuffs, what doublets of white velvet, and plumed caps of antique shape! The six ecclesiastical peers wear only their pontifical vestments; but the six lay peers are marvellously attired: over a vest of cloth-of-gold each wears the ducal mantle of violet velvet, bordered and lined with ermine, and on his head the coronet of gold.

These great parts are played by six Princes of the Blood, Monsieur, the Comte d'Artois, the Duc d'Orléans, the Duc de Chartres, the Prince de Condé, the Prince de Bourbon. The young Duc de Chartres makes a dignified Comte de Toulouse; but the Comte d'Artois carries himself badly and is a poor representative of the Duc de Normandie of tradition. Little he knows that fifty years hence, on the 29th of May, 1825, he will come back to this same church, and that the last coronation at Reims will be his own.

Presently the Sainte-Ampoule is brought from the Abbaye de Saint-Remi, carried by the Grand Prior, who wears a golden cope, and rides a white palfrey caparisoned in cloth-of-silver. The passage of the Sainte-Ampoule makes the expectant crowd more patient. The archbishop advances to receive the phial and carries it to the altar. Immediately upon this the Bishop-Duke

THE QUEEN'S TRIBUNE AT THE CORONATION OF LOUIS XVI.

AT RHEIMS, on the 11th of June, 1775.

From the drawing by J. M. Moreau the younger, in the possession of MM. Delaroche-Vernet.

[illegible] vear-
[illegible] of [illegible]
[illegible] and [illegible]

[illegible] Blood, [illegible], the
[illegible] the Prince [illegible] Condé,
[illegible] a [illegible]
[illegible] badly [illegible]
Little [illegible] that
[illegible] book [illegible]
[illegible] his own
[illegible] Sobaye [illegible]
[illegible] and [illegible] white
the [illegible]
[illegible] advance [illegible] receive
[illegible] the [illegible]-Duke

de Laon and the Bishop-Count de Beauvais raise Louis XVI. from his seat and put the question to the Assembly: do they accept him as King? The assembly acquiesces by respectful silence instead of the acclamations formerly permitted by the ceremonial. The King, seated, and with covered head, then repeats aloud in Latin the traditional oath to maintain peace in the Church of God, to exterminate heretics, to defend his people against rapine and iniquity, and to govern with justice and mercy. He takes the oaths as Sovereign Grand Master of the Orders of the Saint-Esprit and Saint-Louis, and swears to enforce the observance of the edicts against duelling. His emotion in speaking makes the hearers feel that he regards all this seriously and not as a mere formula: when he mentions the extermination of heretics he hesitates and lowers his voice: this, it is said, is a promise he has made to M. Turgot.

The King is led to the altar, and his silver robe is removed; the Archbishop puts the spurs on him and girds him for a moment with the sword. Then they prostrate themselves, side by side, on a square of violet velvet embroidered with fleurs-de-lys. The King remains in this painful posture during the singing of the litanies by the choir and the bishops alternately; this is the humiliation of the Christian, prior to the exaltation of the Monarch. Now he is kneeling before the Archbishop, who has in his hands the paten of the chalice of Saint-Remi, with the sacred balm upon it. The anointing is begun; there are seven unctions, the first of the head, the others on the breast and the arms, which are uncovered successively by the assistant prelates. He is re-clothed with the tunic, the dalmatic, and the mantle; the palms of his hands are anointed; then the Archbishop invests him with the gloves and the ring, and gives him charge of the Sceptre and the Hand of Justice.

The King is consecrated, the "Sacre" is over; the ceremony of the crowning begins.

The Keeper of the Seals of France, discharging the functions of Chancellor, goes to the altar on the Gospel side; and calls up the twelve peers in succession to the side of the King. They range themselves, according to the antique tradition, around their equal of yesterday, their master to-day; they hold the crown of Charlemagne above his head for a few moments, and then, to the grand music of the cathedral organs the Archbishop places it on the trembling brow of the young King. At this moment, there is a stir in the Queen's tribune; every one looks towards it; she is obliged to retire to conceal her agitation. When she returns, she has dried her tears; "vivats" and clapping of hands greet her, and the King's eyes seek hers.

Now comes the enthronement. Louis XVI. is conducted to the jubé and takes his seat upon the throne; the peers, who have followed him, kiss him, and hail the eternity of the Monarchy thrice with cries of: *Rex vivat in æternum!* The trumpets blare, the doors are opened, a vociferating crowd enters, and for some minutes the naves are in a tumult. But the Archbishop is at the altar and now begins the Mass. The symbolical little birds are set free under the vaulted roof, heralds distribute medals of the "Sacre." Outside the Cathedral, discharges of artillery, salutes of musketry by the Guards who line the square, the clangour of innumerable bells from churches and convents, the clamour of the rejoicing city, announce to the country that the son of St. Louis has ascended the throne of France.

In the evening, a traditional festival, regulated in all its details by the monarchical ritual, took place. The Queen witnessed it, with the princesses, from a small balcony in an angle of the hall. At seven o'clock, the King, who had resumed his ordinary attire, joined her, gave her his arm and led her into the wooden gallery which served as a covered way from the Archbishop's Palace to the Cathedral. This gallery, one of the fine designs by Girault which were executed for the Sacre, formed a Doric colonnade painted in imitation of veined white marble and decorated with trophies; it embraced the whole façade of the church, and gave easy access to the square in front. The people and several personages of the Court had gathered there to admire it. The King and Queen forbade the exclusion of any, and came into the gallery without guards, allowing all to approach them. The public in the gallery and those standing in the square outside gave them an ovation, and kept it up for nearly an hour. The affability of the young sovereigns fairly won all hearts. Marie Antoinette was radiant, and the tenderness of the King's manner towards her was generally remarked.

Their Majesties remained some days longer at Reims. The Queen went to see a review of Count Esterhazy's regiment of hussars. Monsieur and the Comte d'Artois in the uniform of the dragoons charged at the head of the squadrons; the Duc de Chartres, the Prince de Condé, and the Duc de Bourbon participated in these military manœuvres. At the ceremony of the Order of the Saint-Esprit, which took place, according to custom, in the Cathedral, the Queen was applauded on entering her tribune, notwithstanding the sanctity of the place. On the day of the cavalcade to Saint-Remi, where Louis XVI. went through the town touching for the king's-evil, the princesses were seated in the balcony of a private house in the Rue Saint Denis. Marie Antoinette "supped full" of popular adoration in those days, the fairest of her reign. She enjoyed the love and admiration of her subjects without the admixture of one drop of bitterness; the heart of that chivalrous people whom God had put into her woman's hand was beating in harmony with her own.

The fêtes of the Sacre were immediately succeeded by those of the marriage of Madame Clotilde. The "solemn demand" was made to the King, her brother, on the 8th of August, by the Comte de Viry, Ambassador Extraordinary of the King of Sardinia, on behalf of the young Crown Prince of Piedmont, Charles Emmanuel. The Prince de Marsan, of the House of Lorraine, and M. de Tolozan, Introducer of Ambassadors, waited on him at his hôtel in Paris, Rue du Cherche-Midi. When the royal carriages returned to Versailles, the French and Swiss Guards were drawn up on each side of the outer court of the Château; the drums were beaten and the officers raised their hats in salute. M. de Viry was ushered into the Hall of Ambassadors on the ground-floor, where he remained until the hour of audience. Then, preceded by his cortège of equerries, pages and Piedmontese gentlemen, the Guards lining the path across the inner or royal court, he proceeded to the marble staircase, where he was received by the Marquis de Dreux-Brézé, Grand Master of Ceremonies.

The hundred Swiss of the King's Guard lined the stairs, in full uniform, slashed breeches, stiffened ruffs, and plumed "toques," holding their halberds; the standard was displayed on the middle landing, and the drummers held their sticks ready for the Envoy's first step upon the stairs. The cortège ascended to the beat of drums, crossed the Hall of the Body-Guards where a company was under arms, and entered the King's "great Cabinet." So soon as M. de Viry began to speak the King put on his hat, and motioned to M. de Viry to do the same. His Majesty then responded to the demand in terms of affection for the Court of Sardinia, and very graciously received the persons belonging to the Embassy who were presented to him.

On leaving the King's presence, the ambassador was conducted to the public audience of the Queen, then to that of Monsieur, Madame, and the Comte d'Artois. On his reception by Madame Clotilde he presented her, on behalf of the Prince of Piedmont, with two diamond bracelets, one containing a miniature of the prince. After this interview he paid his compliments to Madame Elisabeth, and to Mesdames Adélaïde, Victoire, and Sophie. We need not be alarmed at the duration of the task. Walpole tells us that "the whole royal family were *swallowed* in an hour."

This day gave great satisfaction at Versailles. The ambassador had given proof of both magnificence and good taste; his coaches, his dress, and his attendants would have done credit to a more important Court than that of Turin. It was known that he had received seventy-five thousand livres for his expenses, and that he purposed to expend a like sum on his own account. This beginning was a promise of fine fêtes to come, and that promise was fulfilled.

On the 16th of August, the ambassador returned, apparelled as before, for the ceremony of betrothal, and went in the first place to the apartment of Monsieur, who was to represent the future bridegroom, his wife's brother. After an exchange of official courtesies, they went up together to the King's apartment, where they found Louis XVI. seated at a table at the far end of his Cabinet. While M. de Viry was paying his compliments to the sovereign, the Queen, who had been informed of his arrival by M. de Brézé, came in, with the lofty bearing habitual to her on state occasions, by the Galerie des Glaces. She was preceded by the Comte de Tavannes, her gentleman-in-waiting, and the Comte de Tessé, her first equerry. Madame Clotilde followed the Queen, giving her hand to the Comte d'Artois, and the young princess, Madame Elisabeth, carried the train of her mantle of golden gauze. The Comtesse de Marsan, Governess of the Children of France, and the Princesse de Guéméné, reversionary Governess,* accompanied the two sisters. Then came Madame, Comtesse de Provence, and Mesdames Tantes, with their ladies, their gentlemen-in-waiting and their equerries, the Maréchale de Mouchy, lady-of-honour to the Queen, and the Princesse de Chimay, lady-in-waiting. The whole cortège entered the Cabinet, and took their places; the Queen facing the King at the other end of the table, the princes on one side and the princesses on the other. The Comte de Viry was alone in front of the table. M. de Malesherbes and M. de Vergennes, Minister and Secretary of State having the department of Foreign Affairs, then advanced; the latter, having read the beginning of the contract, presented a pen to the royal family, and all the French signatures were affixed in a column facing the signature of the ambassador. Monsieur placed himself on the right of Madame Clotilde, and Cardinal de la Roche-Aymon, wearing his rochet and stole was introduced, accompanied by two of the King's almoners and some of his own priests. The Cardinal Archbishop then performed the rite of betrothal. Afterwards, the ambassador accompanied Monsieur to his apartment, and was himself escorted back to Paris as before.

On the 20th of August, M. de Viry presented to Madame Clotilde on behalf of the King his master, and the Prince of Piedmont, a splendid parure of diamonds matching the bracelets which he had offered her on the day of the "demand." On the 21st, the marriage was celebrated in the chapel of the Château, Monsieur still taking the place of the absent bridegroom. After the ceremony M. de Viry paid his respects to the new Princess of Piedmont, and was afterwards sumptuously entertained

* See preceding chapter.

by the King's officers; this was a select dinner of forty covers in the Hall of the Ambassadors. At six o'clock he repaired to the Gallery where there was "grand appartement," that is to say, a reception open to all who had been presented at Court and where Their Majesties played cards in public. We cannot tell what were M. de Viry's reflections on seeing Marie Antoinette lose five hundred louis at lansquenet that evening, or whether the spectacle inspired him with greater esteem for the Court of France.

On the following day a fancy ball was given in the large theatre which was called the Opera, at the end of the north wing of the Château. The house was admirably adapted to fêtes of this kind, by means of a moveable range of boxes which could be used to shut off the stage, and, with the permanent boxes, formed a perfect oval. It was the most beautiful theatre in France, and the richness of the sculptural adornment, which had been finished just before the arrival of the Dauphine, had already made it famous in Europe. The wood-work was painted to resemble verd-antique marble, with all the reliefs in dead gold, and the draperies were of blue velvet. A modern architect has changed the tints, and unfortunately altered the character of this beautiful theatre, where the National Assembly found a refuge in disastrous later days.

Horace Walpole, still a traveller in his old age, and then in Paris, had gone to Versailles on the day of the ball, and owing to his numerous friends at Court was given a place on the Ambassadors' bench, behind the royal family. He wrote to the Countess of Ossory on the next day, describing the theatre as "the bravest in the universe, and yet taste predominates over expense," and giving the following charming sketch of Marie Antoinette : "What I have to say I can tell your Ladyship in a word, for it was impossible to see anything but the Queen! Hebes and Floras, and Helens and Graces, are street-walkers to her. She is a statue of beauty, when standing or sitting; grace itself when she moves. She was dressed in silver, scattered over with laurier-roses; few diamonds, and feathers much lower than the Monument. They say she does not dance in time, but, then, it is wrong to dance in time... You will want to hear more of the Court.

The new Princess of Piedmont (Madame Clotilde) has a glorious face, the rest about the dimensions of the last Lord Holland, which does not do so well in a stiff-bodied gown. Madame Elisabeth is pretty and genteel; Mademoiselle, a good figure and dances well. As several of the royal family are *drapés* for the Princesse de Conti, there were besides only the King's two brothers, the three elder Mesdames, the Princesse de Lamballe, and the Prince de Condé. Monsieur is very handsome; the Comte d'Artois a better figure and a better dancer." The witty Englishman's remark upon Madame Clotilde is his own version of the following current epigram upon "le gros Madame" à propos of the two Savoyard princesses, Madame and the Comtesse d'Artois:

> Le bon Savoyard qui réclame
> Le prix de son double présent,
> En échange reçoit Madame;
> C'est le payer bien grassement.

The Ambassador of the King of Sardinia responded to the Versailles reception by magnificent fêtes in Paris. On the 23rd of August, in the "Salles" of the new boulevard near the Barrière de Vaugirard, and described by Walpole as "a Colisée erected on purpose," he gave a concert and a supper of three hundred covers to the Ministers and Secretaries of State, to the officers of the Households of the King, the Queen, and the Princes, the ladies-of-honour and the ladies-in-waiting of the Queen, the Comtesse de Provence, and the Comtesse d'Artois, in a word to all the Court. Walpole excused himself, "having no curiosity to see how three hundred persons eat," but he went to the masked ball given two days later, and it is a great pity that he said nothing about it. Six thousand persons came to that ball, also the King and Queen. Paris was illuminated. At eleven o'clock the fête began with a display of fireworks, followed on the arrival of the royal family by a grand concert.

Immediately on her entry the Princess of Piedmont addressed the Comtesse de Viry, and presented her with two bracelets, each containing a portrait, one of the King, the other of the bride herself. The Queen enjoyed the ball immensely: she left the festive scene at three o'clock to return to

Versailles; but the dancing went on until nine o'clock in the morning: this was over-doing it. That evening there was a state performance at the theatre of the Château, and the next day Madame Clotilde set out for Turin.

The newsmongers laid hold of a little adventure of the Queen's at the Sardinian Ambassador's ball. Everybody was bound to wear a domino, even the King had submitted to that obligation. The Queen had accepted it with pleasure, accustomed as she was to the Opera masquerades, and after the departure of the King, she availed herself of her mask to return incognito to the ball, with the Duchesse de Vauguyon, who was masked like herself. A young foreign gentleman, taking them for two ladies of quality, entered into conversation with them rather familiarly, and the Queen amused herself by puzzling him. The fun of the thing was that she knew this gentleman, who was acting in an official capacity at the time, very well. He was the Marchese Caraccioli, the Neapolitan Ambassador. They talked for some time, pleasantly, but not indiscreetly, and with the freedom authorised by the domino. Nevertheless, great was the confusion of the Marchese when the Queen, at the moment of her withdrawal, removed her mask. This scene had witnesses, and although the anecdote is told in a kindly spirit by the narrator, it is easy to perceive how readily it might be perverted and made dangerous to the Queen's reputation.

In the meantime, the whole Court talked of it, and so well did Mercy know that it would reach the ears of Maria Theresa in an exaggerated form, that he was beforehand with the informer, and blunted the arrow by one sentence in his report to Vienna: "The Queen took pleasure in not being recognized at this ball; she had, among others, a conversation with the Ambassador from Naples; he had no notion that it was the Queen who was doing him the honour of talking to him." No doubt the "circle" of Madame de Marsan or Madame de Maurepas was less indulgent.

The departure of the gentle princess who was soon to reign over Piedmont did not deprive the French Court of any element of pleasure or gaiety. Marie Antoinette and her own friends were the sole representatives of youthfulness there; most of the other ladies adopted the austere tone of

Mesdames. During the following years the Queen strove against the dulness that beset the Court, and was assisted in her efforts by a few noble families, for instance that of Rohan-Guémené, who cheerfully spent other people's money while awaiting bankruptcy, lived in great style at the Château as well as in Paris, giving balls, banquets and concerts. Marie Antoinettte added ballets danced in costume to the attractions of the "soirées de Versailles." She gave charming entertainments at her Petit Trianon, and the Princes o the Blood hastened to follow her example.

The fête given by the Queen at her little château in August, 1776, in honour of the recovery of Monsieur and the Comte d'Artois, both of whom had had the measles, was the most brilliant of all. There was a supper, a play was acted in the Orangerie, with verses written for the occasion, and the garden was illuminated. Monsieur made his acknowledgments a few weeks afterwards, at Brunoy, like the intelligent prince and gallant brother-in-law that he was.

Brunoy was a superb residence, which had been built all at one time, in the beginning of the century, according to the ideas of a wealthy financier. It was destined to disappear some years later, with so many other beautiful creations of the same kind. The future King Louis XVIII. was much attached to Brunoy; but, when he returned to France, after the Revolution, he found it easier to restore the ruins of the Bourbon throne than those of his beloved country-house. The remembrance of the fêtes given by Monsieur is all that remains of Brunoy.

The first took place in the autumn of 1776. The Court had left Versailles to go to Fontainebleau, and was making a short stay at Choisy according to custom. Choisy being near Brunoy, Monsieur affected to be availing himself of the presence of Their Majesties in his neighbourhood to invite them to see his house; but there the Queen found a fête all ready prepared for her. A mimic fair with its booths and stage was set up in the grounds: this was a repetition of the fête at the Riding School at Versailles on the occasion of the Archduke Maximilian's visit; but the structure was more picturesque the variety was greater and the success more complete. Monsieur had caused verses and scenes in honour of Marie Antoinette to be added to the "parades" and to the plays, and she was much pleased. Of course these courtesies were not binding on anybody, and Monsieur as well Madame held themselves free, by every underhand means, to attack her whom they made their players laud to the skies as a divinity, and to fight her in the dark.

The prince repeated this fête in November, 1780, and the second is recorded as "the most noble and the most gallant ever given to the Queen." After dinner, Marie Antoinette was taken into the park. The "surprises" began at the first group of trees which she reached; for among them fifty mailed knights lay sleeping, and on their branches hung fifty lances and fifty shields.

From behind the trees came music, and mysterious voices told the story of the sleepers. Ever since the evanishment from the earth of those fair ones who had inspired the doughty deeds of the paladins of Charlemagne, the heroes of chivalry had lain in an enchanted slumber; but on the Queen's appearing, they awoke, arose, and seized their lances. Her coming had brought back to them the old desire for feats of arms. The whole company followed them into a richly-decorated arena, constructed according to the notion then entertained of the inclosure of the mediæval tournaments. Marie Antoinette was led to an estrade under a dais; the steps were already occupied by elegantly attired ladies invited from Paris. Trumpets sounded; fifty pages presented white horses and black horses to the fifty knights, who were ballet-dancers from the Opera. Two camps were formed: the party carrying the Queen's colours, white and blue, was headed by Auguste Vestris in person; the other was commanded by the ballet-master of the Russian Court. There was tilting at the "tête noire," and with the lance, then a combat "à outrance," so well done, that the spectators experienced the sensations of a real tourney. At the end of the fight the triumph of the royal colours was much applauded.

After this diversion came a play, accompanied by a ballet in pantomime consisting of allegorical scenes in honour of the august visitor. The fête ended with fireworks and an illumination: a lofty framework had been erected for the display at the highest spot in the park, the assembly read in letters of fire and under a dark sky: "Vive Louis! Vive Antoinette!" The weather was serene, and the success of the fête was perfect. This magnificent entertainment at Brunoy probably suggested those famous evening fêtes, which were shortly afterwards instituted at Trianon by Marie Antoinette and became the fashion in France.

The most splendid fêtes given by the City of Paris under the old régime were those of the reign of Louis XVI., in 1782. They have fortunately found a chronicler in the younger Moreau, and the municipal body that officially commissioned the engraver to perpetuate the memory of them made, for once, a fortunate selection. The choice of this artist was in itself a compliment to the Queen, for whom the fêtes were given, for she admired and patronized Moreau, and especially bore in mind a medallion portrait surrounded by Cupids, which had popularized her likeness at the beginning of the reign. Moreau felt confident of being still more successful in a series of compositions, all to the honour of Marie Antoinette. His delicate drawings, and the plates on which his graver wrought for many years, are the best witnesses to consult upon the famous days of 1782; they actually convey the sensation of the swarming of the people on the Place de Grève, and the glitter of uniforms and Court costumes under the lustres of the Hôtel de Ville. There are, besides, many written records useful to compare with the artist's faithful recital.

The Dauphin was born on the 22nd of October, 1781. Paris had always rejoiced in an event of this kind, and was doubly rejoiced on the present occasion. The representatives of the capital resolved to thank the Queen for their Dauphin after an unexampled fashion, but a very severe winter soon set in, and it occurred to the loyal gentlemen of the Hôtel de Ville that the season was ill adapted to public rejoicings, and they proposed to put them off. But the Queen asked laughingly whether M. le Prévôt des Marchands and MM. les Echevins meant to wait for the child to be old enough to dance at the fête: upon this, they had to carry out the original project.

Never had fête so much previous criticism to encounter. The public deplored its cost, while the poor were so sorely in need of relief, and the finances of the city were so heavily in debt, that the contractors for the works could not get a "sol" on account of their advances. Dark rumours prevailed : it was said that the Paris thieves had given rendez-vous there to all their brethren of the provinces, so that they might "work" the crowd with safety and success, that English emissaries in the city were to foment disturbances at nightfall, and anonymous placards, posted up in the dark hours, announced that "the four corners" of Paris would be set on fire. The Lieutenant-Général of Police held a consultation with M. Amelot, Minister of the King's Household, and the Maréchal Duc de Biron, Colonel of the French Guards. It was decided at this conference that bands in the open air should be multiplied as much as possible, and the public refreshment stands placed at a distance from the Hôtel de Ville, so as to divide the crowd and prevent it from assembling in a mass at any one point, especially at the moment of the display of fireworks.

The extreme precautions taken to ensure the security of the multitude frightened people still more. Barriers had been erected all along the quays to prevent persons from being shoved into the river by the pushing of the crowd ; the boatmen and the swimmers and divers of the Seine were stationed there with their boats; places of rescue were provided in all the river-quarter; the doctors and priests of the parish of Saint-Jean-en Grève held themselves in readiness to attend injured persons. All this made the Parisians uncomfortable, and the precautions were discussed on door-steps from the Rue Saint-Denis to the new boulevards, in intervals of reading a pamphlet containing a programme of the approaching fête by the sieur Moreau, architect, "director-general of the city buildings and author and director of the plans of the said fête."

Let us take a glance at what the Paris crowd saw on Monday, the 21st of January, 1782, the day fixed for the churching of the Queen and the great fête at the Hôtel de Ville. The Court had arrived on the previous day at the Château de la Muette, to remain there until the Thursday.

The Queen sets out at half-past ten for Notre-Dame, by way of the Quai des Tuileries, the Pont Royal, the Quai des Théatins, the Pont Neuf,

THE ARRIVAL OF THE QUEEN AT THE HOTEL DE VILLE OF PARIS,

on the 21st of January, 1782.

From the drawing by J. M. Moreau the younger. in the possession of MM. Delaroche-Vernet.

the Quai des Orfèvres, the Rue Saint-Louis, the Marché Neuf and Rue Neuve-Notre-Dame. One hundred of the Body-Guards only and a few of the State coaches with eight horses form the cortège. Her Majesty is accompanied by Madame Elisabeth, Madame Adélaïde, the Duchesse de Bourbon, Mademoiselle de Condé, the Princesse de Lamballe and the Princesse de Chimay. Along the whole of her route the Queen, who is radiant, is greeted with enthusiasm, and in her turn acknowledges the welcome of her people with beaming smiles. She alights under the porch of Notre-Dame, with her companions; they are all a good deal embarrassed by their spreading hoops. The clergy of the Metropolitan Church pay their compliments to her. At the end of the nave she kneels down upon the flags, and, like any humble bourgeoise, says the prayers appointed for the Churching of Women, makes her Act of maternal Thanksgiving, then goes up to the Choir and hears Mass.

On leaving Notre-Dame it is the custom to proceed to Sainte-Geneviève. The coaches return to the Marché Neuf, pass over the Pont Saint-Michel and along the Rue de la Vieille-Boucherie, and ascend the hill belonging to the University by the Rue Saint-Séverin, the Rue Saint-Jacques, the Petit Marché, the square of the new church of M. Soufflot, and the Place Saint-Etienne-des-Grès. The Abbé of Sainte-Geneviève receives the Queen at the head of his monks; she venerates the relics of the Saint and returns to her coach. But the people on the left side of the water must also be allowed to see the joyful mother of their Dauphin; so the coaches lumber heavily and noisily through the narrow and ill-paved ways of that gloomy quarter. What a crowd of heads fill up the windows in the streets of Saint-Thomas, Enfer, Vaugirard, Quatre-Vents, La Comédie, and finally the Rue Dauphine. Now the cortège reaches the Pont Neuf again, and presently the sloping roofs and tall chimneys of the Hôtel de Ville of Henri IV. come into view.

At the entrance, the Queen receives an address from the Duc de Cossé, Governor of Paris, and a second from M. Lefebvre de Caumartin, Provost of the Merchants of Paris, who presents the City Corps. She is then conducted to her apartment to await the arrival of the King.

His Majesty, meanwhile, has set out in great state. On his route along the quays the French Guards line the way on one side, the Swiss Guards on the other. With the King are his two brothers, the Duc de Lambese, Grand Equerry of France, the Duc de Coigny, First Equerry, and the Duc d'Ayen, Captain of the Guards. The Princes of the Blood, Orléans, Condé, Conti, offended at not having received a special form of invitation, have abstained from coming. The people hardly notice their absence, however, they are too busily occupied in picking up the small silver coins which one of the King's officers scatters among them. It is said that he also dispenses commemoration medals as large as a crown worth three livres.

The coach arrives at the Hôtel de Ville, leaving vociferous "vivats" and some victims of the crush behind it. It is nearly three o'clock and everybody is hungry. But, before Their Majesties can take their places at the civic table, they must show themselves from the wooden gallery that has been erected facing the river, and there receive, to quote the language of the time, "testimonies of the public joy, very proper to excite their sensibility."

The banquet takes place in this gallery, which is adorned with flowers, lustres and draperies. A sheet of looking-glass at the back extends the view. The table is laid for sixty persons ; the ladies only are seated at it, with the King and the Queen, Monsieur and the Comte d'Artois; the latter are the only men who may eat at the royal table in public. In the drawing by Moreau he has contrived to give a pleasant variety to the long row of feminine forms, with a busy crowd of servants and curious spectators at their backs. Marie Antoinette sits beside the King, who is talking with M. de Caumartin, and seems to compliment him on the magnificence of the reception.

During this time, one hundred and forty persons of the Court were feasting in the Hôtel de Ville itself, and the other invited guests were eating in all the rooms everywhere. But the King remained at table for an hour and a half only, and as there was some delay in the serving of the other tables, and all had to be removed at the same time, there were

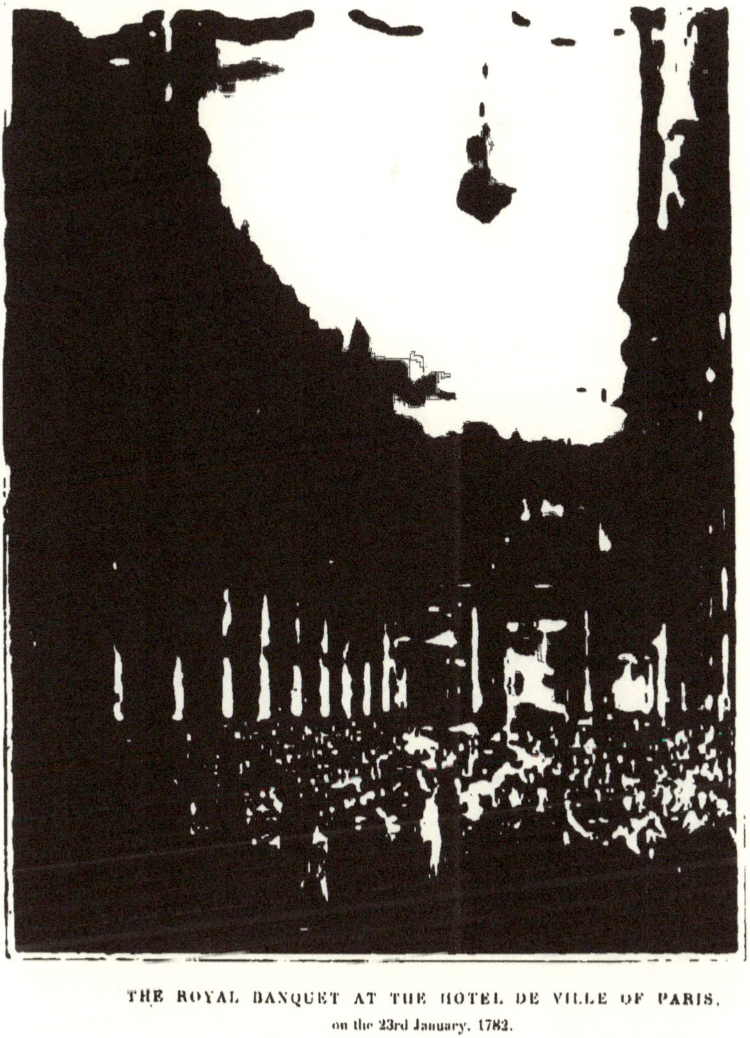

THE ROYAL BANQUET AT THE HOTEL DE VILLE OF PARIS,

on the 23rd January, 1782.

Drawn by J. M. Moreau the younger, in the possession of MM. Delaroche-Vernet.

[illegible] Majesty [illegible] Garde [illegible] Lambes [illegible]

[illegible] order to the [illegible] and curious [illegible] who [illegible] the [illegible]

[illegible] were [illegible] were [illegible] at table for [illegible] of [illegible] there were

a good many malcontents; the dukes and peers in particular had dined on butter and radishes.

The company moved into the Salon de Jeu, and when it was dark, returned to the wooden gallery. A box, richly draped and canopied had been prepared for the King and Queen, with tribunes for the Court on either side; those intended for the municipality were placed against the wall of the illuminated Hôtel de Ville. The square swarmed with people. At half-past six the show began, with Bengal fire on every side, and the first rockets went up amid shouts of admiration from the crowd. The set piece represented the Temple of Hymen raised on a high basement of rocks, with fountains which threw columns of sparkling water into the air, and figures symbolical of the welcome of France to the Dauphin. Some rain had fallen during the day, and a few of the effects were spoiled, but the fountains and cascades were set on fire with entire success, and two fiery pillars in front of the Temple held aloft the royal crown, to the special admiration of the people.

The illuminations were general and the crowd pervaded Paris until late at night. The interior of the court-yard of the Luxembourg was particularly admired, with its longs lines of light upon the façades. Monsieur took good care to let the public see how much he rejoiced at the birth of this Dauphin, who came to destroy his secret hopes. The Queen's milliner, Bertin, opposite the Cloître Saint-Honoré, had distinguished herself by going to greater expense than her neighbours. In the meantime the fête at the Hôtel de Ville had been brought to a close by the show of fireworks. Their Majesties had graciously thanked the Governor, the Provost, and the Echevins. On their return the cortège passed through the Rue du Roule and the Rue Saint-Honoré, in order that the royal party might see the illuminations. The Queen's carriages made a brief pause at the Hôtel de Noailles, where the Marquis de la Fayette, who had recently arrived from America, was staying. Marie Antoinette, who had just been told this by the Marquise, was pleased to permit the young hero to salute her at the door of her coach. The cortège afterwards proceeded to the Place Vendôme, the Rue Saint-Honoré, the Rue Royale, and the Cours-la-Reine. A great crowd was assembled in the Place Louis XV., where the illumination of the colonnades, facing the Palais Bourbon, on the other bank of the river, which was also illuminated, produced a splendid effect. As the cortége passed slowly to the Palace gates loud acclamations greeted the King and Queen; shouts of "Vive le Roi! Vive la Reine! Vive Monseigneur le Dauphin!" accompanied and followed it. Alas! Where were these good Parisians eleven years later, and what was the popular cry in the same place, on the same day of the year, the 21st of January, 1793?

The first fête was then indisputably successful. The precautions taken by the Municipal authorities had prevented any accident, and the typical bourgeois of Paris, who had been so terribly frightened, willingly acknowledged "that the day was worthy of being recorded in the annals of the nation." All had shared in the rejoicings. In the previous week the Queen had sent one hundred thousand livres to the Curés for the poor. In all the principal places open-air orchestras and dancing-halls were erected. Bread, wine, and meat had been distributed everywhere.*

The second fête, a masked ball, given on the 23rd of January, was not so faultless. The arrangements for arrrival and departure were imperfect. Carriages could not be brought up to the doors of the Hôtel de Ville, and the guests having passed those doors, found thenselves among a disorderly crowd which included the scum of Paris. Thirteen thousand tickets had been distributed officially, but a great number of these were used several times, and many persons had procured others, so that the crowd was greater than the vast building could contain. The refreshment tables supplied almond biscuits, brioches, bonbons, dried fruits, oranges, pressed apples, ices, orgeat, lemonade, syrups and wine; towards morning capons and rice were served; "but," says the chronicler of these details, "the greedy crowd of people of the lowest class who had been too easily

* An immense number of turkeys, each divided into four portions, formed a part of the provisions; this gave rise to the following punning compliment: "Il n'y avait aucun reproche à faire à ces messieurs de la Ville, qui s'étaient mis en quatre pour regaler le public."

allowed to get in, and who never left off eating, made it difficult for respectable persons to approach the refreshment tables."

There was, however, one grand moment in the evening, the arrival of the King and Queen. Their presence was not expected; but they had been so pleased with the Monday's fête that they wished to go to the popular entertainment in order to thank the people of Paris. They supped at the Temple with the Comte d'Artois, and reached the Hôtel de Ville at half-past twelve. The Queen dressed at the abode of the City Treasurer, and entered the ball-room, followed by forty ladies, with her mask hanging on her arm. She found it difficult to get through the crowd; at one moment she cried out that she was suffocating, and the King had to force a passage for her roughly with his elbows. But the rumour that the King and Queen were present spread quickly, and way was then made for them to pass freely through the ball-rooms. Marie Antoinette surveyed the spectacle presented by the Place de Grève, from the upper part of the same gallery from whence she had witnessed the show of fireworks at the Monday's fête. She was recognized, and instantly greeted by "vivats" and clapping of hands. She then returned to the ball-rooms, beaming with smiles, delighted with this festival where all eyes were turned upon her. In the engraving by Moreau we see her as she walks, smiling, behind the King, who is always grave, and turning towards the Comte d'Artois with the proud and gracious movement of a happy woman.

A few days after the celebration of the birth of the Dauphin by the City of Paris, the Body-Guards in their turn gave a superb ball to the Queen at the Versailles Opera House. The fête had been retarded on account of the illness of the Comtesse d'Artois; but this had given time for leisurely preparations, for testing the lighting of the theatre and making its decoration a masterpiece of taste. The Memoirs of the time are eloquent of praise; some remark that "the refreshments were in profusion and there was enough for everybody;" others, that "a rare and sustained politeness reigned during the whole entertainment." The Body-Guards' ball is contrasted maliciously with that of the Hôtel de Ville, and the City Provost having come there "to gape," as the chronicler impertinently puts it, an insolent mask asked him whether he came to learn how to give fêtes?

There was a "double" ball, full-dress and masked. The first began at five o'clock and ended at eleven; the second and most splendid, began at one o'clock and lasted until seven in the morning. All the Court was present. Light silks and rich laces mingled with the glittering uniforms, and formed a brilliant display against the dark background of the boxes. There was a great deal of dancing. The King and Queen moved about through both balls. It was the custom that the oldest officer of the Guard should open the balls with the Queen; this honour fell to M. de Prisy, who walked a minuet with her. But, to do the greater honour to her dear regiment of blue-coats, Marie Antoinette was pleased to give a contredanse to a junior member of the corps. She chose one of those who were doing the honours of the fête, M. de Mouret, of Tarbes, one of the handsomest men in the company of the Duc de Noailles. The young gentleman was rather shy at first, but the kindness of his sovereign's manner soon put him at his ease; he danced with her, "transfigured with joy," and his comrades in their enthusiasm cried "Vive la Reine!" "It was as much as they could do," says a sly spectator, "to keep from crying 'Vive le Roi!'"

This was one of the Queen's brightest days. But there are points of comparison all along the course of her history which suggest themselves irresistibly to our minds. These brilliant narratives of the past, written by contemporaries, without misgiving or reservation, in the spirit of the moment, summon up the phantoms of the future, and amid the music of the festival we hear the muffled distant tread of menacing Nemesis. The theatre, for instance, where the Body-Guards are celebrating the birth of their Dauphin, recalls that other memorable fête, their banquet of the 1st of October, 1789. Then the evil days had come, and when Marie Antoinette with her son entered the noisy banqueting-hall, where every man wore the white cockade of fidelity, the "vivats" that welcomed her

THE MASKED BALL GIVEN AT THE HOTEL DE VILLE OF PARIS,
on the 23rd January, 1782.
Drawn by J. M. Moreau the younger, in the possession of MM. Delaroche-Vernet.

The

there

the spirit of the

amid the

Nemesis The

rating the birth of

banquet of the

and, when Marie

ball, where every

that welcomed her

had another meaning than those of the earlier time: they told the Queen that her partners in the dance of 1782 were going to die for her, as indeed they did die, on the 6th of October and the 10th of August.

In the spring of the same year, both the Court and the City were occupied with the arrival and stay of the Comte and Comtesse du Nord at Paris. Under this strange name the Grand Duke of Russia, who was afterwards Paul I., and his wife, a princess of Wurtemberg, were travelling. Baroness Oberkirch, her friend, has given interesting reminiscences of the Grand Duchess Marie to the world: she was in attendance on Her Imperial Highness, and was present at all the fêtes.

On the 20th of May, the Grand Duke and his consort made their entry at the Château. While the prince was being received by the King, the Comtesse de Vergennes, wife of the Minister of Foreign Affairs, conducted the Grand Duchess to the Queen's apartments. Marie Antoinette received her in her sleeping-chamber with all her ladies. So curious was everybody to see the future Tsaritza that the youngest daughter of the Duchesse de Polignac got leave from the Queen to slip in close to the royal couch. The Grand Duchess was rather stout, but had agreeable, simple manners. She wore very fine jewels and was richly attired. It was said that her first visit in Paris had been to the Queen's milliner, Mademoiselle Bertin, who had dressed her most splendidly in a brocade gown edged with pearls; the petticoat was stretched on a hoop six ells in circumference.

Marie Antoinette did not like the imperial family of Russia, and knew how hostile Catherine II. was to her; but she was charmed at once by the amiability of the Grand Duchess; after a few moments she talked to her like a friend, questioned her about her children, and the education she was giving them, enquired into her tastes and what could be done for her pleasure. The Grand Duke appeared, and then the conversation turned on the recent visit of Their Imperial Highnesses to the Emperor at Vienna, their journey, and their stay at Venice, where they had been so brilliantly entertained. The ice was broken, and the Queen, when her guests took leave, pressed them to visit her often.

A small apartment on the ground-floor, looking on the lawn of the Orangerie, had been placed at the disposal of the imperial pair. Marie Antoinette attended in person to every detail of the preparations for them, following her brother's careful instructions precisely. The Grand Duchess had a harpsichord and heaps of flowers in her room; the Grand Duke had plans of Versailles and its neighbourhood, and portfolios of engravings which he liked to turn over, in his. They retired to this apartment after the presentations, and received visits from some persons of the Court. They dined aftewards with the royal family in the King's apartment, and Louis, who had as usual been rather stiff during the morning interview, was more at his ease, while the Queen resumed her air of affectionate welcome, and enchanted the Grand Duke. After dinner they went to her apartment, and the whole Court assembled in the Salon de la Paix for a concert. Legros, from the Opera, sang, and also Madame Mara, from Saxony, who was the favourite singer of the year. Persons who had been presented, but had not been specially invited to the concert, were accommodated with folding-stools in the Galerie des Glaces, so that they might hear the music. The Château was illuminated as on drawing-room or "grand appartement" days.

"A thousand lustres," says Baroness Oberkirch, "hung down from the ceiling, and candelabra with forty wax lights in each stood on all the consoles. The orchestra was placed on tiers of benches. No idea can be given of the splendour and the richness of it all. The toilettes were miraculous. The Queen, beautiful as the day, animated the whole with her brightness."

Our illustrious foreigners wanted to see everything in Paris; the theatres, the churches, the Bibliothèque du Roi, the Parliament, the Academy, the Invalides. They visited the Sèvres Porcelain Manufactory, the picture-gallery belonging to the Duc de Chartres, the "Folie Boutin," and even the *petite maison* of Mademoiselle Dervieux. They went to the Opera ball one night with Marie Antoinette. They dined at Sceaux with the Duc de Penthièvre, the Comte d'Artois gave them a concert at

Bagatelle, the Prince de Condé a shooting-party by torchlight at Chantilly. But the Court and the Queen brought them back continually to Versailles. Baroness Oberkirch went thither for whole days on her own account: when she was not retained by her august friend, she was to be seen going about from one apartment to another, invited everywhere, dining with the wife of a minister, witnessing Court functions, or writing her name in the book of one or another of the official ladies. The baroness, who was enchanted at being so warmly received, and slightly intoxicated by French life, gives, in her rapid and flattering sketches, a picture of the Court of France as it appeared to those travellers who had no time to learn its realities. Such spectators see nothing but the outside of things, but they sometimes see that outside thoroughly.

Let us ask this witness of ours, for instance, to tell us about one of the plays that were given at the theatre of Versailles for the Comte and Comtesse du Nord. The Queen had caused the baroness to be placed in the King's small private box behind her own, and had spoken to her several times; we may be sure that everything seemed faultless to the foreign lady on that evening: "The opera," she says, "was *Aline ou la Reine de Golconde*, taken from a story by M. le Chevalier de Boufflers, to whom, it appears, something of the kind happened. The words are by the Sieur Sedaine, the music is by M. de Monsigny, and the arrangement of the ballets is by M. de Laval, ballet-master to the King. The music is charming and was admirably executed. The dances charmed me most; to what a pitch of perfection has that voluptuous art been brought! Those in the first act are by the elder M. Gardel, those in the second by M. Vestris, and, lastly, those in the third by M. Noverre. The scenery was extraordinarily fresh and real-looking; one would have wished to be Aline to reign over such a delightful country."

After these plays, the baroness would sup with the Princesse de Chimay or Madame de Mackau. Sometimes, she returns to Paris at three o'clock in the morning, again taking that nocturnal drive which all the Court ladies found so trying. She has a headache, and being no longer afraid of crushing her gown, or bringing down the edifice which forms her head-dress, she sleeps, overpowered with fatigue, in the carriage. But in spite of all this she is delighted, enchanted, and the next day when she makes notes of the excursion, in which trifling conversations with the Queen occur frequently, the most charming expressions flow from her pen.

Marie Antoinette was profuse in her kindness and attention to the Grand Duchess. At Sèvres she was shown a magnificent toilet service of lapis-lazuli porcelain mounted in gold, a recent masterpiece of the royal manufactory; this she greatly admired. The mirror was supported by the three Graces at whose feet exquisite little Cupids played. "That is for the Queen, of course!" exclaimed the wondering princess at her first glimpse of the service; but on a close approach she recognized her own arms on every piece. The service was a gift from Marie Antoinette. On the occasion of the first play given at Versailles for the imperial guests, the Queen said to the Grand Duchess: "It seems to me, Madame, that you have the same defect as myself, rather short sight. I correct it by a glass set in my fan; will you try how this one suits you?" She presented a fan ornamented with diamonds to the princess; who tried the glass and found it perfect. "I am so glad," said Marie Antoinette, "and I beg you to keep it." "I accept it with pleasure," answered the Grand Duchess, "since it enables me the better to see Your Majesty."

The two princesses went together to Marly, where the fountains played for them the whole day and they exchanged confidences. A few days later the scene of meeting was Trianon, but this time at a great fête, for which the most sumptuous toilettes of the season had been reserved. At six o'clock in the morning Baroness Oberkirch was awakened by her maid to have her hair dressed and to be put into full Court costume. "I tried for the first time," she says, "a thing very much the fashion but very uncomfortable; small flat bottles curved to the shape of the head, containing a little water to moisten the stems of the real flowers and keep them fresh in one's head-dress. This was not always successful, but when one did manage it, the effect of spring flowers on one's head in the midst of powdered snow produced an incomparable effect." The Comtesse du Nord also had a singular head-dress, a little bird in precious stones set on a spring hovered above a rose with every movement of the wearer. We shall return to this fête, one of the finest ever given by Marie Antoinette, when we follow the Queen to Trianon.

The last entertainment for the Comte and Comtesse du Nord was a ball at Versailles in that great Gallery whose innumerable mirrors had so often reflected the changing images of the Court of France since Louis XIV. The ladies who danced wore white satin dominos with small hoops and trains. The princesses gathered about the Grand Duchess to get a close view of her famous chalcedonies, the finest in Europe. Marie Antoinette danced with the Grand Duke. The latter, whose fortunate facility for saying the right thing at the right moment had already gained him a reputation for wit in Paris, made a singularly àpropos speech to the King when walking through the Gallery. The company naturally collected about them, and Louis XVI. remarked aloud, in a tone of displeasure: "We are too much crowded here." The Comte du Nord stepped back slightly, with all the rest, then said immediately: "Pardon me, Sire, I reckoned myself among your subjects, and like them, I thought I could not approach Your Majesty too closely." Louis XVI. gave his hand, with his kindly smile, to this flatterer of a novel kind.

On leaving the official ball, Their Imperial Highnesses went to supper at the apartment of the Princesse de Lamballe, at the end of the Château. There was only a small party. After supper the royal family played at loto; then a lady took her seat at the harpsichord and the Queen danced a contredanse. This little ball was much more lively than the other, especially after the departure of the King, who merely put in an appearance. "Madame d'Oberkirch," said the Queen that evening, "do speak a little German to me, so that I may know whether I remember it." When the baroness had obeyed her, she thought a while; then said: "Yes, I am glad to hear the old Teutonic tongue again; but the French! It seems to me, spoken by my children, the sweetest language in the universe." A few days afterwards the Comte and Comtesse du Nord left Paris to return to St. Petersburg, and their departure put an end to the intimacy of the two princesses, which had grown up amid the shady groves of Marly and Trianon.

The plays that offered one of the chief attractions to the foreign princes who visited Versailles, were not exceptional pleasures for the Court. During the whole of the winter, from December to Easter, the three companies from Paris theatres under the administration of the Menus-Plaisirs gave performances at Court alternately. On Tuesdays, the company of the Comédie-Française gave tragedy, on Thursdays, comedy; Wednesdays were devoted to the Opéra-Comique associated with the Comédie-Italienne. The Grand Opéra company played six times each winter, on Wednesdays. In summer there was no such regular rule, but the Court, even while moving about, could not do without plays and actors.

The Court had them then, plays and actors, everywhere; at Fontainebleau, at Choisy. At La Muette the theatre was a wooden building only, at Marly it was roofed with slates, and had been erected in a hurry in the Bosquet de Bacchus, on an occasion when the Queen was impatient for a play. Little stages which could be put up and taken down easily, enabled improvised representations to be given in the apartments or the gardens of the various royal residences. This was done more than once at Versailles, in the Orangerie. After the birth of Madame Royale, a stage which she could see from her bed was erected in front of the door of the Queen's room. This was pushing the love of the drama very far. The Opéra de la Cour (or great theatre) was seldom used, as the least important representation there involved enormous cost; almost all the plays took place in a much less spacious theatre which had been erected at the Queen's request, in the right wing of the Cour Royale. Gabriel, the architect, had destroyed the harmony of that wing, which was of the Louis XIII. and Louis XIV. order, by his mock Greek style. The premises were commodious, the stage was spacious and well-contrived, and the decoration very rich; the boxes were hung with blue silk.

The number of the performances was considerable. In the year 1777 it amounted to ninety-three : forty-eight by the Comédie-Française, twenty-four by the Comédie-Italienne, seven by the Opéra, two parody-plays, two proverbs, and ten ballets, apart from plays. The theatre, including the stage itself, was lighted by wax candles only, at very great cost. The orchestra on the contrary consisted merely of the musicians of the Chapel Royal, and was not always in unison with opera airs. The performances at Fontainebleau were the most costly : in addition to the journeys of the theatrical companies and carriages for their use, their lodging and maintenance for several days had to be paid for. The average cost of the whole "service" amounted to two hundred and fifty thousand livres annually : this was indeed very far from the millions at which it was rated by malevolent malcontents; but the fortuitous aid of mourning, as imposed by etiquette, which came in more than once, and the vigilance exercised by the Menus at all times, were urgently required to reduce the sum to this figure.

The Intendant at that time, M. de la Ferté, was quite equal to his task. He utilised old scenery and decorations, had the old costumes which were laid by in store repaired, and opposed unnecessary journeys and superfluous gratuities. But he had to contend against the purveyors, whose interest it was to promote waste in every way, against the actors, always insatiably greedy for money and suppers, but especially against the First Gentlemen of the Chamber. Each of these personages, the Intendant's immediate chiefs, was on duty one year in four. They were supposed to execute the orders of Their Majesties, and most frequently they suggested those orders. None of all these courtiers was inclined towards economy : they wanted as much expense as possible to acquit themselves worthily of their functions.

It was, however, possible to induce a reasonable man like the Duc de Fleury, or a sincere lover of art like the Duc d'Aumont, to consent to some reforms. With the Maréchal de Duras this was not the case; the agreeable academician, who was organizer-in-ordinary of the Court fêtes, took special pleasure in doing things on a grand scale, and his extravagant liking for plays and player-people always led him farther than the forthcoming funds permitted. The Maréchal de Richelieu made life still more difficult for poor La Ferté. When he touched things theatrical, the conqueror of Port Mahon was nothing more than a meddling and blundering Jack-in-office or an undignified old beau who made the débutantes of the Comédie-Italienne rehearse their trifling rôles at his abode. The two reversionary First Gentlemen of the Chamber, the Duc de Villequier and the Duc de Fronsac, who also had to provide for the amusements of the Court and the public, resembled their respective fathers in character to some extent: the former was accommodating and judicious like the Duc d'Aumont, while the latter was as quarrelsome as Richelieu, and equally lavish with the King's money.

Although she had so noble a staff to watch over her pleasures and keep them constantly renewed, Marie Antoinette occupied herself with the organization of the Court plays, and even interested herself in theatrical affairs in Paris. As we know, she had a passion for everything connected with the stage. Before she appeared in person on the boards at Trianon, she took a vivid interest in the Paris theatres, in the chronicles of "behind the scenes," in the success of the new pieces and the small rivalries of actresses. She occasioned some surprise by taking the side of Mademoiselle Raucourt against her fellow-players without much reason.

During the first half of the reign, the Queen came constantly to Paris, in the evening, to hear a singer or to see a piece. She considered herself under special obligation to defend Gluck's operas by her presence, and afterwards those of Sacchini, against the constantly recurring action of a cabal.

The pleasure of being admired and applauded had also something to do with this, and when admiration and applause had failed her, she came less frequently. At length she passed almost unnoticed, and although her presence was remarked one evening in October, 1785, it was observed only to be criticised, for she was accompanied by her daughter, Madame

Royale, who was just seven years old, and it was not the custom, people said, for princesses so young to be taken to theatres.

Marie Antoinette did not lack opportunity to gratify her tastes. She could have "the play," at Versailles itself in the town theatre, a new building erected on ground belonging to the Château. Boxes were reserved for the Court, and thither the pages resorted, to criticise the literature and quarrel with the pit. With such facilities the Queen, at certain Carnival times, went to the play every evening when there was not a ball.

The repertory intended for the Court was submitted to her, and was for the most part regulated upon her suggestions. Sometimes a tragedy was acted for the first time before the sovereigns, for instance the *Menzikoff* of La Harpe, and the *Azémire* of Marie Joseph Chénier. The King liked tragedy, and would recite whole scenes from Racine, with his pages for audience. Marie Antoinette preferred ballets and musical pieces; it was she who chose these, imposing her taste upon the administration of the Menus. Her least wishes in such matters were obeyed. The entire programme for Fontainebleau was made out according to her fancy; she named the pieces and the actors; she intervened in the discussions between the Menus and the artists, always with a disposition to settle difficulties to the advantage of the latter, and to treat them with a familiarity which made them more exacting. For the sake of keeping Picq, then first dancer at San Carlo, a few days longer in Paris, and having him one evening at Trianon, she made him break a Carnival engagement with the State of Venice. The dancer received a gold watch, a gratuity, and many promises, but Mocenigo, the Ambassador, was placed in a difficulty between the duties of his post and his desire to please the Queen; the Most Serene Republic claimed the capers it had bargained for, and a diplomatic correspondence arose from this incident.

The Queen was actuated by a more praiseworthy motive when she insisted upon the performance of Gluck's *Iphigénie* at Fontainebleau, in 1777, notwithstanding the expense involved by the execution of the opera, which was rather out of date and had to be almost entirely remounted. She desired that performance because the maestro was to be present; it was for the purpose of doing honour to him once more; it was to be a cherished recollection on his return to Germany. In such a case Marie Antoinette never hesitated; she insisted that her pleasure should be done, but was excused by the fine feeling that prompted her.

The history of the stage at the Court of Louis XVI. has been written, but not that of the balls, and the latter would be a more attractive narrative, a more accurate mirror of the vicissitudes of a reign. Marie Antoinette's balls have so large a place in her life that a sketch of them must be given here. All Europe talked of them, and the Prince de Ligne, twelve hundred leagues from Versailles, in the snow, and fighting the Turks, wrote, with a sigh, one winter's evening: "The Queen's balls begin to-day, perhaps!"

At the termination of the Court mourning, with the close of the year 1774, these balls were formally inaugurated. In general there was one ball a week from the beginning of the year until Lent, given by the King to the Queen, and the Queen invited the guests. None but ladies who had been "presented" were eligible, but foreigners passing through Paris were dispensed from that formality, and Marie Antoinette invited them with pleasure.

The balls took place either in the state rooms or in a theatre on the ground floor, which dated from Louis XIV., and had been abandoned because it was too small. Sometimes, however, the fête was held in the Salle d'Hercule, one of the finest ball-rooms imaginable. Marie Antoinette selected the place, and the Intendant of the Menus had it arranged by the upholsterers to the King, on each of these occasions. First-rate decorators, such as Mazières or Bocciardi, were employed, and did wonders in a few days. For instance, the Queen's "great" antechamber was given an Ionic Greek aspect by twenty wooden pilasters in imitation of marble, their bases and capitals were adorned with flowers, and painted garlands cheated the eye successfully and agreeably. A similar effect was produced by baskets containing various kinds of fruit, and by white marble groups which completed the decoration.

...made at ... on the ... ber, ... presence of ... Majesties
From an anonymou[illegible]raving.

A Monsieur de Faujas de St. Fond, de Plusieurs Académies

Masked ballets and quadrilles were all the fashion at the Queen's balls, and continued to please. This was the doing of Marie Antoinette herself; in this more than in any other form of pastime she enjoyed the pleasure of realising her ideas. On several occasions in Carnival time, the Queen and her friends invented a new diversion. Now it was a ballet danced by Laps or Indians, again it was a quadrille of the Four Seasons. The idea would arise in conversation; then the clever designers of the Menus, Bocquet at their head, would be summoned in haste to the Château; their opinion would be asked, the scheme would be discussed, adopted, and all the wardrobe people would be employed day and night in furnishing the desired series of costumes by a fixed date. Out of their workrooms came in endless variety little marvels of form and colour, which had the charm of a dream, and won the fleeting renown of fashion. These modest artists held themselves rewarded for their labour when, in order to show her satisfaction, the Queen commanded the Opera dancers to wear the same dresses at Versailles or at Fontainebleau which had been worn by the Court at the ballets "des appartements." Preparation for these quadrilles occupied Marie Antoinette from one week to another, and the dancers came to her private rooms every day for rehearsal. Mercy perceived one good result of this engrossing pursuit; the Queen had no time to go to Paris, so that her health was no longer exposed to the risk of cold drives by night, or her reputation to the gossip of the Opera-house.

At first the Queen's balls were very well attended, and the new Court welcomed them eagerly. Horace Walpole describes one of the ordinary balls in a letter to the Countess of Ossory, already quoted: "There were but eight minuets," he writes, "and except the Queen and princesses only eight lady dancers took part in it. I was not so struck by the dancing as I expected, with the exception of a *pas de deux* by the Marquis de Noailles and Madame Holstein. For beauty, I saw none, or the Queen effaced all the rest. After the minuets were French country-dances, much encumbered by the long trains, longer tresses and hoops.

In the intervals of dancing, baskets of peaches, China oranges (a little out of season), biscuits, ices, and wine and water, were presented to the royal family and dancers. The ball lasted but just two hours. The monarch did not dance, but for the first two rounds of the minuets, even the Queen does not turn her back to him; yet her bearing is as easy as divine." (*The Letters of Horace Walpole, Earl of Orford;* Bentley, 1857.) The principal attraction of these fêtes, as we readily perceive, was Marie Antoinette in her own person, in the prime of her beauty and her youth, unused as yet to tears.

These first balls ended at an early hour. Towards ten o'clock it was permissible to retire. Sometimes, the Queen's guests remained much later, but then the ball-room was forsaken for the card-tables. All the women wore powder: it was the epoch of monumental head-dresses, absurd vagaries of French taste. Marie Antoinette adopted rather than led the fashion. In the evening she did not wear on her head the preposterous "poufs" which were constructed—an English garden, with its grass-plots and streams, was one of them: these follies were reserved for races or sleighing-parties. But her ball feathers were stuck upon the scaffolding of hair which has so ridiculous an effect in the famous print by Janivet. The Court ladies not only followed this example, but vied with each other in going beyond it. These head-dresses gave the salons an extraordinary appearance, and required a great deal of bloom and beauty, not always forthcoming, to make them pleasing.

Masculine costume at the same period tended, on the contrary, to simplicity. The dancing men only made an exception, and even they did not wear the prescribed costume; several of them chose the black coat embroidered in jet which had a fine effect in the brilliant light; gold and silver embroidery being forbidden even to ladies. The feathered Henri Quatre hat was worn, and kept on the head while the wearer was dancing. The young men of the Court had obtained leave to wear these feathers by a comic petition to Marie Antoinette containing phrases of the following kind, which must be given in the original, as the play upon the word "plume," with its two-fold meaning, "pen" and "feather," cannot be conveyed in English: "C'est avec une plume que nous demandons des plumes à Votre Majesté, et si elle daigne exaucer nos vœux, cette même plume nous servira, tant que nos doigts la pourront soutenir, à célébrer la bienveillance de Votre Majesté." The request, presented in January, 1775, was signed by La Marck, Coigny the elder, Etienne de Durfort, Ségur the elder, Noailles de Poix, Coigny the younger, Noailles, Lafayette, and the Comtes de Provence and d'Artois. The list is curious; these thoughtless young men, solely on pleasure bent, are the cream of the Queen's first "circle," and several of their names give us pause as we remember the fate that was awaiting them.

The receptions, which had been so brilliant early in the reign, soon fell off. A sufficient number of young women to form the quadrilles could not be found, and the most picturesque of the ballets had only the musicians for spectators. Nothing could be more chill and depressing than a ball in the great salons of Versailles with ten or twelve ladies dancing. Marie Antoinette was profoundly hurt and grieved, and did not conceal her feelings. It was, however, she herself who had brought about this state of things. Did she not show marked preferences in public? Was it not observed that she always sought out her own intimate associates at the official entertainments? Had she not offended many by causeless exclusion? The King expressed his regret on a certain occasion that one of the gentlemen of the Court whom he held in special esteem had not been invited. "He dances too badly," cried the Queen. "Must I also stay away then?" asked the King.*

In the winter of 1777, Versailles was entirely deserted. Mercy explains this fact as follows: "By degrees the ladies of Paris are losing the habit of going to Versailles, because of their uncertainty as to the days and hours when they may succeed in being admitted to pay their court to the Queen, for this always depends upon her very uncertain disposal

* The letter from which an extract is given in page 64 was written on the 23rd of August, 1775. On September 16th, Horace Walpole writes (again to the Countess of Ossory): "The charming Queen is gone out of fashion, so I am no longer in love with her."

of her mornings and evenings. Besides, Her Majesty having hitherto adhered to her system of having a rather restricted society of ladies, almost invariably nominates the same persons for invitations to the private suppers. This favour is shown to five or six favourites whose age and rank would not merit such a preference, and other ladies of the greatest distinction are excluded from an honour to which they have the clearest right. Added to this, there are now hardly any women at Versailles who keep up an establishment: the Superintendent (Madame de Lamballe) attracts very few persons to her abode, so strict are her rules of etiquette, and so much is she wanting in tact and social experience; while the Princesse de Chimay has not sufficient fortune to keep open house. From these unfortunate circumstances it ensues that ladies summoned from Paris to the Queen's balls arrive at Versailles to stay there in full dress until ten or half-past ten, and have to return to Paris in the dark night to get their supper. Now, as all this fatigue fails to procure them any share in the distinction of the 'cabinet' suppers, the aforesaid ladies are much displeased, and dispense, so far as they can, with the Versailles balls."

Before long the ruinous play at Court completed the alienation of the great families, and the "nouvelles à la main" spitefully opined that Marie Antoinette ought now to be satisfied, since she was reduced to the society of her friends only.

Then she understood the fault she had committed, and how much need sovereigns have to be surrounded and supported by fidelity of every kind. She began to receive her invited guests more warmly, to ask a more numerous company to the private suppers, to treat people according to their rank or their merit, and not merely according to the sympathy with which they inspired herself. At the same time the high play was moderated a little, and at the end of 1780 the Court was again crowded and the fêtes were resumed.

This revived movement was arrested only for one season by the death of Maria Theresa, and Marie Antoinette might well believe that royalty had recovered its former prestige. Those last winters at Versailles did indeed so strongly impress the remembrance of their elegance, magnificence, and taste upon certain contemporaries that the deepest impressions of the revolutionary period have been powerless to efface it.

In 1780, balls took place in the long-disused theatre on the ground-floor of the Château. The pillared vestibule which now forms a passage to the Cour des Princes occupies the former position of that building. Light wooden pavilions, which were kept in store at the Menus, and might be decorated and set up in a few hours, were easily brought down to Versailles, and placed on the garden side of the theatre, thus giving space and variety. The theatre ball-room of 1786 was especially effective, and Madame de Staël, who danced there as Swedish Ambassadress, calls it "a fairy palace." We are indebted for a description of it to a young Page of the Chamber, who made his first appearance at a Court ball there, and no doubt his first conquests also.

"On entering," he says, "we found ourselves in a green bosquet adorned with statues and rose bushes and terminated by an open temple where billiards were played. The dark green of the bosquet enhanced the brilliant effect of the illuminated billiard-room. On the right were little paths leading to the dancing and card-rooms; and, in order to allow the card-players to see the picture formed by the dancers without letting cold air into the beautiful salon, one of the doors was formed of a large unsilvered mirror, so transparent that a sentinel had to be placed on the spot to prevent people from attempting to pass through it. The ball-room was a long square, reached by a few steps. There was a gallery all around it, so that those who were not dancing might move about freely without intruding on the dance, which was distinctly seen between the pillars; it was indeed from thence that persons not presented, and only admitted to the boxes which surrounded the dancing space, had a view, and the pages took care to have refreshments served to them. At the far end of the dancing-room was the buffet, in a semi-circular recess. Enormous baskets of fruit and pastry were placed between tall antique urns containing liqueurs. From four marble shells rose jets of water which played all night, and diffused a pleasant coolness through the dancing-room, while the other apartments were warmed by hot water pipes."

The balls were prolonged to a much later hour than formerly, and it had become the custom to sup at midnight. A great number of tables of a dozen covers were laid, and the guests made up their own parties. The royal family frequently supped at one of these tables, with the exception of the King, who did not appear until after he had supped in his own apartment at nine o'clock. He played at trick-track, and retired about one o'clock. Thereupon etiquette was sensibly relaxed and additional animation prevailed. The "old young people" who affected no longer to care for balls, joined the rest in their turn. The classic minuet appeared no more and was replaced by the new dances.

The Queen moved about among the groups with the proud and elastic tread, the graceful gait, and the winning bearing which were hers alone. From the tip of her fan she waved to the young gentlemen who loitered in corners talking politics, an order which sent them to the ladies. Although she herself had already left off dancing, she would set the example if it were necessary to enliven the proceedings: she allowed herself a contredanse or a "colonne anglaise," and she was still beautiful—though her figure was not so slender as in former years—owing to her dazzling complexion which seemed made for festal light to shine upon it and surpassed the bloom of the youngest there. Madame Elisabeth, who had never danced much, also allowed herself to be tempted at those latest, liveliest, and most enjoyable hours of the Queen's balls.

The years pass, the Court balls cease, the Versailles plays are suspended, the Queen is hated. The end of the reign draws near in gloom, for it is shadowed by the deficit, the poverty of the people, and popular disturbances. The assembled notables have declared and defined the malady that is preying upon the country. It is believed to be curable; a remedy has been found, and the King has been persuaded to try it. This

MADAME ELISABETH, THE KING'S SISTER.

Drawn by L. S. Boizot, engraved by Marie Louise Adelaide Boizot.

[illegible]

[illegible] with [illegible]
[illegible] fearing [illegible]
[illegible] would in the young [illegible]
[illegible] where them [illegible]
[illegible] among the [illegible]

[illegible]

remedy has been imposed upon the Court, and the curtain of 1789 rises on the scene of the States-General, to the sound of the applause of Paris and the provinces; all are expecting the completion of the reforms that have been inaugurated.

It is the 1st of May, and a cavalcade passes along the streets of Versailles such as they have rarely beheld. The heralds and the king-of-arms of France, wearing their surcoats of violet velvet embroidered with fleurs-de-lys in gold, and mounted on white horses, advance, preceded by trumpeters of the Grande-Écurie and a detachment of the French Guards. At all the cross-roads, the king-of-arms proclaims the command of the King and the opening of the States.

It is the 4th of May: early in the morning the streets are hung with tapestries from the Garde-Meuble, and all the town prepares for the procession which is to entreat the enlightenment of the Holy Ghost for the great Assembly.

Since yesterday, the open places and the avenues are crowded by a multitude of people who have come from Paris. Whole families have failed to find lodgings: they have slept under gateways and porches, or stood on their feet all night, in spite of the rain, to keep their places for a sight of the procession as it passes. The dawn has promised a clear day. Windows have been let for great sums, and the roofs are covered with spectators, especially in the vicinity of the Church of Notre-Dame, from whence the procession is to set out, and where the deputies of the three Orders are already assembled, with their wax tapers in their hands.

There is a long wait, but at length, about ten o'clock, the arrival of the Court is announced. The entire Household of the King, the Equerries, the mounted Pages, and the Falconers, hawk on wrist, precede the huge state coach. The King has Monsieur on his left; the Comte d'Artois sits in front of them; at the doors are the Duc d'Angoulême, the Duc de Berry, and the Duc de Bourbon. The coach occupied by the Queen and the princesses is followed by all the Court coaches, bedecked with the high-plumed harness of state. The King's coach passes; he is saluted by cries of "Vive le Roi!" Then there is a great silence. The royal family alight before the door of the Church, and pass into the Choir, where they await the formation of the procession. M. de Dreux-Brézé and his assistants are very busy on the steps at the entrance, and have great trouble in inducing the deputies to fall into the order of their going and to assort themselves by bailiwicks.

The procession begins to move. The banners of the parishes, the Franciscans and the clergy of Versailles are in front, and the uniforms of the civic authorities make a framework for the surplices and chasubles. The road is lined so far as the Church of St. Louis by the French and Swiss Guards, who keep back the crowd. The Third Estate walk in two parallel lines; they are in black, and, in conformity with the orders issued by the Grand Master of Ceremonies, wear short silk cloaks, white muslin cravats and hats turned up on three sides; one Breton peasant appears in the costume of his province. The whole of the Third Estate is cheered, the deputies who are known are pointed out, especially "that" M. de Mirabeau, with his insolent ugliness. A wax taper in his hands surprises everybody, but the rôle he plays is already popular and many "vivats" are for him.

Now come the Nobility, and the applause ceases; nevertheless that Estate makes a fine show, with gold lace and embroidery on its cloaks, its large hats looped up in the style of Henri IV., and covered with white feathers, such as it wears at the Queen's balls. One deputy of the Order of Nobility is cheered, it is the Duc d'Orléans, who had refused to take his rank in the royal family, and walks with the bailiwick of Crespy-en-Valois. In him the crowd salutes "the friend of the people," and still more the adversary of the Court, the enemy of "the Austrian." The Order of the Clergy comes next, in two groups, the Curés are separated from the Bishops by the royal band. A detachment of the Body-Guard and the Swiss Guard precedes the canopy. The cords are held by Monsieur, the Comte d'Artois, the Duc d'Angoulême, and the Duc de Berry. The Sacred Host is carried by the Archbishop of Paris.

The King follows, in coat and mantle of cloth of gold, carrying like everybody else a wax taper, and surrounded by the great officers of the Crown. The Queen walks a little behind, on the left, heading the line of princesses and Court ladies. The line on the right is headed by the young Duc de Chartres, then come the other Princes of the Blood and the dukes and peers. The procession advances, in the spring sunshine, by the way of the Rue Dauphine, the Place d'Armes, and the Rue de Satory, to the Church of Saint-Louis where it is to receive Solemn Benediction.

At the spot from whence the procession is seen to the greatest advantage, a balcony of the Petite-Écurie, a sick child, pale and thin, lies on cushions, looking at it languidly. This child is the eldest son of Louis XVI., Louis, Dauphin of France. His eyes, dim and haggard with pain and weariness, grow animated for a moment as the strange spectacle unfolds itself before them. The sick child is taking his last pleasure, for in a month he will be dead. And his mother (who knows that he is doomed) raises her head in the midst of the cortège as it glitters on the Place d'Armes, and looks up at the little Dauphin's balcony with a smile.

She walks on, downcast now, and wears that air of lofty sadness which contemporaries remark. The crowd, keeping silence, follow her with their eyes; she feels the covert hostility of a whole people. Suddenly, a shout is raised alongside of her: "Vive Orléans! Vive le Duc d'Orléans!" They are women come down in a body from Paris who salute her with this insult: and what hatred there is in the tone of it! That odious "vivat" is a death cry! The King feigns unconsciousness, but Marie Antoinette, struck to the heart, turns pale, stops, and staggers. The princesses have to support her so that she may recover sufficient strength to drag herself to the end of that sad journey.

On the day after the procession, the opening of the States took place. The great Hall with Doric colonnades had been constructed two years previously for the Assembly of the Notables, in the court of the Hôtel des Menus. Louis XVI., wearing the famous diamond called "the Regent" in his hat, was seated in the centre of an estrade which occupied all the upper part of the Hall, beneath an immense canopy of violet velvet with fleurs-de-lys in gold and long golden fringes. On his left, below the throne, sat the Queen, in a violet velvet "coat" and white skirt spangled with silver; a heron's plume and a slender band of diamonds formed her head-dress. The princes and the officers of the Crown surrounded Their Majesties: the Court ladies, seated on benches at either side of the estrade displayed superb costumes furnished by Madame Éloffe and called "les toilettes d'États généraux." At the King's feet stood the Keeper of the Seals. Lower down the Ministers and Secretaries of State occupied a bench placed before a large table covered with violet velvet; among the Ministers of Sword and Gown was M. Necker in plain every-day attire. On the right of the Hall, the Clergy; on the left the Nobility; at the back, the dark mass of the Third Estate, as numerous in itself alone as the two privileged Orders. In the spaces between the pillars and in the galleries were nearly two thousand persons: ladies in full dress occupied the front seats.

The King spoke in a clear steady voice. All the assembly stood bare-headed in the softened light that fell from the embayed windows upon the hangings, the pillars and the rich canopy and carpet of the estrade. The spectacle was imposing and symbolical. The nation, such as the later ages of monarchy had constituted it, was well represented there. On high, the Throne, surrounded by the Court and upheld by its two supports, the Clergy and the Nobility. Below, the "Third," wearing no ceremonial dress, without plumes or broidery, but strong in its numbers and in its rights: the Third which now was hardly anything in the State, and to-morrow was to be everything.

For the last time Marie Antoinette appeared in a public ceremony as Queen after the order of the old régime. She seemed to divine something of this, and failed in entirely concealing her emotion under official smiles and gracious bendings of the head all round. While the King was delivering his speech, which promised justice and devotion to his people, while Necker was making his long statement on the condition of the

[illegible]

[illegible]

[illegible]

[illegible]

whom she vaguely [illegible]
the question to herself, [illegible]
assemblage, how many among [illegible]
inheritance of her children at the [illegible]
encountered the mocking glance [illegible]
and each time the [illegible] of the [illegible]
[illegible] gone back to her [illegible]

finances to hearers who listened to him with eager attention, the Queen was thinking of the new era for royalty which was dawning on that day. Her eyes wandered over the faces of those unknown persons who had come from every corner of France, who represented the nation, and in whom she vaguely felt the power of the future. In her disquiet she put the question to herself, how many friends might she have in all this assemblage, how many among them might be trusted to defend the inheritance of her children at the decisive hour? But she constantly encountered the mocking glance of the Duc d'Orléans turned upon her, and each time the cry of the day before, that insulting cry of the women of Paris, came back to her like a threat.

[illegible]

THE QUEEN'S PRIVATE LIFE.

At the end of the Grande [illegible]
Above the chimney-mantel [illegible]
giving Peace to France,' a triumphal [illegible]
of [illegible] The walls are covered with [illegible]
[illegible] paintings by Lebrun. [illegible]
[illegible] on the terrace [illegible]
the [illegible] reflected in the [illegible]
is the [illegible] "great apartments" of [illegible]
Marie Antoinette

The salon, [illegible]
Louis XIV., and [illegible]
of the latter. [illegible]
withdrawn on the [illegible]
Paix was used for [illegible]
There, too, presentations [illegible]
foreigners of distinction [illegible]

THE THIRD CHAPTER.

THE QUEEN'S PRIVATE LIFE.

At the end of the Grande Galerie at Versailles is the Salon de la Paix. Above the chimney-mantel is a panel by Lemoine, representing "Louis XV. giving Peace to France," a triumphal peace which is not that of the Treaty of Paris. The walls are covered with mirrors, marbles, and bronze trophies; above these are paintings by Lebrun. Three windows look upon the "Grandes Eaux," three others on the terrace of the Orangerie, where, behind the balustrade, the woods are reflected in the Pièce d'eau des Suisses. Such is the horizon of the "great apartments" of the Queen, and we are "chez" Marie Antoinette.

The salon, in fact, is nothing but a prolongation of the Galerie de Louis XIV., and in its present unfurnished state it has the majestic dreariness of the latter. Under Louis XVI., a moveable door and hangings, which were withdrawn on the great reception days, separated the two. The Salon de la Paix was used for concerts and especially for the Queen's card-parties. There, too, presentations to Marie Antoinette took place in general, and foreigners of distinction were received with grace and kindness never forgotten by them. Nicholas Venier, a Venetian patrician, who frequently sat at the Queen's round table, speaks of her spirited play and praises her desire to make the game interesting. The familiarity of Versailles, as it was in those days, comes into view in the records of those card-parties. At the time of the States-General, Drawing-Rooms were held at Court and the public "jeu de la Reine" took place several times in honour of the deputies; a great number of whom attended, and a simple country Curé, in an old soutane, was seen leaning unconcernedly on the back of Her Majesty's chair and watching her play. Marie Antoinette also passed through the Salon de la Paix in going to the Chapel. On days of solemn observance, she left her room at the hour of Mass by the gilded door, and entered the gallery followed by the whole of her household, her clergy, and the princesses of the royal family, who were accompanied in their turn by their attendants and ladies of honour. The public always mustered strong in this place, and could get a close view of the Queen. Her majestic bearing, as she advanced with a firm and harmonious movement which could not escape notice, impressed the crowd, and she would pass on, addressing a pleasant word to some gentleman whom she knew, but without stopping, or whispering a jesting remark to Madame de Mailly about something that her glance had lighted on by the way.

The bedroom occupied by Marie Antoinette had been appropriated to the queens or the dauphines since the time of Louis XIV. Maria Leczinska had changed the decoration of this splendid room. Camaïeux by Boucher had been placed in the ceiling, among the high reliefs in gold in which the escutcheon of France and Navarre alternated with the Austrian eagle. The door-tops were adorned with works signed by De Troy and Natoire. The whole room was hung with magnificent Gobelins tapestry, divided only by three wall-mirror frames representing palm-trees festooned with flowers; each had an opening at the top which contained portraits. The bed was placed on an estrade behind the balustrade; on its rich canopy, sculptured amorini holding copper lilies sported amid garlands of flowers. At the side stood the King's arm-chair; on this his sword was laid every night; then came the toilet-table, the handsomest piece of furniture in the room; it was

[illegible] portrait [illegible]

[illegible] on its rich [illegible]

[illegible] of flowers [illegible]

La Reine annonçant à M.me de Bellegarde, des Juges, et la
liberté de son mari; en mai 1

rolled into the centre at noon. The sofa and the folding-stools for the "grandes entrées" were ranged along the walls.

In front of the Louis XIV. fire-place, a small white bed was put up on four occasions for Marie Antoinette, at the birth of her children. We see the windows which Louis XVI. forced open with all the strength of his wrists at the birth of Madame Royale, when the Queen gasped for air in a room full of people, and the doctor was alarmed for her life. The scene has often been related; but a narrative, written by the Swedish envoy, M. de Stedingk, for Gustavus III., on the very day of the Dauphin's birth, is not so well known, and must be given without the omission of a single word, so true and vivid is its tone and so picturesque the note of feeling.

"The Queen gave birth to a Dauphin to-day at half-past one o'clock. Madame de Polignac was summoned at half-past eleven. The King was starting for the hunt at the moment with Monsieur and the Comte d'Artois. The coaches were already filled and several parties had set out. The King went to the Queen's room and found her suffering, although she would not admit it. His Majesty countermanded the hunt; this was the signal for everybody to hasten to the Queen's apartment, the ladies, most of them in extreme 'négligé,' the men just as they were. The King, however, had changed his hunting-dress. The doors of the anterooms were shut, contrary to custom; this was a great improvement. I went to the apartment of the Duchesse de Polignac, she was with the Queen, but I found there Madame la Duchesse de Guiche, Madame de Polastron, Madame la Comtesse de Gramont the younger, Madame de Deux-Ponts, and M. de Châlons. After a cruel quarter of an hour, one of the Queen's women comes in, all wild and dishevelled, and cries: 'A Dauphin! But it is not to be told yet.' Our joy is too great to be restrained. We rush out of the apartment, which opens into the Queen's guard-room. The first person whom I meet is Madame, hastening to the Queen's room. I call out: 'A Dauphin, Madame! What happiness!' I only said this at hap-hazard and in my excessive joy; but it caused some amusement seemingly, and it is related in so many ways that I am much afraid it will not help to make me a favourite with Madame.

"The Queen's anteroom was charming to see. The rejoicing was great indeed; every head was turned by it; people who hardly knew each other were alternately laughing and crying together. Men and women embraced each other, even those who cared least for the Queen were carried away by the general joy; but it was quite another thing when, half an hour after the birth, the folding-doors of the Queen's room were thrown wide open and M. le Dauphin was announced. Madame de Guémené, radiant with delight, held him in her arms, and was carried in her chair through the Queen's apartments to her own. Then the assembled company broke out into acclamation and clapping of hands which reached the Queen's room, and certainly her heart. All strove to touch the child, or even the chair. They adored the infant, they followed him in a crowd. When the duchess had entered her apartment, an archbishop wanted to have the Dauphin invested at once with the blue ribbon, but the King said he must first be a Christian! The baptism took place at half-past three in the afternoon.

"At first they had not ventured to tell the Queen that it was a Dauphin, lest she should be too much agitated. All who surrounded her were so composed that the Queen, observing their constraint, thought it was a daughter. She said: 'You see how reasonable I am; I ask you nothing.' The King, observing her anxiety, thought it was time to put an end to it. He said to her, with tears in his eyes: 'M. le Dauphin wants to come in.' They brought her the infant, and those who witnessed the scene say they have never beheld anything more touching. She said to Madame de Guémené, who took the child: 'Take him, he belongs to the State; but I also take back my daughter.'"

Nothing in that now disfigured room would recall the memory of these great events of the Court of France, were it not for the portrait of Marie Antoinette by Madame Lebrun, which has been placed there. In this portrait, painted in 1788, the Queen wears a white gown and a blue toque and mantle. The forehead is already marked by lines of care, which tell of the first sorrows of the mother and the first anxieties of the Queen.

The door opens on the "Room of the Nobles," where Marie Antoinette had to submit on Sundays to the custom of "grand-couvert," or eating in public with the King, which she detested. Even her bedroom was a place of intolerable representation, where every movement was regulated by etiquette. There, for instance, she had to shiver on cold winter mornings, as she sat waiting with bare shoulders for the chemise which the princesses and the ladies-in-waiting, in the order of their arrival, passed from hand to hand. Can we not easily understand her having curtailed the ceremonies of her toilet, and at length abolished this clothing in public? Thenceforth, after her hair was dressed, she retired to her cabinets, and had herself attired at her ease and to her taste.

The Queen's cabinets formed the refuge of her private life, and, outside the fixed audiences, her women allowed none to enter them but certain privileged persons of whom they had a list. For a hundred years they have been unguarded by the Queen's women, and traversed by the careless public. Let us try to tell what they have seen, and what they recall of the dead past.

Two narrow doors, hidden under the hangings of the bed-chamber, give access to the cabinets. By one of these doors the Œil-de-Bœuf may be reached through the Queen's dressing-closet, and it also leads to the King's apartments. But a secret passage, constructed underneath the state rooms crosses the entresols of the ground-floor; it is lighted by lamps day and night, and leads from one bed-chamber to the other: this is invariably used by the King. It was upon the representations of Mercy that the secret passage was constructed. The distance between the suite of apartments occupied by the King and Queen respectively made it a difficult piece of work, but it was necessary, for otherwise neither could reach the private rooms of the other without crossing the Œil-de-Bœuf which was always full of people. This subway was called "The King's passage."

The second door, on the right of the Queen's bed, opens into the prettiest boudoir in the Château, a little cabinet, with a low ceiling and panelled walls, one containing a fire-place, two others transparent glass doors. A master of the carver's art, Gouthière or Forestier, has twined the stalks of a rose-bush around these; and we find their delicate foliage on the panels of the wood-works, with the eagle of Austria and the attributes of Love, lakes, torches and arrow-pierced hearts. The bolts bear the initials of the Queen. Between the doors there is a mirrored recess in which the image of the person seated on the sofa is reflected on all sides.

A portion of the cabinets had been put up for Marie Antoinette on her arrival in France as Dauphine, but this boudoir dates only from 1781. She commissioned Micque, her architect, to build it, and he had the drawings made. It is a marvel of French taste, a very pure example of the Louis XVI. style, and the latest in date of the rooms associated with Marie Antoinette that have been preserved. Light indeed is wanting to make it entirely perfect; but it is not the fault of the Queen that the outlook is on the dull and sunless courtyard which we see from the window. This was the only corner of all the big Château de Versailles that she had been able to reserve for her private life, the only corner where she was permitted to pull down, to rebuild, in short to meddle with the cumbersome majesty of the old palace.

Alongside the boudoir was that library of which our contemporaries have said too much; in addition to serious works and important collections, it contained all the literary novelties of the time, bound and bearing the Queen's arms. There were numbers of presentation copies of books, and from authors not likely, one would think to offer their "hommages." For instance, a certain student of physics named Marat, an obscure person at the time, sent a copy of his *Recherches sur le Feu* to his sovereign. Marie Antoinette left the purchases for her library to M. Campan, her private secretary. It was he who furnished the shelves; but he fulfilled that delicate task with the unscrupulousness of a man of pleasure, without a thought that the books chosen for his personal amusement might one day serve to stain the memory of the Queen.

The catalogue indicates many of the licentious poems and novels produced in great numbers in the eighteenth century, and these we would rather not find there. The conclusion to be drawn is, however, the simple one that Marie Antoinette may have erred in this respect, like the women of her time, whose reading, like their speech, was very free.

Probably she herself did not know what books her library contained. "Except a few novels," says Besenval with very slight exaggeration, "she never opened a book;" and Maria Theresa reproaches her daughter, through Vermond, her mouth-piece, for neglecting both the cultivation and the adornment of her mind. She attempted, however, as a duty and to please the Abbé, to study big and heavy books, such as Hume's "History of England;" but the effort was as transient as it was meritorious and it never was renewed. It is not even certain that the Queen looked though the beautiful folios of the *Voyage pittoresque de Naples et de Sicile*, which was dedicated to her by the Abbé de Saint-Non with a head-piece by Fragonard, in the best style of that painter who was "galant" par excellence.

Although Marie Antoinette treated the frivolities chosen by Campan and the too serious works prescribed by Vermond with equal contempt, her library increased very fast notwithstanding, and although portions of it were taken to Trianon and elsewhere, it soon became necessary to enlarge the book space at Versailles. A room, hitherto reserved for the Queen's women, at the side of the library, with its elegant bookcase and drawers for prints with the two-headed Austrian eagle as handles, was transformed into a second library, and the doors were adorned with imitation book-backs after the fashion of the time. The bath-room was close by. The Queen seldom used the bath there, she preferred the "sabot" or slipper-bath which was rolled into her room when she rose. All was very simple and convenient; adjoining the bath-room there was a "resting room," just large enough to hold a bed. At the birth of each of the Queen's children this was occupied by Madame de Lamballe, in her capacity as Superintendent of Her Majesty's Household. The chief among all those little rooms is that called "The Queen's Cabinet." Let us consider it as in occupation for a moment. The decoration, like that of all the others, is white and gold, but it is more rich. The uniform panels shew us winged sphinxes standing in front of tripods which are wreathed and smoking as for a sacrifice to Love; underneath are amorini, blind-folded. Facing the mirror which divides the windows is a mirrored recess larger than that in the boudoir, and its arch is draped with silk. The furniture of this retreat in which Marie Antoinette passes the greater part of her time, is delicate, slim, exquisite. A harp, a desk laden with music, and a harpsichord by Taskin, always open, tell of her favourite pursuit. Her deep arm-chair is surrounded by low chairs for her work-baskets and her bags of wool for the "tapestry" or, as it was called in later days, the Berlin-wool-work in which she excelled.* The white marble consoles, the red marble mantel-piece, and a large marquetry table are crowded with souvenirs, Chinese curiosities, and small art-objects. The miniatures are by Siccardi, Liotard, or Campana; these comprise family portraits, those of her brothers, her sisters and the Princesses of Hesse-Darmstadt, who were her companions in childhood; there is also a corner reserved for her French friends. In the midst of this feminine museum stands a large jar of Chinese porcelain surrounded by a number of small vases, crystal, Sèvres or Venetian, filled with flowers which are constantly renewed. So dearly does Marie Antoinette love flowers that it is the sole function of one of her women to attend to the adornment of the Queen's apartment with them; she has to place them everywhere, especially in the "grand cabinet."

The Queen gives private audiences here; the women-in-waiting announce the persons thus honoured and introduce them by the second library. One day Madame Campan was on duty and had just admitted the Duc de Lauzun. Lauzun was one of the "set" of Madame de Guéméné, a handsome fop, but not devoid of brains, and well received by Marie Antoinette. A few days previously he had sent to the Queen a superb heron's feather which he had worn one evening at a reception at the apartment of the Governess of the Children of France, where Her Majesty had much admired it. Marie Antoinette, embarrassed by the gift which she had brought upon herself, wore the feather in her head-dress once, at dinner, and graciously enhanced her thanks by saying that she thought it became

(*) Note 6. See Appendix.

her. The matter rested there and the feather was seen no more. But the young duke, who was used to easy conquests, thought proper to regard this little affair as a mark of special interest on the Queen's part. For some time already he had been boasting both at Versailles and in Paris of the favour in which he imagined himself to be held, and he had asked for an audience of the Queen simply for the purpose of pushing this supposed advantage. He had been in the room only a few moments when the door was flung open, and the Queen, greatly disturbed, appeared on the threshold. With an angry gesture and in a harsh tone she exclaimed: "Begone, Sir." Lauzun bowed low and withdrew. The Queen, pointing to him, said to her waiting-woman: "That man is never again to be admitted!"

Lauzun did not return. Afterwards, when he had become Duc de Biron, he found the Queen obstructing the path of his ambition, and from that hour his wounded vanity assumed the right to be implacable. He joined the Duc d'Orléans: he had the same vices, he adopted the same enmity. The Queen had no more remorseless enemy. He assailed her even in death, and it is the testimony of Lauzun and his like that is now invoked by her enemies when they desire to resuscitate the slander that pursued her in life.

The Queen's Cabinet has, however, certain recollections of a more cheerful kind; let us evoke some of these. In front of this very mirror she held those prolonged conferences with Bertin, from which the milliner used to go forth full of pride, and there in the later days of economy and prudence she arranged with Madame Éloffe for the repair of her satin shoes and the mending of her gowns. Here, with her own hands, the Queen dressed the pretty Comtesse de Polastron, sister-in-law of Madame de Polignac, on the day of her presentation. This harpsichord recalls her passion for the only art she ever really loved. To its accompaniment she sang, in her pleasing but uncertain voice; on it she played airs from the works of her favourite composers, Mozart, whose name recalled Schœnbrunn and her childhood, Grétry, whose daughter was her godchild, above all, Gluck, the innovator of his time, whom she, "the little Dauphine," had made France accept. Why, the maestro himself, he of the scornful lips and rude speech, had been seen seated at that harpsichord, humble and docile, accompanying his royal pupil! German musicians were particularly well received by Marie Antoinette; this was the only special taste of her fatherland which she retained; she had forgotten its language. The harpist who gave her lessons was a German, one Hinner, whom she lent to her sister Marie Caroline of Naples. The young Steibelt, whose wonderful voice sent the Court ladies into hysterics, Salieri, who was chapel-master to the Court of Vienna, have performed their music in this little salon, which was large enough for the private life of a queen.

Marie Antoinette patronized not only the singers who rejoiced in the favour of Paris, all the rising stars were encouraged by her. The Duc de Penthièvre and Madame de Lamballe came expressly from Anet to Versailles to bring her a little prodigy seven years and a half old who was then enchanting their province. This boy was Martin Pierre d'Alvimare, who became, under the Empire, a composer of fashionable "romances" and taught the harp to Joséphine. Garat, who was presented to Marie Antoinette towards the close of 1782, was fond of describing, in his old age, his reception at Versailles at the outset of his career. The smallest details of the event remained indelibly impressed upon his memory.

His father, a magistrate of the Bordeaux Parliament, accompanied him. In the Queen's Cabinet were the King's brothers with the whole of the Queen's intimate society, and Salieri awaited Garat at the harpsicord. "How is this, Monsieur Garat,". said the Queen, "you bring your son, an excellent musician, an accomplished singer, to Paris, and you have not sooner presented him to me?" The father excuses himself on the plea that his son's talent is but immature, and the latter protests in his turn that he has learned nothing whatsoever of music; all he knows is the patois songs of his province. ".Very well then," said Marie Antoinette, "let us have your Gascon songs." Garat, who was not shy, obeyed, translating each of the little poems into French, as he sang. The result was a striking success, and the Queen enquired whether he did not know something of French

TO THE QUEEN.

Drawn by J. M. Moreau the younger, engraved by Lemire.

[illegible] Parliament, [illegible] like [illegible] brothers with the [illegible]
[illegible]

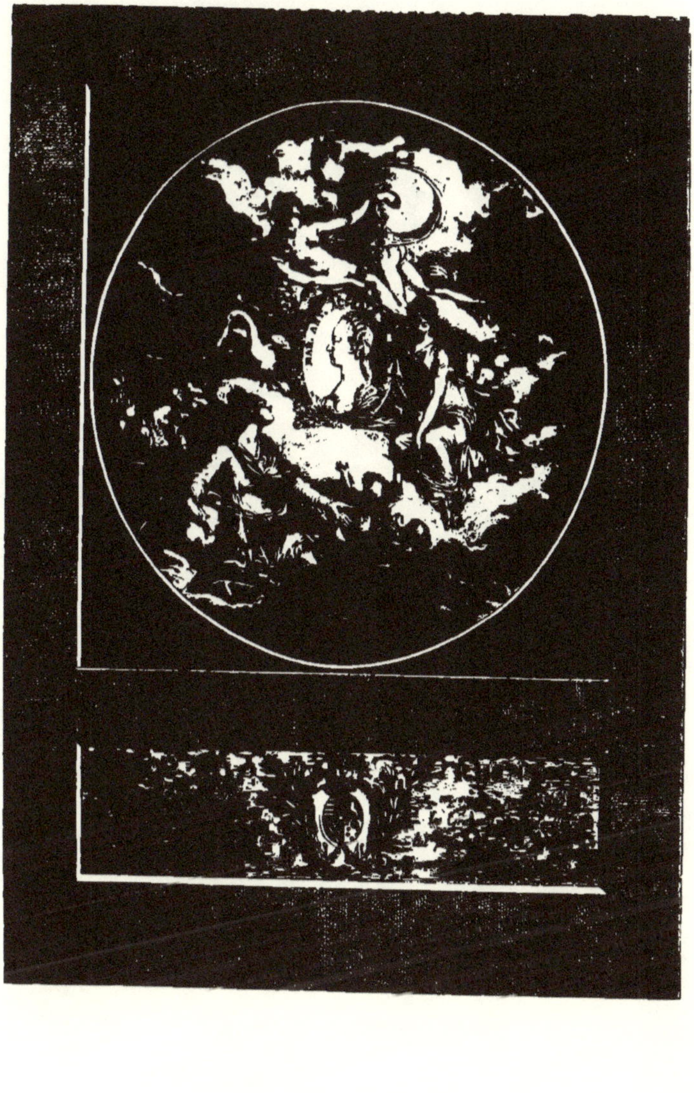

Photogravure Goupil & Cie

opera. "I have not learned anything, Madame," said he, "my father has only allowed me to lose my time over the study of law." "What, nothing else?" resumed Marie Antoinette, laughing. "But, Madame, I went yesterday to the Opera, notwithstanding; I heard *Armide*, and perhaps I may remember something from it." "Let us see. M. Salieri, will you take the score and accompany M. Garat?" Without a single failure of memory the youth from Bordeaux sang the best solos from the opera. The Queen, who was astonished, gave the signal for applause. "That is very good," said the Comte d'Artois, "and when he has learned music—" Salieri sprang off the music-stool: "He! learn music, Monseigneur! But he *is* music itself!" Garat left Versailles an enthusiast for Marie Antoinette. "We shall meet again, Monsieur," she said to him; and indeed he returned often, and was always well received, in spite of his southern familiarity, for he was necessary to the Queen's concerts, nobody singing Gluck so well as he.

The few artists who were permitted to take the Queen's portrait from life worked in this same salon, the most convenient and best lighted of the private rooms. The place was quiet and suitable for long sittings, but had Marie Antoinette time to devote to that purpose? With the morning came the endless details of Court etiquette; with the afternoon, walks, drives, hunting-parties, changes of dress, the uncalculated demands of pleasure and amusement upon time, so that the best part of her days was always taken up, and more than once the artist coming from Paris had to return thither without having seen his model. Thus it happened that the good portrait for which Maria Theresa begged with touching supplication was delayed for months, even years. "I want to have your face and your Court dress... Not to inconvenience you too much it will be enough for me if I have the face and the bearing which I do not know and which please everybody so much. Having lost my dear daughter when she was very small and childish, this desire to know her as she has grown-up must excuse my importunity, arising from strong maternal tenderness." The Empress obtained the fulfilment of her desire only one year before her death; but she had good reason to be satisfied : the artist whom the Queen employed to paint her portrait for Austria was Madame Vigée-Lebrun.

The details of the sittings at Versailles which Madame Lebrun has left give us a fresh view of the Queen's character. Marie Antoinette very soon began to treat her portrait-painter affectionately. Having heard that the latter had a good voice she sang duets by Grétry with her in the intervals of "pose." She even allowed the artist on one occasion to get a glimpse of her private troubles, when in reply to a compliment upon the noble and imposing carriage of her head, she said hastily, as though wounded by a remembrance : "If I were not a queen, it would be called insolent, would it not?"

Madame Lebrun was with child at this time, and one day she felt unable to keep an appointment with the Queen : on the next she hastened to Versailles to make her apology. In the court-yard she saw the carriage ready for the Queen's drive, and on reaching the private apartments she was rudely addressed by Madame Campan in a harsh voice : "It was yesterday, Madame," said the waiting-woman, "that Her Majesty expected you. To-day she is going out and certainly will not sit." Poor Lebrun replied mildly that she had come to take Her Majesty's commands for another day. She was introduced. The Queen was in her dressing-closet, finishing her toilet, and hearing Madame Royale a lesson, book in hand. "My heart beat," says Madame Lebrun; "I was all the more frightened that I was in the wrong. The Queen turned towards me and said gently : 'I expected you yesterday all the morning : what happened to you?' 'Alas, Madame,' I answered, 'I was so ill that I was not able to fulfil Your Majesty's commands. I have come to-day to receive them and I am going back at once.'

"'No, no! do not go away,' replied the Queen; 'I will not have you come all this way for nothing.' She countermanded her carriage and gave me a sitting. I well remember that in my haste to respond to her kindness I snatched at my colour-box and overturned it; its contents, with my brushes and pencils fell out on the floor. I stooped to repair my awkwardness, but the Queen said: 'Stop, stop! you are too far advanced to stoop'—and in spite of my protest, she picked up everything herself."

Madame Lebrun was truly *the* painter of Marie Antoinette. After the first portrait, which was painted in 1779, and which was popularized in a celebrated engraving under the erroneous name of Roslin (the Queen, standing, has a rose in one hand) she devoted several of her best pictures to that noble face. These works undoubtedly do not possess in any instance the absolute, the so-to-speak documentary sincerity of the medallion by Nini or the portrait by Wertmüller; but they convey the special charm of a beauty which was at once incomplete and sovereign, the pride and sweetness of the Queen's look, the elegance of her bearing, the dazzling bloom of her complexion; while they lessen the faults of her face, the round big eyes, the "Austrian" lip. In these pictures a purely feminine brush has fixed the ideal portraits, probably the truest, of the brilliant Queen of Versailles upon the canvas for ever.

When Marie Antoinette received her own select society and there was no music, what did they do in her private rooms? They played and they talked. That talk, although some there possessed wit and information, never rose above drawing-room gossip. It was for a long time a failing of the Queen that she could not bear grave matters. The theatre, "that convenient resource of superficial minds," was a constant theme of conversation: she wanted to know all about the performances at which she had not been present. "Were many people there?" was a never failing question, and frequently some one would answer with a bow: "Madame, there was not a cat." This did not mean that the "house" was empty, probably it had been crammed, but then merely with financiers, bourgeois and provincial people.

Such was the tone of conversation in the Queen's circle. Her own, according to Besenval, was desultory, and rambling from subject to subject. Her taste was for the current anecdotes of the day, especially for gossip as it was supplied at Court. Madame Campan asserts that the new songs and the latest little scandalous stories were the chief topics of conversation around Marie Antoinette, and Madame Lebrun was present during a sitting of her august model, when the Baron de Breteuil devoted the whole of a visit to the Queen to speaking ill of all the women of his acquaintance. Her unfortunate tendency to ridicule, which made so many enemies for Marie Antoinette, was thus developed by her surroundings; she was naturally kind and good, but she yielded readily to the malicious spirit of fashionable life, and Besenval himself, who poses for being shocked by this, was the first to urge her to it and to compromise her by it.

Apart from music and the drama, art held a lesser place than might have been expected by those about the Queen. Notwithstanding the accepted tradition, it is certain that she was not interested in painting, sculpture or poetry. In vain did artists, other than musicians, reckon on the taste of the young queen.

M. Davy de Chavigné, auditor at the Cour des Comptes, had a superb plan for a monumental fountain to be called "The Fountain of the Muses" engraved, "in commemoration," says the print, "of the patronage bestowed by Her Majesty upon literature and the arts." But Marie Antoinette was not entitled to be represented under the helmet of Minerva by this amateur architect, and there is only one correct symbol in the whole design: "Apollo, god of music, rendering homage to Her Majesty for the progress of music in France." In the same way, at the beginning of the reign, Cochin, the engraver, had dedicated *The Homage of the Arts*, an anticipative and hopeful allegory, to her; posterity considered their acknowledgment too hasty.

As for painting, the Queen, ever and in all things a woman, cared only for "genre" pictures and portraits which she recognised. Louis David made her pay dearly for slighting his big productions at the Salon, as though she could prefer scantily-attired Romans to the fascinating shepherdesses of Madame Lebrun. Hubert Robert pleased her, not by his pictures, but by his skill in landscape-gardening; this she turned to account by getting him to construct the rock-work of the Bains d'Apollon in the gardens of Versailles. Among the artists of the day there was one man of genius.

— THE HOMAGE OF THE ARTS.

Drawn by C. Cochin, engraved by A. L. Prévost.

HOMMAGE DES ARTS

Jean Houdon; he made an admirable bust of Louis XVI.; how was it that Marie Antoinette did not commission him to make one of her?

It is but just to the Queen to admit that she never pretended to a taste for literature; she knew nothing about it and preferred to leave it undiscussed. Nevertheless, she always treated talent with respect, and was very willing to credit her friends with possessing it, on their own mere word. She patronized the Abbé Delille, procured a pension for Chamfort, and attempted to get Voltaire received at Court in his old age, in spite of the reluctance of Louis XVI. A bookseller issued a new edition of the works of Metastasio at her expense. She encouraged the appearance of Collin d'Harleville on the stage. True, she applauded a bad tragedy by M. de Guibert and a ridiculous comedy by Dorat-Cubières; but she was to be excused in the case of the comedy: the reader who had interpreted it in her cabinet was Molé, one of the Comédie Française company, and his fine diction had misled the Queen and her friends.

The favourite literature in the Queen's circle really consisted of epigrams by Boufflers, and of those charming letters which were regularly addressed by the Prince de Ligne to the "set" of the Comte d'Artois, but which always found their way to the Queen at last. There were exquisite pages in the prince's epistles, but of a light kind, and the author was advised to make them as little "gay" as possible, "the Queen not liking them too lively." Thus were art and wit understood by the women of Versailles. André Chénier, who was unknown to the Court, and is the only poet of the period whom posterity will remember, was thinking, it seems, of their Queen when he wrote his verses on Frivolity:

> Mère du vain caprice et du léger prestige,
> La fantaisie ailée autour d'elle voltige. .
> La Reine, en cette Cour qu'anime la folie,
> Va, vient, chante, se tait, regarde, écoute, oublie,
> Et dans mille cristaux qui portent son palais,
> Rit de voir mille fois étinceler ses traits.

Although Marie Antoinette did not care for serious subjects, yet, when she did touch them, she exhibited good sense not at all common among her associates. She was not always caught by fashionable fads. Her reply to Ségur, then a young man, who was enthusiastic about Mesmer's "tub" is a case in point. "How can you expect us to listen to your foolish talk," she said, "when seven commissioners of the Academy of Sciences have declared that your magnetism is only the product of an excited imagination?" But let there be too much discussion of the American "insurgents," the parliamentarians, or the economists, and Marie Antoinette pouts, turns the conversation and carries off the whole party from the salon through her cabinets: presently the narrow staircase leading to the billiard-room is crowded with rustling silken gowns. The Queen takes up her pretty ivory cue, made from an elephant's tusk and topped with gold; her favourite game atones to her for the wearisome dissertations she has had to endure.

What would not we give to have a conversation with Marie Antoinette, were it ever so insignificant, exactly reported, with the accent, the light tone, the playful piquancy, the grace and the charm of the woman. We have half-authentic sayings of hers, or arranged "causeries;" but of the latter none give a living expression of her mode of speech except those related by her page Tilly, that captivating scamp, whose memoirs tell too much of his "bonnes fortunes." The Queen thought it her duty to watch over the conduct of her pages, and the youthful Tilly gave her no small cause for solicitude. She was continually receiving complaints of him: he was always going to Paris, he was on familiar terms with Champcenetz, the loosest talker of the Court; he contracted debts for his clothes. "Do dress more simply," said the Queen to him; "you have had two new embroidered coats in a few days; your fortune will not be sufficient for you if your tastes outrun it. Why is your head dressed in that way, and why do you wear those *crochets*. Are you going to the play? Simplicity does not make people remark you, but it makes them esteem you." These maternal counsels touched the young rake, but did not convince him, and the Queen determined to try severity. She was not very hard on him, however. One day when Tilly asked leave to "place himself at her feet in order to present a petition," she replied: "Come to me before five o'clock." At the hour named, the page waited in the Salon of the nobles, and the Queen appeared. "Good day," she said, "where have you dined?" "With Madame de Beauvilliers, Madame." "*My* Madame de Beauvilliers?" "No, Madame, Madame Adelaïde's." "Does she give dinners?" "Yes, Madame, to me at least; she has known me from a child, and does not mind me?" "If M. de Champcenetz had been at Versailles, you would have dined with him. You are keeping good company!" "Madame, he is witty and has such high spirits!" "Ah! that is charming! He will get on with those! Well, Monsieur, what is it you want? Come in." "I entreat the Queen to hear me with a little indulgence, because I shall perhaps take more time than I ought." "But, of course I will hear you." "Madame, a gentleman..., a sort of magistrate, has come here. My parents and I myself are his well-wishers; he wants to obtain a place at Alençon, it is vacant; here it is on a bit of paper. It depends on M. de Miromesnil; my gentleman is an excellent fellow. One word from the Queen to the Keeper of the Seals, and it is clear." "Well, it is clear?" "Yes, Madame, that he could not refuse." "Is that all?" "Yes, Madame." "I will write. Give me that paper; come back to-morrow at half-past three, the letter shall be ready. Adieu." "I do not know how to express all my gratitude to the Queen." "By conducting yourself properly." And the Queen dismissed the page, who bent low before her, with a motion of her hand.

This simple dialogue is not only an example of the ready kindness of Marie Antoinette, who could not refuse anybody; we seem to feel the vivacity of her speech, and even the clear tone of her voice, in the short sentences.

The personages who shared the private life of the Queen and who absorbed her entirely for many long years, are well known to us. The memoirs of their friends or their adversaries, official documents, and private letters tell us so much of them that they present themselves to our fancy to-day, each with his or her own particular physiognomy, special quality, or chief defect, in the precise place, important or non-important, that each of them filled in the society of Marie Antoinette.

Unfortunately, the least worthy occupied the first rank there. This was the Comte d'Artois, who imitated the conduct of his grandfather, Louis XV., and surpassed it in public scandal. His friends, and they were warm friends, for he was liberal and faithful, were pleased to liken him to Henry IV., whom he assuredly did resemble in his vices. He was readily intoxicated by praise, and for one frank outspoken servant such as the Bailli de Crussol, he had a hundred flatterers and satellites like the Prince d'Hénin. He was careless of his own dignity and heedless of how he compromised the dignity of the Queen. His portraits make us thoroughly acquainted with this big boy, with his saucy air and his half-open mouth; his pervading look of robust health and wild spirits. He was incapable of moderation or reflexion, and his pleasures were always enhanced by open defiance of public opinion. The Comte d'Artois, whose follies contributed to the destruction of the Monarchy, is only entitled to receive justice at the hand of history; its respect is due solely to the expiation of Charles the Tenth.

There was not a gentleman near the Queen so worthless as this Prince of the Blood. The elder Coigny, the duke, was an old friend. He was a "fidèle" of Chanteloup, and this led to his being made First Equerry on the accession of Marie Antoinette, and afterwards Lieutenant-General of the King's Armies and Governor of Choisy. At one moment he had a sufficiently strong position to fight Madame de Polignac, but not to defeat her. He possessed high intelligence and fine manners, and, avoiding all intrigues, he confined himself to representing the ever-present influence of the Duc de Choiseul in the Queen's Cabinets. His heart was sound, unspoiled by his worldly elevation. He had neither enmities nor enemies, and if his affection for Marie Antoinette was misinterpreted, many people regarded the calumny as a tribute to his merit and personal charm.

The Duc de Guines, who was of the same age as Coigny, and turning grey like him, also belonged to the Choiseul party; but, being an adroit

CHARLES PHILIPPE DE FRANCE, COMTE D'ARTOIS.
From a contemporary portrait Musée de Versailles).

[illegible] the [illegible] impor- [illegible] of Marie [illegible]

[illegible] the first [illegible] the Comte [illegible] of his grandfather [illegible] The Comte d'Art- [illegible] monarchy, is only [illegible] at the head of [illegible] due [illegible] of Charles the Tenth.

There was not a gentleman near the Queen [illegible] of the [illegible]. The elder Coigny, the duke [illegible] of Chanteloup, and this [illegible] the [illegible] of Marie Antoinette, [illegible] Armies and [illegible] sufficiently strong [illegible] enemies [illegible] people [illegible] charm [illegible] and [illegible]

schemer, he made his position at Court safe by transacting an intimacy with the Polignacs. He was ambitious on a large scale, and aspired to the Ministry; it is even said that he hoped to replace Maurepas, in spite of the very damaging record of his embassy to London. His persuasive way of talking was for a long time influential with the Queen; he even submitted written memoranda to her suggesting a sort of reform of the Court, which was on the point of being carried out. That the plans of M. de Guines were not without merit, Mercy himself acknowledged; but they assigned the leading rôle to the duke, and the Ambassador opposed him in an underhand way. Guines, feeling the unexplained resistance, wanted to force things on, to complete his success and get rid of the Mentor; but Marie Antoinette, who was so easy to lead so long as she did not know it, would not even submit to be advised. On one occasion, when the Court was at Marly, Guines was so ill received that he went away abruptly under pretext of an attack of gout; returned to Paris, and for a whole week closed his doors. When he made his next appearance, he found that he might esteem himself lucky to have escaped exclusion from the society which he had aspired to lead.

The Polignac family, whose reign was thenceforth undisputed, was agreeably composed in respect of both the men and the women, but in each household the man held the second rank. The Duc de Polignac was aware that he did not owe the title and honours showered upon him to his own merit, and he carried the burden with a simplicity which was in excellent taste. He tendered his thanks to the duchess by leaving her in entire freedom, kept aloof from the coteries of her salon, and was described in a word by a contemporary, who says that he had met M. de Polignac by chance, and the latter "wanted to talk of affairs; this does not suit him."

M. de Guiche, the duke's son-in-law, was at the feet of the duchess to whom he owed his good fortune, if not happiness. The brother, M. de Polastron, was not so amiable, and would not even try to appear so; when he was at Versailles he played the violin at the Queen's receptions, and when he was with his wife he passed his time in pining for his regiment. The husband of Madame de Châlons, in his anxiety to avoid causing embarrassment to his wife, carried his gallantry to the extent of applying for such distant diplomatic posts as Venice and Lisbon. M. d'Andlau, a less discreet diplomatist, who was made Minister of the King at Brussels, usually transacted his business in the salon of the duchess.

There were several Polignacs at the Court, but they were not of the "society." Among these were the old Marquis de Polignac, first equerry to the Comte d'Artois, and that disedifying Bishop of Meaux to whom the Queen, out of sheer complaisance, gave the post of her first almoner, or chaplain, fortunately a purely honorary function. The Vicomte de Polignac, the father of Jules and the head of the family, was sometimes invited, but not frequently, because he was stupid. His incapacity had always kept him out of public affairs until his daughter-in-law one day discovered in him the stuff whereof ambassadors are made. On this recommendation the Vicomte de Polignac represented the King at the Swiss Cantons for several years.

The Comte d'Adhémar was a more animated and interesting personage. He was not born to fortune, but his ambition was boundless, and he had gifts which make for the satisfying of ambition. He was of a mild and propitiatory disposition, sufficiently agreeable to please, not brilliant enough to startle or to arouse jealousy, and above all he thoroughly understood the times, and that the favour of women was the way to success. This favour he well knew how to win, indeed he was an adept. He had married a Lady of the Palace, Madame de Valbelle, who was very wealthy, but of whom nothing was heard after she became Madame d'Adhémar. The count wanted nothing from her but her money; he utilized another woman for his advancement. Madame de Polignac had been captivated by the middle-aged beau's good looks, by his humility, his attentions, his little "society" accomplishments (M. d'Adhémar sang and made pretty verses) and the constant politeness of a man who was always to be found behind the ladies' chairs. She resolved to do him an important service, and she had him sent as Ambassador to England. He came constantly to Versailles to see his friend; she even crossed the Channel to visit hers, and M. de Polignac accompanied her.

Two men held foremost place in the Queen's "society;" these were Besenval and Vaudreuil. The former, who was of Swiss origin, had served the King splendidly during the Seven Years' War, with the dashing and intelligent bravery of a French soldier. At the lucky moment he won the favour of the Comte d'Artois, who brought his deserts to light, and introduced him into the Queen's circle. He was no longer young, although he could assume the appearance of youth readily; but with his intellectual suppleness, which could fawn or bite, his facility in the art of false frankness and wisely-calculated imprudence, his rough speeches introduced as though inadvertently into a conversation and withdrawn suddenly with graceful ease, his flattery and his rudeness, he personified the disturbing and dominant man whom women dread and seek.

The Queen was all the more taken with him because he displayed a quite Helvetian fidelity to the dismissed Minister. This confidence was not altogether safe for her. Mercy had long since made her observe that the Baron and Madame de Polignac had, on several occasions, "been guilty of a sort of treason, by misrepresenting what the Queen had been so good as to say to them, and by misusing the influence which they had gained for themselves to their own advantage or that of their friends." Vain were his words: Marie Antoinette went so far as to entrust Besenval with those domestic secrets which it is always better strictly to keep, because they confer on those who hear them undue rights and too much authority.

Besenval has left memoirs admirably written, which are among the most valuable documents concerning the end of the eighteenth century. The author makes his partiality so evident that his prejudices are powerless to mislead the reader. He has been accused of ingratitude towards the Queen, and of a fault still more grave. The first accusation does not lie very heavily on the memory of a courtier. The second originates in a story of the grey-haired baron at the feet of the Queen told by Madame

Campan: but her statement strongly suggests the waiting-woman's inventive spitefulness. Marie Antoinette's well-known pride and loftiness of soul were ample security for the discretion of one whom she favoured. We do not care to defend Besenval otherwise than on this point, nor do we forget that he was depicted in one sentence: "No man ever was more amiable or less moral."

Madame de Polignac was led by M. de Besenval, but only just as M. de Vaudreuil desired. The latter, who was the closest friend of the Comte d'Artois, was also the real ruler of the favourite's salon. There he exercised his rights with a sickly despotism which is accounted for by his languor, his "vapours," and his blood-spitting, and was pardoned in consideration of his goodness of heart. Besides, when he chose, he could be irresistibly fascinating, and he knew how to talk to women in the tone of tender, gay, and respectful gallantry that was already a lost, or at all events a rare art. He, a Creole, the son of a Governor of Saint-Domingo, was almost the only man at the Court of Versailles who preserved the traditions of French conversation. To those he added spirit and vehemence, which made everybody listen to him everywhere, and when he spoke, his face, terribly disfigured by small-pox, turned handsome and shone. He would extol his friends warmly, and was prompt to defend them; he was also hot in attack, would flare up at the least contradiction, and give way to short-lived anger.

Besenval and Vaudreuil came into conflict rather frequently; they had, however, certain tastes in common which availed to unite them when the "rivalry of the salon" disturbed their relations. Both were collectors and men of letters. Besenval had himself painted by Dauloux leaning on his mantel-piece, in a cabinet full of pictures and art furniture. Vaudreuil interested himself in the whole of the intellectual and artistic movement of his time with the fervour which he carried into everything. His fortune enabled him to play the Mecænas, and, when he outran it the King's coffers paid in his name. He gave financier's fêtes, but only clever people were his guests. He had a collection of pictures by the best masters, a theatre at his country seat, and the artists whom he patronized longed to see him in the only State post that would befit him, that of Director General of the King's Buildings. He frequented studios and "behind the scenes." He was intimate with Chamfort and he patronized Lebrun-Pindare.

So refined a sceptic was this gentleman who lived on the Court and the Throne, that he keenly enjoyed the most daring attacks made on both with that lethal weapon, the pen. He introduced more than one of these effusions into the royal circle, and one day Marie Antoinette said to him, being rather startled at an ode by Lebrun which he had given her to read: "Do you know that this man strips us all?" At all events he shared the Queen's personal regard for a woman who had nothing but the name in common with the revolutionary poet, and equally admired her talent as an artist. Madame Lebrun, whose salon he visited frequently, speaks of him with affectionate gratitude in her *Souvenirs*. Vaudreuil took especial pleasure in her society and circle, and when he had righteously discharged his duties at Versailles as a friend and a courtier, would escape as quickly as possible from the futilities there, to the intellectual sphere which he had left behind in Paris.

Such were the principal gentlemen of the Queen's society at the period of her great intimacy with Madame de Polignac, when her friend composed the royal circle of such elements as she chose. Some other names must be added: Count Edward Dillon, who was called the handsome Dillon and was said to be too well aware of the fact, Bailli de Crussol, the Comte d'Avaray, the Duke of Dorset, British Ambassador, whom the Queen called a "good woman" and received graciously, Count Esterhazy, whom she treated even better, for she paid one hundred thousand livres of debts for him; lastly, a more illustrious foreigner, the Prince de Ligne, who, though born in the dominions of Maria Theresa, was pleased to regard himself as a subject of Marie Antoinette.

This great traveller, an habitual wanderer about the European Courts, reserved several months in each year for the Court of his predilection. He writes, speaking of Versailles: "My taste for pleasure brought me there, and my gratitude brings me back." He was supplied with news of the little circle by the Chevalier de l'Isle, who was a captain in the Champagne regiment. It was he who came in first after dinner at Madame de Polignac's receptions, to make visitors who arrived later believe that he had dined with the Queen. The Chevalier also corresponded with Voltaire, and had a happy knack of writing satirical ballads and songs. He addressed verses to Marie Antoinette. The following lines, set to the air of *Joconde*, are curious on account of their tone of familiarity; the author threatens the Queen with making her known at the masked Opera ball; this, it seems, is her great dread :

Dans ce temple où l'incognito
Règne avec la folie,
Vous n'êtes, grâce au domino,
Ni Reine, ni jolie...
Sous ce double déguisement,
Riant d'être ignorée,
Je vous nomme ! et publiquement
Vous serez adorée.

The boundary line of gallantry that no man ever passed, is marked here. It is important to note the fact, for the familiarity of Marie Antoinette has been much exaggerated. "Her tact," says Prince de Ligne, "was as imposing as her majesty. It was as impossible to forget what she was as to forget one's self." Let us borrow a few more traits of her character from the same witness, for he is the only authority on these private details. "Marie Leczinska," he says, "who was prematurely old, and rather ugly, —sometimes asked the theatres to give pieces *a little strong*. The ultrapious ladies also liked that sort of thing, and when their tastes were gratified, we sometimes said : "This play belongs to the Queen's repertory." "Add at least," said Marie Antoinette, "that it is the *late* Queen's." The prince goes on to say that "none ventured on speech too free, stories too gay, or gossip too malevolent in her presence." They made up for this self-restraint, it is true, when she had left the room, and they had no longer to fear offending the "white soul" of the Queen.

"Women reigned then, the Revolution has dethroned them." So says one of those whose royalty was the gentlest. The women who surrounded Marie Antoinette had some claims to dispute her sceptre in point of beauty and grace. They were almost all related to the Polignacs. The Comtesse de Polastron, born d'Esparbès de Lussan, had beautiful pensive eyes, destined to much weeping; her low, plaintive voice bespoke a romantic, timid, and retiring disposition, requiring to be sought in order to be understood. Very different were the other women of the family: the Comtesse d'Andlau (she was the daughter of Helvetius) who was called "the brilliant d'Andlau," one of the loveliest of the Court ladies, "idolized" by many, and especially by the Duc de Coigny, who afterwards married her; lastly the young Duchesse de Guiche, handsome like her mother, and whom her intimate companions called "guichette," as they called Madame de Polastron "bichette." Some agreeable Parisian ladies whom the Queen liked, would occasionally come to Versailles as visitors to the Jules de Polignacs; among these was the Comtesse de Sabran, whose letters to M. de Boufflers reflect all these Court people in the mirror of an indulgent mind.

Two women held the chief place in the Queen's circle, the Comtesse Diane, and the Duchesse Jules, that is to say, wit and beauty. Diane de Polignac was ugly and scorned any artificial alleviation of the fact. She possessed such sure and certain powers of fascination as made her preferable to the most beautiful. Into this group of women melancholy not seldom stole its way, and although the Queen herself laughed much, she had not naturally high spirits: it was Diane de Polignac who brought life and movement among them. She was the heart and soul of the Court, she was the sunshine of the rainy days; she did what all around neglected, she cultivated her intellect by much reading. Her turn of mind was ironical, but she was also tender-hearted; would blush readily, and yet be prompt and bold of speech like a man; none but she could get the better of M. de Vaudreuil and make fun of his womanish fits of temper with impunity. Her invulnerable spirit knew no fear of anything or any person; she saw every ridiculous point, seized it on the instant, and always had ready a verbal dart which struck home, avenged, and killed. She was said to be intriguing, designing, false, scandalously ill-conducted and indecently immoral. These are big words, and doubtless came from persons whom she had offended. Nevertheless, Louis XVI. certainly did make a singular selection in placing her at the head of the Princess Elizabeth's household; he might have found, without much seeking, a more virtuous lady.

Such a foil served to enhance the attractions of the Duchesse Jules, just as the somewhat formal charms of her daughter, Madame de Guiche, made her simplicity and natural sweetness more pleasing. The favourite was very beautiful; hers was the beauty of the brunette with blue eyes; and no portrait, not even that by Madame Lebrun, adequately conveys the charm on which all contemporaries dwell, and to which even her enemies submitted, while they cursed it. "Hers," says the Duc de Lévis, "was the most heavenly face that eyes could behold. Her glance, her smile, all her features were angelic. She was like a painting by Raphaël in which a spiritual expression is combined with infinite sweetness." All witnesses are agreed upon the special charm that rendered her beauty so captivating: "her bearing," says one of them, was marked by a fascinating repose which distinguished her from the other women of the Court, who had only the restlessness of pride and vanity." "In all her movements," says another, "there was a negligent grace which made her remarkable among the very fairest."

It was this novel and rare attribute which conquered Marie Antoinette. The "negligent grace" of Madame de Polignac was accompanied, besides, by sound moral qualities. The Queen loved her from the first for her sincerity, her clearness of judgment, and her freshness of mind, no less than for her taste for music, which was that of a musician, and the caressing tones of her voice, and she at once gave to her all the hoarded tenderness that she had not been able to lavish on other friends. Then there arose between them one of those pretty friendships which come into young lives "à vingt ans," with exchange of confidences, impressions, likes and dislikes, and, although they do not always last into the years of grave things, leave their perfume in the heart of life. The ardent and trustful soul of Marie Antoinette was to learn more surely than any other, what happiness and what disappointment such an affection may produce.

We know how irreparable was the harm done to the Queen by this intimacy, and the abuse of power to which it led. In these pages we need not stain the memory of a friendship which was disinterested at first, and might perhaps have so remained but for the various contending interests which traded upon it; for Madame de Polignac herself displayed no great eagerness to profit by her good fortune, and was indolently indifferent about maintaining it. But that very indolence — the apathy of her nature — was a force in the case; it stimulated the Queen's generosity, and constantly set her upon trying what new pleasure would induce her friend to smile, what unexpected bounty might force her to gratitude.

The first favour, and the most dear to the two friends, was the fixing of Madame de Polignac at Court by finding a post for her husband. The Queen had an apartment given to them immediately; it was very small but very near her own. At the first opportunity, this apartment was enlarged, so that Marie Antoinette might be received in it. Soon she passed all her time there, and the salon of Madame de Polignac became a repetition of the royal salon, with the same company, the same amusements, the same associations. There was a sufficient number of pretty women to make the Comte d'Artois oblivious of his actresses in Paris for days together. The King himself came frequently of an evening. The august presence of the Sovereign was an honour for the host and hostess, but it rather repressed the general enjoyment, and more than once, as he was known to be very punctual, and always retired at ten o'clock, some wag furtively pushed on the hands of the clock. The King having gone away, the Queen would remain as long as possible, and it would be very late when, wrapped in her furs, she returned to her own apartment and crossed the guard room where the guards dozed around their big fire-place.

The same thing went on at Fontainebleau, where also the favourite was domiciled close to the Queen. Very soon the latter could not do without her. When Madame de Polignac was in childbed at Passy, the Queen arranged a "little journey" of the Court to La Muette, so as to be near her friend. She came to the young mother's house at ten o'clock in the morning, dined there, and stayed all day. Under similar circumstances she showed the same kindness to the Duchesse de Guiche, prolonging another sojourn at La Muette in order to share the maternal anxiety of Madame de Polignac. The Chevalier de l'Isle speaks of this to the Prince de Ligne: "I am writing to you from the villa Jules, at the side of the newly-made mother. Her mother is there also, and salutes you. The Queen has just gone, she who hardly ever goes; the best nurse-tender in France."

Nevertheless this close tie was loosened. Marie Antoinette has been wrongfully accused of inconstancy; she had passing fancies, no doubt, but her affection remained ever faithful. After years of self-deceiving she had to endure a cruel disenchantment. The favourite had become the instrument of her coterie, and had taken with zest to her rôle of place-provider and maker of Ministers. She no longer made requests, she imposed what she desired, and often without employing as a medium the Queen, who discovered by degrees that Madame de Polignac was sacrificing her to her friends, and that for the most part her own too great generosity had merely created a large number of ingrates. At first she refused to believe in her own discovery, she repented of her first recoil under the stroke of conviction, and the duchess had only to make a pretence of intending to quit the Court to see a queen in tears at her knees entreating her forgiveness for a suspicion. But those outspoken and truth-telling persons, Mercy and Vermond, had a thousand opportunities of convincing Marie Antoinette, and their vigilance was sharpened by their jealousy. They availed themselves especially of her antipathy to M. de Vaudreuil.

The place in her heart which Madame de Polignac assigned to her "too intimate friend" had been a grievance to Marie Antoinette for a long time. This rivalry, in which she always felt that she was beaten, shook even her affection at last, and the recoil was accelerated by the intrigues of Vaudreuil, by his equivocal behaviour in the affair of *Le Mariage de Figaro*, and his avowed campaign in favour of Cardinal de Rohan. It was to him the Queen alluded one day when she said that she regretted to meet certain persons who were unpleasing to her in Madame de Polignac's salon. The duchess actually ventured to reply : "I do not think that Your Majesty's being pleased to come into my salon is a reason for claiming to exclude my friends from it." Marie Antoinette said to M. de la Marck at a later period, when she repeated this speech to him : "I do not resent this to Madame de Polignac; at heart she is good, and she loves me, but her surroundings have got the better of her."

By degrees the Queen withdrew from her friend. She only visited the apartment of the Governess of the Children of France for the purpose of seeing the Dauphin, and from a motive of self-respect, in order to palliate the disaster that had befallen her feelings in the eyes of the world. Externally, nothing, or very little, was changed : the friendly attentions of the Queen were hardly diminished; but she no longer reposed trust or invited counsel; she did not speak of her plans or projects until she had decided upon and arranged them. This new attitude pleased neither Besenval nor Vaudreuil. The latter especially was disappointed, he had actually ventured to aspire to the post of Governor to the Dauphin. Madame de Polignac on the contrary, the recipient of a favour which she had not sought, let it pass away without clinging to it; for she was sure of the public advantages that would still be hers. She sacrificed neither her ease nor her friends to the jealous affection of Marie Antoinette. Each time that the Queen proposed to pass the evening in the salon of the duchess, whom people still persisted in calling "the favourite," she was obliged to send a footman beforehand to ascertain the names of the persons who were to be there; if the list did not suit her, which was frequently the case, as she had no longer the right to change it she stayed away.

How sorrowful it must then have been to perceive, as in memory she recalled the better years, that the sacred fire had been kept alight by herself only! The outbreak of the Revolution alone sufficed to rekindle this extinct affection. When the Queen was on the verge of the abyss, did Madame de Polignac recognise that she had driven her to it? She did at least feel that she must love her better and tell her so more warmly. The Queen, on her side, forgot her own danger, thinking only of the peril of her servants, and of getting the Polignacs out of the reach of the infuriated populace. At the moment of their final separation, on the day after the fall of the Bastille, something of the past was born again in the two hearts, but in that strife of tenderness the one who won was again the friend who wore a crown.

During the whole of the close of the reign Madame de Polignac continued to hold the "circle" of former times in her official apartment as Governess, at the angle of the Château on the terrace of the Orangerie. On Sunday she received the Court and Paris, the rest of the week some friends only; these were always the same. It was a sort of country life that she and all about her led, a life full of peace, and the Duc de Lévis, who had enjoyed it, refers to it in his *Souvenirs* in a tone of singular regret. He describes the winter salon, the great wooden gallery with a piano on the right, a billiard table at the back, and a "quinze" table on the left. These were the Queen's favourite games; but, from this pleasant place where nothing seemed changed, one person only was missing, and that person was the Queen.

Marie Antoinette, however, could not do without friendship. As the difficulties of her royal life grew and multiplied, she felt more and more strongly the need of private confidence and support. It might be thought that she would resort once more to a forsaken friend, that Princesse de Lamballe, formerly so much loved by the Dauphine and the Queen, and whom the more intelligent and attractive Madame de Polignac had replaced.

LOUISE MARIE ADELAIDE DE BOURBON-PENTHIÈVRE,
DUCHESSE D'ORLÉANS.

From the portrait painted by Madame Vigée-Lebrun Musée de Versailles.

But the princess was no longer there. She had not been able to content herself with the second place; her delicate health had served her as a pretext for gradual withdrawal from Court; she never remained there for a longer time than her duties as Superintendent of the Queen's Household required, and she saw Marie Antoinette only at fêtes and under official circumstances, or when she received her in Paris, at the Hôtel de Toulouse "en grand souper." The rest of the time she lived with her sister-in-law, the Duchesse d'Orléans, or her father-in-law, the venerable Duc de Penthièvre. She went with him to Eu, Crécy, Anet, Rambouillet, Aumale, and Vernon. She took part in his works of piety and charity, and presided at those singular meetings of Masonic Lodges where the academic candidature of the Chevalier de Florian was arranged, under the leafy shades of Sceaux.

Nevertheless, Madame de Lamballe deeply loved the Queen. In the troublous days she will reappear at Court; on the morrow of the 6th of October she will fly to the Tuileries, then become a perilous place and deserted by the courtiers, bringing "her heart that does not change," that heart which is to be faithful even to imprisonment, even to massacre.

In the meantime the Queen had formed more intimate relations with a few noble women who will not forsake her in danger, the Duchesse de Fitz-James, and her daughter, the young Duchesse de Maillé, the Princesse de Tarente, the Marquise de Tourzel. But the friend whose salon replaces that of Madame de Polignac to the Queen is Madame d'Ossun, her lady-in-waiting.

Geneviève de Gramont, Comtesse d'Ossun, was the niece of M. de Choiseul and the sister of the Duc de Guiche. Her relationship with these personages had long before brought her close to the Queen, who had attached her, from 1780, to her personal service, and had always treated her with affection and confidence. It required a certain time to appreciate and like Madame d'Ossun, for she was not attractive in appearance, nor was she intellectually gifted; she was a complete contrast to the fascinating Polignac; but she had solid worth of character and no hidden ambitious designs. Marie Antoinette, now matured and taught by experience. had chosen a friend more wisely this time.

When she formed the habit of visiting her lady-in-waiting regularly, the Queen offered Madame d'Ossun a sum of money to defray the expenses of a daily reception. The countess, whose means were not large, named only a few thousand livres monthly, and never asked for anything beyond that for herself or others. The happiness of having her queen with her was enough for Madame d'Ossun, and, if she did receive a royal pension afterwards, it was Marie Antoinette who insisted upon her accepting it. The state of the public finances did not permit the Queen to do for this friend what she had done for the other; but Madame d'Ossun did her best to procure similar pleasures for her. She received her at dinner with four or five persons only, who made it pleasant without restraint. She arranged small dances, and concerts for which she engaged the fashionable singers, after the Queen ceased to attend the Opera. By a strange coincidence, Madame d'Ossun occupied the apartment at the château that had formerly been assigned to Madame de Polignac; every corner was full of recollections sweet and sad for Marie Antoinette.

There she met the Duchesse de Bourbon, mother of the young Duc d'Enghien (of tragic memory) and they "made music" together, the duchess finding an echo of the sorrows of her own stricken life in the melancholy moods of the Queen. Only a few men formed part of this private circle, which was chiefly composed of distinguished foreigners. M. de Mercy, whom Marie Antoinette treated with almost filial respect, and to whose advice she gave more heed than formerly, was a member of it, the Comte de la Marck also, who was thus brought into relations with the Queen, which led afterwards to the negotiations conducted by him between Her Majesty and Mirabeau; then the brilliant group of Swedes, whose long stay in France had made them half French, Count Stedingk, Count Axel Fersen, and others; occasionally, too, the new Ambassador from Sweden joined them. This personage was M. de Staël-

Holstein, who owed his marriage with Mademoiselle Necker to Marie Antoinette.

The Queen had not relinquished the habit, which did her so much harm, of shutting herself up within a small private circle. Although her friends were better selected, this exclusive disposition of hers discouraged more than one who would have brought goodwill and devotedness to her service. Young Schomberg, who had the honour to be invited to a royal supper, writes to his mother: "The Queen treated the Chevalier de Puységur, who was there, with the greatest kindness, before me, and I can see, as I have been told, that she is extremely amiable to the persons of her own society. It is very unfortunate that so much care and pains are required to enable one to approach that circle." Many other gentlemen left Versailles with the same feeling, and thus valuable adherents were lost to the Monarchy! We can discern, however, the source of the Queen's instinctive shrinking from any extension of her private circle; she explained it indeed in a sentence by a word to some one who had pointed out to her the objections to a too-evident preference for foreigners. "You are right," she said with a sad smile; "but it is because they do not ask me for anything."

The old favourites, those who were always asking, never forgave Marie Antoinette for having given them up. Notwithstanding the extreme reserve of Madame d'Ossun, the Polignac salon pelted the rival salon with epigrams. In some of these most malignant allusion was made to the Queen's dancing Scotch reels with the young Lord Strathavon. One of the men on whom she had showered her bounty composed some odious rhymes upon the subject; these, after they had been received with smiles in the salon of the Governess of the Children of France, raised an outcry in Paris against the Queen. What was not said of her regard for Fersen? What openly cynical or underhand slander did not that sentiment of hers give rise to? The answer is to be found in the despatch addressed by Count Creutz, the Swedish Ambassador, to his sovereign, after Fersen's first stay in France. The following is the document, which belongs to this history and must not be severed from it.

"I must confide to Your Majesty that the young Count Fersen has been so well received by the Queen, that several persons have taken umbrage. I own that I cannot help thinking she has a liking for him; I have seen indications of this too plain to be doubted. The young Count has behaved, under these circumstances, with admirable modesty and reserve, and his going to America is especially to be commended. By absenting himself he avoids danger of all kinds; but it evidently required firmness beyond his years to resist such an attraction. During the last days of his stay the Queen could not take her eyes off him, and as she looked they were full of tears. I entreat Your Majesty to keep their secret for yourself and Senator Fersen (the father of Count Axel). When the approaching departure of the Count was made known, all the favourites were delighted. 'How is this, Monsieur?' said the Duchesse de Fitz-James, 'You forsake your conquest!' 'Had I made one,' he replied, 'I should not forsake it; I go away free, and unfortunately without leaving any regrets.' Your Majesty will own that the Count's answer was wise and prudent beyond his years."

Marie Antoinette did then feel something more than friendship for a foreigner: a blush tinged her brow, her eyes fell before the glance of a man whom, had she not been a queen, she might have loved. Yes, all this is true, but only this. He whom she thus distinguished proved himself worthy of a royal heart, too proud to make offer of itself, too weak to dissimulate. Count Fersen, who is represented to us as tall, reserved, serious, so different from the Parisian fops and the Versailles courtiers, was in truth the ideal hero for this romance, all made of silence and of sacrifice. His return to France during the Revolution, his chivalrous devotion to the royal family, lend greater lustre to his noble memory; the poem of his fate ends only with his tragic death at Stockholm at the hands of the mob. Fersen was generous and brave, and it is to the honour of Marie Antoinette that she recognized his character instantly. But the women who wear crowns are not like other women? Are not their most private, most delicate, most sacred feelings destined to be the prey of calumny sooner or later?

Marie Antoinette's life was shared by one person, the King. The King! To the nation he was the incarnation of its strength and its glory, the representative of justice and divine right, the father and the master; to the Queen he was the husband. It was a heavy task for a mere ordinary man to have to keep up this double prestige in the eyes of a woman and a nation, itself feminine, and given, beyond all other nations, to crises, humours, exaction, and caprice.

Louis XVI. has been hunting at Saint-Hubert or Rambouillet; he has supped at one of the hunting-lodges, and has gone to sleep in the carriage that takes him back to Versailles. On his arrival at night at the Château, he has to be awakened. He gets out of the carriage, still sleepy and stumbling like a drunken man; the servants have to support his massive and clumsy form, and the guards, who observe the scene, laugh among themselves and think the King is the worse for drink. In the morning he rises early; no sooner has he got rid of the ceremonial of the "lever," than he escapes by an inner staircase, and goes up to his forge, which is set up in a workshop in the attics where Gamain, the journeyman locksmith, is in attendance. There he makes keys, bolts, iron boxes, nothing in fine metal, but just rough blacksmith's or locksmith's work, for which he occasionally gets slanged by his comrade-like apprentice. If he interrupts the work at all, it is because he has seen from the window some masons mixing plaster, and runs down to help them, with his shirt-sleeves turned up.

This was what France knew of her King; this was the guise in which Marie Antoinette contemplated her husband, trowel in hand, or his big face still red from the forge fire, when he has to resume his embroidered coat to receive ambassadors, or to give his hand to ladies at the balls;

the temperament and the habits of a workman are to be recognised in this singular descendant of Saint Louis; in his thick hands, his ungraceful movements, his clumsy jesting with men, his embarrassment under the scrutiny of women.

Neither the nation nor the wife find in him that superiority which is equally essential to the sovereign and the husband. France turned him into ridicule, the Queen smiled at him. She wrote to an Austrian friend that the rôle of Vulcan pleased the King, but that he would not like her to play that of Venus, and tells how it is that she manages to obtain all she wants from him, and to lead "the poor man" as she desires. "The poor man!" that word, written thoughtlessly no doubt, is destined to go the round of Europe and to do equal injury to the husband and the wife. "Could anything," says the Emperor, scolding his sister, "more imprudent, more unreasonable, more unbecoming be written?" The Queen was only a girl then, and she promised to guard her pen; but for a long time after that she continued to disdain the King, and prefer the society of agreeable and superficial men to his. Thinking herself superior to him, she liked to make him feel it, not harshly by any means, but with that petty, half-unconscious cruelty which is woman's revenge for conjugal bondage, and the King, dazzled, intimidated, and in love, accepted the smallest favours from her thankfully.

With years, reason, and maternity, all this was altered by degrees. The last was the great factor in the change. It cannot be doubted that the Queen suffered severely when the fishwives pursued her with their coarse jibes in the salons of Versailles after the Comtesse d'Artois had given birth to her eldest son, * and demanded that she should give a Dauphin to France, and that her childlessness made her irritable and impatient. But children came at length, and the heart so long unquiet was tranquillized. Then the Queen began to appreciate the character of the King. Her serious-minded husband, who had seen all her girlish and womanish follies, and with the tact lent by love had never uttered a reproach which cou

* The Duc de Berry.

wound her; that husband who had done violence to his own personal tastes to adopt hers, and who had acquired some degree of polish from contact with her faultless grace; that husband whose attention to her wishes was unremitting, and who paid her debts so discreetly, did he not deserve some gratitude in return? Was his absolute fidelity to her not to be rewarded, could she be indifferent to love which no rival might ever assail with a chance of success?

As King, had Louis XVI. no merit? Was not his strong sense of duty admirable and admired by all? He was a hard-working sovereign, too; he studied all documents himself, he required his Ministers to keep him fully informed of all the affairs of their several departments, and when he had expended the surplus of his physical activity in his forge, he would devote long hours to his library, where his table might be seen with its load of papers, maps, and volumes open and annotated. Is a duty-loving, hard-working king, who did not confine himself to good intentions, but did more good to the country in a few years than Louis XV. in the whole of his reign, to be very severely reproached for his intermittent weakness and his irresolution? As Marie Antoinette increased in wisdom these reflexions occupied her more closely, and by dint of esteeming Louis XVI., of placing confidence in him, and feeling that she was adored by this man of vulgar exterior but sure and stedfast heart, she also came, at last, to entertain a sentiment that was almost love. At least she became—as her mother had desired for her happiness—"the King's best friend."

This transformation was discernible in the outward bearing of the husband and wife, and in the unison of their life. Joseph II., when he visited France for the second time, in 1781, remarked a "considerable change for the better." In the Queen's letters also it is discernible: she does more and more justice to her husband, and mentions, at certain moments "attentions and thoughtful acts of affection which she will never forget in her life." A girl, the youngest of the women of the royal family, did much to strengthen this union; that woman was the King's beloved sister, Madame Elisabeth.

When Madame Clotilde left France, Madame Elisabeth could not as yet replace her. The King's second sister had held her rank at Court only from 1778, when she was handed over to Louis XVI. by her governess, Madame de Guéméné, and a household was formed for her. The princess was not pretty; her irregular features, her short stature, her nose, which was Bourbon to excess, deprived her appearance of anything like majesty; but her fresh complexion, mild blue eyes, and kind sweet smile, made her pleasing. She was already serious-minded, highly informed, full of sense, readiness, and prudence. Marie Antoinette, who had never regarded her sister-in-law otherwise than as a child, was much surprised to discover how charming she really was. Madame de Bombelles, the confidant of Madame Elisabeth, refers in her correspondence to the awakening of this new sentiment. She writes on the 22nd of April, 1779: "Madame Elisabeth came back yesterday from Trianon. The Queen is delighted with her; she tells everybody that the princess is amiable beyond anything, that she had not hitherto known enough of her, but that now she has made a friend of her, and that it will be for her whole life." In character, tastes, and education, indeed in every respect, the queen of twenty-three and the princess of fifteen years of age were different; but this contrast did but draw them more closely together; in spite of intrigues against it their attachment grew and strengthened day by day.

It is to be regretted that Marie Antoinette had not been brought in contact with Madame Elisabeth at an earlier period. The affectionate heart which had been fully satisfied in the home at Vienna, where it had so many to require and requite its tenderness, was very sad and lonely on arriving at Versailles. No woman of the family that was thenceforth to be hers was worthy of Marie Antoinette. These women were narrow-minded, jealous, and suspicious; there was no warmth, no youthfulness in them. Was it surprising that she should seek elsewhere, that she should resort to strangers who gave her the reality, or at least the semblance of affection? We may fairly believe that Madame Elisabeth, a few years older, would have filled the place in her life that was taken by Madame de Polignac. Such a companionship, being free from the drawbacks of private favour, would have largely aided in the formation of the Queen's character. She was very susceptible of external influence, and although that of Madame Elisabeth came late into her life it made itself felt. The princess saw the Queen's heedlessness and that she chose her friends ill, but did not think herself entitled to censure her; her example alone was, however, a reproach which Marie Antoinette understood.

We can divine the rôle of Madame Elisabeth, and her unseen action, from her letters. She was one of those unselfish and amiable girls who maintain the peace and unity of family life. She moderated and strove to dispel the displeasure of Mesdames with the Queen. The King had not forfeited her sisterly confidence by his opposition to her religious vocation; that she sincerely admired him her touching words attest: "My brother," she writes, "means so well; he so truly desires to do good, to make his people happy; he has kept himself so pure, it is impossible but that God must bless all his good qualities with great success.... He is very good, and much superior to all the Court put together."

Such sentiments could not fail to quicken and strengthen the Queen's growing appreciation of her husband, and to outweigh the scornful criticism and irreverent comments which were whispered around her. In this, as in everything, Madame Elisabeth was the guardian angel of the royal House.

Her distinguishing trait among the ladies of Versailles was piety. The Court of the Most Christian King was wanting above all things in religion. Outward practices, which were matters of etiquette or good-breeding, were not abandoned; but the age of unbelief had affected these feminine heads; the women read Voltaire and often worse than he, and most of them had serious private reasons for not living like Christians. The Queen undoubtedly did not come to this, but her associates tried to make her, and forced conversations upon her which were equally dangerous to faith and morals. Mesdames were deeply scandalized, and showed what they felt. The Abbé Vermond reproached her with having become "very indulgent as to the reputation of her friends, male and female." She was warned by all, even by Joseph II. who was far from being devout, of the moral danger she was incurring and of her falling-off in her religious habits. In reality, Marie Antoinette had not departed in anything from her former faith; her very first taste of suffering sufficed to revive it; she did not wait until her supreme trials came upon her to bow down her spirit to Christian resignation, to charity, and to forgiveness. But it is not a rash conclusion that the influence of Madame Elisabeth was active in the Queen's return to the fervour of the Faith in later years.

The piety of the princess had nothing narrow or gloomy about it; but was of the only kind that could attract the Queen; for it was allied with youth, gaiety, a liking for harmless pleasure, and the graces of society. It did not prevent Madame Elisabeth from riding on horseback for hours together, being an ardent billiard player, and even indulging in keen satire on occasion. Her religious practices, which were frequently severe, never made her unamiable. Education had corrected the defects of an impetuous temper, but allowed her to retain a charming vivacity, and this she put into everything, and above all into the relief of poverty and suffering. She was tolerant, never resenting difference of opinion from herself in any one. For instance, she loved and respected a Court lady who was her opposite in everything, although she had been placed, by a mistake, at the head of her household. Assuredly, the princess prayed to God for the conversion of the Comtesse Diane or any other friend of the Queen, but she supposed it would be easily accomplished: that soul, whose goodness was so absolute, believed in the goodness of every other soul.

Two foreigners on their travels, who had an unparalleled opportunity of

MARIE CHRISTINE, ARCHDUCHESS OF AUSTRIA,
DUCHESS OF SAXE-TESCHEN, GOVERNESS GENERAL OF THE LOW COUNTRIES.

From the portrait by R[illegible] engraved by Bartolozzi.

[illegible] vast [illegible] supreme [illegible] imagination. [illegible] the influence [illegible] the fervour of [illegible]

[illegible] endowed with [illegible] of society, [illegible] from riding on horseback [illegible] billiard player, and [illegible] as practices, which [illegible] Education had [illegible] of an [illegible] vivacity, and [illegible] into the midst of poverty and [illegible] of opinion from [illegible] a Court lady [illegible] although [illegible] by [illegible] any other [illegible] accomplished [illegible]

[illegible] opportunity of

MARIE CHRISTINE
ARCHIDUCHESSE D'AUTRICHE
DUCHESSE SAXE TESCHEN
GOUVERNANTE GENERALE
DES PAYS-BAS

forming a correct judgment, closely observed the private life of the royal family during the summer of 1786. The distinguished strangers were Marie Christine, Archduchess of Austria and Duchess of Saxe-Teschen, the eldest of the Queen's married sisters, and her husband. The visit of the Duchess had been planned several times, especially since she had been appointed Governess of the Low Countries in the name of Austria and had made Brussels her official residence. It would have pleased Maria Theresa much that the Duchess should have gone to Versailles after the birth of Madame Royale and brought her back all the particulars respecting her daughter and her grand-daughter which feminine observation could collect. Certain difficulties of etiquette relating to the reception of Marie Christine were raised, however, and unfortunately the Queen's reluctance was added to these. Marie Antoinette did not care to see a sister whom she had hardly known, who was very much older than herself, and to whom she attributed a part of the reports and comments concerning her which were sent to Vienna. Whatever the fabricators of autograph letters may assert, she never had any familiar correspondence with Marie Christine. She had a greater regard for Marie Caroline, Queen of the Two Sicilies. Her sympathies, which were often ill directed at Versailles, also went astray on crossing the frontier.

Marie Christine would have been far more deserving of those sympathies than the Queen of Naples. She was ill made, but her face was agreeable, her conduct irreproachable, and her mind cultivated; she was fond of drawing and she drew well; she loved beautiful books and fine works of art. There is a series of compositions to illustrate Don Quixote done by her which gives her a place among artists. Her memory is associated with the library and the collection of prints which were formed by her husband, and are numbered among the artistic treasures of the imperial family of Vienna. These were tastes unshared by Marie Antoinette. Her prejudices had been partially overcome before her sister and brother-in-law actually did make their journey, and their visit tended to remove them altogether.

The Duke and Duchess of Teschen travelled like private individuals, without formalities and without a suite. On arriving at Versailles, they were taken to their apartments by the Escalier des Princes. The first thing that struck them was the dirt of the entrance, and the shabby little shops set up on the landings. This bad impression was modified by the Queen's welcome. They found her in bed, for she had recently given birth to her fourth (and last) child and the allotted weeks of her "couches" had not yet expired. After the first few words, the sisters,—both on the defensive—exchanged explanations. The utterance of their mother's name, the recollections common to both, their affection for the Emperor and the frankness which characterised them, disposed of some of their respective grievances. The Queen's amiability did the rest. No great cordiality between them was indeed created, but there was an end to their hostility. An hour passed before the King arrived; he apologized for his late appearance, saying that he had been detained by some members of the parliament of Paris who had audience. The visitors were somewhat surprised by his lack of distinction, his shyness, his clumsy figure, and his "big smith's" aspect; but they soon discovered that the King of France was not wanting either in intelligence or knowledge. This first interview lasted long, and it was nearly ten o'clock before the duke and duchess took leave. They declined the rooms prepared for them at the Château, and went to an inn, as Joseph II. had done.

The next day they were visited by the Comte d'Artois and the Abbé de Vermond, who had had the honour of knowing them at Vienna. At noon they again visited the Queen and dined in her room, alone with her and the King. The three children were presented to them; Madame Sophie, the new-born infant, was in her nurse's arms. The afternoon was occupied in doing their manners to the rest of the family; then they resumed their freedom and returned to Paris.

The Emperor had told them about everything that they ought to see and learn in that city which he described as an "abode of pleasure and folly." They went to the best places without loss of time, and at a sitting of the Academy they were so lucky as to see the ladies shedding tears over a report upon the Prizes for Virtue, which was read by Chamfort, and to have the sons of the Duc d'Orléans, with Madame de Genlis, their "Governor," pointed out to them. They paid their respects to the Duchesse d'Orléans, who did not go to the Academy; they met the old Maréchale and the former Court (of Louis XV.) at the hôtel of the Princesse de Conti, and at the little fête which M. de Richelieu gave them at his own. They were anxious to avoid offending anybody who represented any kind of power, so, certainly by the advice of Marie Antoinette, they went to see Madame Louise at Saint-Denis, and Madame Necker at Saint-Ouen.

Versailles took up several of their days. This was not because Marie Antoinette wished to see her sister often. "My brother-in-law," she wrote to Mercy, "hunts with the King on Monday. Let it be quite understood, if possible, that I reserve those days to myself for my own affairs and that I like to be alone, so that *she* may not ask to come, for that would worry me (*me gênerait*) very much." Her outward demeanour was of course correct on all occasions of receiving her kinsfolk. She carefully selected the customary presents made by the King, tapestries, carpets and porcelain. She did not give entertainments, her health and the too recent emotions of the Necklace trial forbade any such effort. Marie Christine and her husband witnessed only two State spectacles, the "Saint-Louis," with the Chapter of the Knights of the Order held in the Chapel, and the ceremonial of the "relevailles." The latter was very simple: all the ladies, in Court dress and wide hoops, crossed the room in single file, making three curtseys, in front of a couch on which the Queen reclined. The sovereigns of Saxe-Teschen could not derive an idea of the magnificence of the Court of France from these examples; on the other hand, they became well acquainted with its ordinary life.

Each morning, the Queen's chairmen came to the inn and carried them to the Château "in their walking cages." While the duchess went to her sister, at her toilet, the duke presented himself at the King's "lever." They afterwards dined in private, the table being laid for four, except on the day of the dinner in public, a spectacle which astonished our foreigners not a little. After dinner they went into the great park, and visited Trianon and Montreuil, and the delightful garden which was Madame Elisabeth's Trianon; they went to Saint-Cyr later, and the princess joined them and did its honours. One day they went to Bellevue with the Queen, to dine with Mesdames and admire the view of the valley of the Seine, which is commanded by the château built by Madame de Pompadour. They also passed an afternoon with Madame de Polignac, and there they found her "society." The official position of the Governess of the Children of France explains this visit; and moreover, Marie Antoinette was resolved to spare her friend's pride and to conceal the extent of the change in her own feelings from her family.

In the evening the Queen took them to the theatre in the town, or gave them performances of proverbs, charades, and short plays in the Salon de la Paix. The day's proceedings ended with a supper in the apartment of Madame. The various households of the royal family sent their supper there, and the last touch was given to the dishes in the kitchens. This family meeting for the evening meal was a patriarchal custom established by Marie Antoinette. At nine o'clock precisely everybody was seated at table; the windows of the dining-room opened upon the parterre, and very often the repast would begin with a special soup made from little birds which Madame herself caught in a net. This soup was the triumph of the princess, who indeed could hardly hope for any other. After supper the conversation was continued, but the guests did not leave the

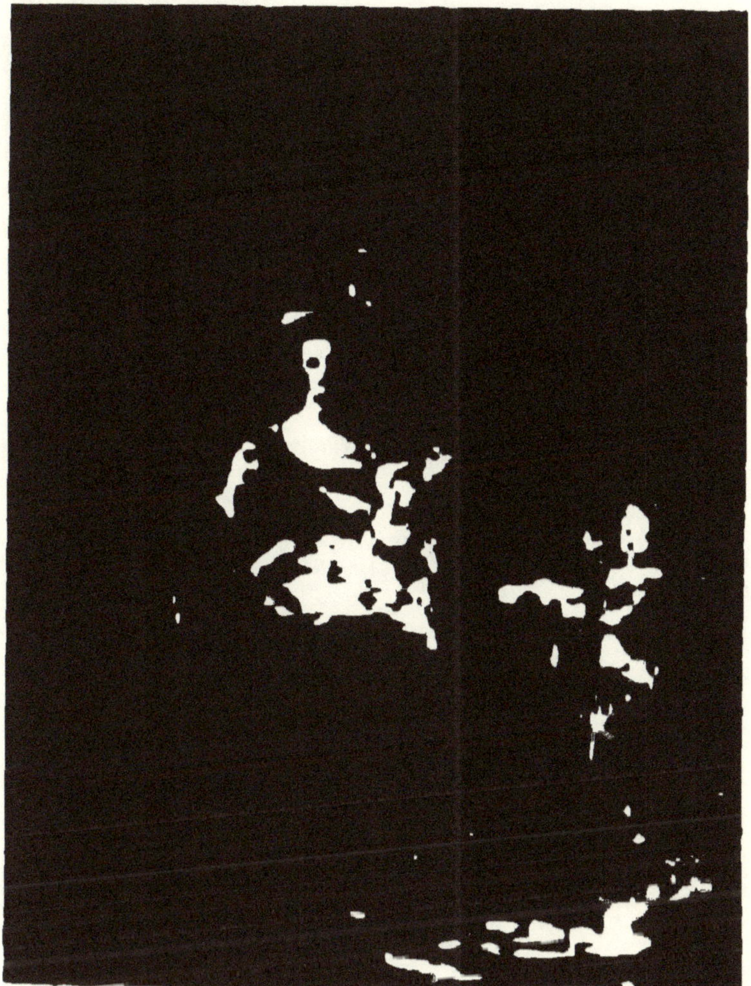

MARIE ANTOINETTE, QUEEN OF FRANCE, AND HER CHILDREN (1787).
From the portrait by Madame Vigée-Lebrun (Musée de Versailles).

[illegible] Whit[illegible]

presented himself [illegible]

[illegible] the noble being

[illegible]

table; when they began to feel sleepy the King would give the signal by rising, and all would retire to their several "lodgings" in the vast building.

In short, life at Versailles at the close of the reign had nothing brilliant about it, and was very like what Marie Christine had always seen at the imperial Court. The princess carried away an agreeable recollection of her sister; the only thing she condemned was her too evident desire to please, and this she indicates in a letter to Joseph II., who saw her meaning at once: "Yes," he replied in a clumsy phrase, "she is rather frenchified, and only the face of the good fat German remains." Let us leave it to the Emperor and the Archduchess to regard the fact as a defect.

The Queen's serious and elevated view of her maternal duties, so fully verified by Marie Christine, must strike even the most prejudiced inquirer into her history. In the later years she lived for them only, and she found consolation in them for all the unhappiness of her life. The maladies of her children were her great troubles, their education was her chief care. The Dauphin's household was selected by her. She did not hesitate to oppose the family authorities in order to secure a Governor whom she could trust for her son, and she carried the appointment of the Duc d'Harcourt against the rigidly pietistic objections of Mesdames. She did more: after the birth of her second son, she desired to have her daughter near her, and she lodged Madame Royale with Madame de Mackau, the under-governess, in her "petits appartements" on the ground-floor of the château, reserving only a few rooms for herself. When the Dauphin was removed from the care of the Governess and her subordinates, the Queen required Monsieur and Madame to vacate their handsome apartment, close to those of the princess, and sent them, in spite of their grumbling, to the other end of the Château. The Dauphin was installed in their place, with the Harcourt family.

The two elder children were now as close to their mother as possible;

staircases and inner doors enabled her to enter their several dwellings from all sides; she could go to them for kisses whenever she liked. She became more and more attached to those "petits appartements" which placed her children within her reach and were level with the terraces, so that she could see the Dauphin at play, and she planned a maternal nest still more private than her cabinets, for herself. A large bath-room, a resting-room and a library had been already added for her use, and several new improvements were projected The 5th of October found the works still in progress there.

The Duc de Normandie only remained in the charge of Madame de Polignac: their mother was Governess to the other children. Her mornings were given to them; she was present at their studies with their masters, and sometimes heard them repeat their lessons herself. The leisure hours which she formerly gave to pleasure were now devoted to these new duties. The Queen's capacity to form the minds of her children may be judged from her own account of her method. "They are accustomed," she writes, "to have great confidence in me, and, when they have done wrong, to tell me of it themselves. And in reprimanding them I always show that I am more pained and grieved about what they have done than angry. I have made them all understand that *yes* or *no*, spoken by me, is irrevocable, but I always give them a reason within reach of their age, so that they may not think it is temper on my part." The whole of this "instruction," which was addressed, a little later, to Madame de Tourzel, who replaced Madame de Polignac, ought to be read. No mother ever studied her children with ideas more just or affection more clear-sighted. The document also makes us feel the moral progress of Marie Antoinette, and enables us to divine what she would have become, as queen, in less troubled times.

This education in honour and rectitude bore its fruits, and rewarded the wise tenderness to which it was due. Madame Royale "begins to become a personage " and a charming companion for her mother. She accompanies her in her visits to the orphans who are brought up by persons of the Queen's household at her expense, and to the old and infirm servants whom she either pensions or places at Trianon. She trusts the practical exercise of charity to correct the " little something of pride and obduracy " that is a defect in the princess.

Not much was heard of the little Duc de Normandie, "a real peasant's child, big, rosy, and fat," says Marie Antoinette with pride ; but the Dauphin gave promise of a generous and intellectual prince. He was thoughtful, precocious, and profoundly serious, after the manner of children who read more than they play. His sayings and doings were beyond his years. One of his young companions had broken a china cup which the Queen prized highly ; the culprit having gone away, the Dauphin was accused. He did not defend himself, although the punishment was severe ; he was to be deprived of his cherished excursion to Trianon for three days. The other child came back and spontaneously confessed his fault. Everyone expressed astonishment that the prince had said nothing : " Is it for me," he replied, " to accuse any one?"

The maternal happiness of Marie Antoinette did not last long. Her youngest daughter, Madame Sophie, died at eleven months ; and almost immediately afterwards the Dauphin's health broke, and his state suddenly became serious. " My eldest son," writes the Queen to Joseph II., " gives me great anxiety. Although he has been always delicate and weakly, I was unprepared for the crisis that has occurred. His figure has got out of shape, one hip is higher than the other, something is wrong with his spine, the vertebræ are loosened a little and stick out. For some time past he has been feverish every day, and he is very thin and weak.... The King was very weak and sickly during his childhood ; the air of Meudon proved very salutary to him ; we are going to send my son there." This was an unfounded hope inspired by the doctors, who also persuaded the child's mother that the chief cause of the malady was his cutting his teeth with difficulty. It was the Queen's destiny to be deceived, and these were the only beneficent falsehoods that ever were told to her in all her life.

The removal of the Dauphin to Meudon did no good. In the spring of 1789 the truth could be hidden no longer; the child was dying, and he knew it himself. The young Comtesse de Lage went to see him, one afternoon, with Madame de Lamballe, and returned from Meudon in great emotion: "It is heart-rending," she said, with sobs, "his endurance, his sense, his patience go to one's heart. When we arrived someone was reading aloud to him. He had taken a fancy to lie on a billiard table, and mattresses had been laid there. We looked at each other, my princess and I, with the same idea, that it resembled a mournful bed of state after their *(leur)* death. Madame de Lamballe asked him what he was reading: 'a very interesting moment of our history, Madame,' he replied, 'the reign of Charles VII.; there are a great many heroes in it.' I ventured to ask whether Monseigneur read on and on, or only the most striking parts: 'On and on, Madame,' he said, 'I do not know enough about it to choose, and it is all interesting to me....' His beautiful dying eyes turned towards me as he said this."

The countess speaks also of the mother, of that mother who was said to have shrunk from her son's death-bed with childish repugnance! "The poor child's sayings are almost beyond belief; he rends the Queen's heart; his affection for her is extreme. The other day he entreated her to dine in his room; alas! she swallowed more tears than bread."

The end was approaching. Paris had been in a political ferment for some weeks; nevertheless, it was affected by the thought of the child whose birth it had hailed with rejoicing seven years previously. People told each other about the royal child's suffering and courage, and enquired anxiously concerning the progress of his illness. On the second of June, at ten o'clock in the evening, the great bell of Notre-Dame rang for the devotion of the Forty Hours' Prayer; on the third, there was Exposition of the Blessed Sacrament in the morning in all the churches; on the fourth, between six and seven o'clock in the evening, after the first act at the Théâtre Français, the curtain went down; the death of the Dauphin had just been announced. While the city was full of the rumour of the event and the comments upon it, the Revolution was forgotten for the moment, and in a room in the Château de Meudon a weeping mother kneeled beside the couch whereon so many hopes lay dead.

[illegible] hope inspired [illegible] child's [illegible] the chief [illegible] his teeth [illegible]

[illegible]

[illegible] political [illegible] thought of [illegible] previously [illegible] courage and [illegible] anxiously concerning the progress of his illness. On the second of June, at ten o'clock in the evening, the great bell of Notre-Dame rang for the devotion of the Forty Hours' Prayer; on the third, there was Exposition of the Blessed Sacrament in the morning in all the churches; on the fourth, between six and seven o'clock in the evening, after the first act at the Théâtre Français, the curtain went down: the death of the Dauphin had just been announced. While the city was full of the rumour of the event and the comments upon it, the Revolution was forgotten for the moment, and in a room in the Château de Meudon a weeping mother kneeled beside the couch whereon so many hopes lay dead.

THE FOURTH CHAPTER

TRIANON.

During the closing days of April 1789 the [illegible] to Trianon was thronged with unwonted [illegible] barristers and attorneys from the provincial [illegible] long coats, and country curés in short cassocks [illegible] were the deputies of the States General who had just arrived at [illegible] town of Versailles and were visiting His Majesty's gardens in the [illegible] of escape from their official functions. Their first visit was to the [illegible] Château, the famous Trianon, so constantly mentioned in the [illegible] pamphlets and songs in circulation in the provinces.

The visitors, on arriving at the gates of the small [illegible] there, much surprised by the modest aspect of the [illegible] consisting of two storeys, with a five-windowed [illegible] perceived for themselves that the gentlemen's [illegible] were far more lordly. Nevertheless they [illegible] inside of this dwelling: wonders respecting [illegible] many believed that the Queen had expended a large part of the [illegible] of

THE FOURTH CHAPTER.

TRIANON.

During the closing days of April, 1789, the road that leads from Versailles to Trianon was thronged with unwonted visitors. There, at all hours, barristers and attorneys from the provincial Courts of Justice *(baillinges)*, in long coats, and country curés in short cassocks, were to be met. These were the deputies of the States General who had just arrived at the royal town of Versailles and were visiting His Majesty's gardens in the intervals of escape from their official functions. Their first visit was to the Queen's Château, the famous Trianon, so constantly mentioned in the newspapers, pamphlets, and songs in circulation in the provinces.

The visitors, on arriving at the gates of the small court-yard, would stand there, much surprised by the modest aspect of the house, a square building consisting of two storeys, with a five-windowed façade and a flat roof. They perceived for themselves that the gentlemen's residences in their own villages were far more lordly. Nevertheless they went in, being curious to see the inside of this dwelling: wonders respecting it had been told to them, and many believed that the Queen had expended a large part of the fortune of

France on it. Their astonishment increased when the attendant conducted them into the rooms, where the decoration and furniture were no doubt very elegant, but not very rich: instead of the lavish luxury that they expected they found only good taste. The deputies could not understand this. They wanted to be taken into every part of the house, even the servants' quarters; several of them went into particulars, and insisted on seeing a salon draped in diamonds, with curved pillars studded with sapphires and rubies. It did not occur to their guide to inform them that the salon in question never had existed except as a theatrical "property," and that the precious stones were bits of coloured glass. So simply true an explanation would not, however, have convinced anybody, and the visitors would have gone out, had it been given, as they actually did go out, convinced that the principal rooms in the house had been concealed from them.

Such was the notion of the Queen's little château generally entertained in France. These prejudices, originating in the Court slanders, and exaggerated by the foolish ignorance and folly of the masses, were gradually causing the modest country-house to be regarded by the mass of the public all through France, as "the Austrian woman's den of debauchery," the phrase which had been applied to it by the already menacing mouth of the Revolution. We shall see presently what the "den" was, and what constituted the "debauchery."

Little Trianon has a history before the time of Marie Antoinette. In 1749, Louis XV. had annexed a private domestic menagerie, a kitchen garden, and the famous botanic garden in which Bernard de Jussieu worked, to the park of the old Château de Trianon, built by Louis XIV. At the same time a salon for cards and conversation was put up near these new creations, and it still exists in the middle of the "French garden." People then began to say "Le petit Trianon" in opposition to "le grand Trianon" of Louis XIV. The King, who could find no pleasure anywhere, seemed to like the place, and Madame de Pompadour made it attractive by constantly varied amusements. She soon persuaded him to build a pleasure-house there. Gabriel sent in the plans in 1762, and the building was completed in 1768.

LITTLE TRIANON.

From a photograph.

It was not the Marquise who gave the house-warming; she was dead when all was ready "to the last nail," and Louis XV. had long ago forgotten her for Madame Du Barry, who figures largely in the recollections of "le petit Trianon." During the last years of her feminine reign she frequented the house and gardens, and frequently supped there with the King and their friends. A mechanical table ready-served rose from beneath through a sliding aperture in the floor, which opened and closed in a few seconds; at each course the centre of the table detached itself, disappeared, and rose again bearing fresh viands: four dumb-waiters within reach of the guests supplied the place of servants, and secured the absence of indiscreet spectators.

Little is known concerning those Du Barry suppers, but rumour had attached an ill-fame to them, and when Marie Antoinette thought she had redeemed the place by her presence, calumny seized upon the evil recollections attached to it, and with fell purpose confounded the two women of Trianon in the popular imagination.

Louis XV. was taken ill at Trianon in the spring of 1774, and died at Versailles; Madame Du Barry left the Court never again to appear there, and the young Queen begged her husband to give her the little château for a country-house. The King has been credited with a gallant speech on this occasion: "Madame, this lovely place has always been the abode of the favourites of Kings; it ought therefore to be yours." It would have been very unlike Louis XVI. to suggest such an association of ideas, especially as his dislike of Madame Du Barry was notorious. Marie Antoinette received the present with childish delight, and amused herself by telling the King that he was to come to her own house only on invitation.

This fancy indicates by one stroke the new life that Marie Antoinette intended to make for herself in her new residence. As Dauphine the Court had wearied her; she wanted now, as Queen, to escape from it as much as possible. She liked privacy, informal play, and gardening; and she was now to be enabled to gratify her tastes within a few steps of solemn Versailles. The simplicity of the manners and the pleasures which she had known in her childhood, and so deeply regretted since, was to be restored at Trianon.

Like the women of her kingdom, she too would have the government of a house and a garden, and she intended to banish censorious, evil-speaking, and importunate persons, to make a selection among her courtiers, and to admit only her friends.

At first the Queen had only family parties at Trianon. Louis XVI. was constantly there with her. After the 6th of June, she received him at dinner with the royal family. Very soon she gave suppers and had plays performed in the Orangerie. But, apart from these littlé fêtes, which displayed her refined taste, and skill in organization, she made a genuine country-house home of Trianon. She constantly went thither in the afternoon, accompanied by two ladies only, and even supped there sometimes, before returning to Versailles.

Besides, how grave were the affairs which required the presence of the young châtelaine, and kept her on the spot! She decorated Micque, her architect, with the title of "Intendant and Comptroller-general of the Queen's buildings," and that novel function was not to be a sinecure. She had grand projects for Trianon. How could a woman think herself really and truly at home, unless she had set the seal of her fancy and her own taste on everything around her? The Queen wished to have an entirely new garden, on a plan of her own selection, and this was to be her greatest recreation. The botanic series of Bernard de Jussieu, the hot-houses filled with exotic plants, the large monotonous squares which covered nearly the whole of the garden ground of Little Trianon, and whither naturalists came to study, made up too sombre a whole for the girlish possessor. A word from her lips, and the collections were "bundled up" and carried away to the Jardin des Plantes in Paris, the trees were uprooted, and the soil was upturned. This transformation coincided with that of Versailles. The King ordered the fullgrown, growing, and ornamental timber about Versailles and Trianon to be sold together, and the highest bidders were bound to clear the ground for replanting in less than six months.

This curious hurry is worth noting. All that Louis XIV. had done in horticulture, and that Louis XV. had preserved and enlarged, was swept away

IN 1775.

From a painting by Hubert Robert (Musée de Versailles).

in the first year of his successor's reign. The new society brought with it a new order of taste. The day of straight interminable avenues, leading to nothing unexpected, was ended; nobody cared any longer for the pompous artificiality and majestic stiffness of the geometrical trees and dark armies of clipped yews ranged everywhere about the parks in regular lines; everybody wanted gróves less formal wherein to read Gessner's idylls and the poetic declamation of Rousseau upon "the man of nature" at ease. The changes in the art of Le Nôtre are explained by the literature of the time. Versailles was only partly transformed, perhaps out of respect for the recollections of the great reign, but much more certainly from want of money: the most considerable work done there was the erection of the cascade rock, with Marly's horses in the heroic style, and Girardon's Apollo and the Muses placed on it with just passable skill. At Little Trianon, on the contrary, almost everything was swept away. In one corner a few parterres and quincunxes of the old style were preserved; the rest was replaced by groves, winding paths, and mown lawns, which suited the fancy of the day.

The picturesque part in the plan of the new garden would do credit to Hubert Robert. The painter had no hand in it, however; it was suggested by an amateur gardener, the Comte de Caraman. The Queen had visited the Anglo-Chinese gardens which had been laid out from the Count's own designs for his hôtel in the Rue Saint-Dominique; she had been charmed, and had asked for his ideas on Trianon. On reflection, she rejected several and retained only those which were in irreproachable taste: no hermitage, no mock ruins, but two really elegant buildings only, the Belvédère and the Temple de l'Amour, to furnish and adorn the perspective.

These two "dreams" of Marie Antoinette are still standing: under the light cupola supported by a Corinthian colonnade, Bouchardon's Cupid (no longer the original marble, it is true), goes on cutting his bow out of Hercules' club, and the Belvédère with its fine outline, still dominates the artificial lake between the hills.

But, if we would behold this scene, which is like that of a stage ballet as it was in the past, we must refer to the works of the Chevalier de Lespinasse. The noble engraver has launched a flotilla of boats, with a feminine crew, upon the lake; he has peopled the alleys with fair ladies, walking or sitting on the grass, by the side of the water, in straw hats, with the eloquent fan between their fingers.

The creation of all these pretty marvels was not accomplished without some difficulty, and it took more time than the Queen had expected. The resources of the Treasury could ill bear the cost; M. Turgot objected, and the Queen's architect encountered financial obstacles at every new project. Nevertheless, his sovereign lady got the better of the Minister by degrees; the soil was turned into rose gardens, winding alleys surmounted the lake, cascades made music as they tumbled over the rocks brought from afar, and the grotto offered its cool shade and mossy couch for silence and repose.

Such were the early delights of Trianon for the young Queen, and the first changes which she made there. The theatre and the Hameau were to come soon, but she already had a little domain of her very own, where she passed her afternoons, and rambled in the grounds with her friends. She longed to go and live at Little Trianon for a few days, or at least to sleep there, the real taking possession of a dwelling. But how was she to leave the royal abode? On what pretext could she evade the etiquette that bound her to sleep under the same roof with the King. The spring of 1779 brought about the desired opportunity. A few months after the birth of Madame Royale, the young mother had the measles, and the doctors desired that she should be removed from Versailles for the period of her convalescence. Trianon was chosen, naturally, for her residence, and the Queen wrote to Maria Theresa: "I am going to-day to establish myself at Trianon, for change of air, until the end of my three weeks, when I shall be allowed to see the King. I have prevented him from shutting himself up with me; he has never had the measles, and especially at this moment, when there is so much business, it would have been unfortunate had he taken the infection."

The good reasons given to the mother by the daughter did not half satisfy Monsieur de Mercy. A departure from custom which might soon become a habit made him uneasy. And then, the inconvenience of it! The entire household of the Queen accompanied her. As the little château could only accommodate a part, the rest had to be lodged in the out-buildings, and in the great château: this meant considerable expense in fitting up rooms. Lastly, Marie Antoinette had either chosen singular nurses, or she had been persuaded into accepting the services of four gentlemen who were to watch her day and night. Mercy had great trouble in making them take their departure at eleven o'clock, p.m., to return to Versailles.

These favourites, the Duc de Coigny, the Duc de Guines, the Comte Esterhazy and Baron de Besenval, for whom all the customs of the Court were violated, and who would hardly allow the lady-in-waiting and the lady of honour a few minutes for the performance of their respective parts, belonged to the Queen's particular set. The indiscreet zeal of the four personages was severely censured; there were complaints of the Queen's familiarity with courtiers too highly honoured; the ladies in attendance protested against the exclusion to which they were subjected, and it was maliciously asked: supposing the King were to be taken ill, who would be the four ladies to have charge of him.

The Queen's first sojourn at Little Trianon had not, however, the ill-consequences that Mercy feared. Marie Antoinette, whose main purpose was to amuse herself, also gave a portion of her time to her royal duties. She received the Duchesse de Cossé and the Maréchale de Noailles, both grave personages, and for the first time learned the worth, and appreciated the charming mind of her sister-in-law, Madame Elisabeth.

We know exactly what was the Queen's mode of life during her stay at Little Trianon: "Her Majesty went out only at the hours of the day proper for taking exercise, and she retired regularly at eleven o'clock. Although etiquette was dispensed with in the ordering of the Court, the different times of the day were duly observed in the fitting order; all the Queen's following (*alentours*) assembled at a déjeuner which took the place of dinner; general conversation, and some walking filled up a portion of the afternoon, and led to the time of evening and supper, which was always served early."

The Queen had other amusements. The Comte d'Artois, like herself, did not care for the Court, and had taken a fancy to Trianon. One day he brought Nicolet and his company, called "les grands danseurs du Roi," to the château. The two stars were Placide, who played pantomimes composed by himself, and "le Petit Diable de Hollande," an extraordinary rope-dancer who dispensed with the balancing-pole and danced on eggs without breaking them. Marie Antoinette was so much pleased with their performances that her brother-in-law, who was himself a proficient in bodily exercises, was jealous of the triumph of his protégés, and resolved to earn a share of it. The following year, the Court was greatly puzzled by his conduct; every morning he went to Little Trianon and remained there in the pursuit of some mysterious occupation for several hours. At length the grave purpose to which the Prince devoted his leisure was made known. "In the greatest secrecy," says a contemporary, "he took lessons from Placide and 'le Petit Diable,' heroes most in renown for rope-dancing; then, when he was sufficiently advanced to shine in the art, he displayed his talents to the eyes of the Queen in a select company, and everybody agreed that his performance was admirable."

And this personage was the only friend that Marie Antoinette had in the House of France! To put against the grumbling hostility of Mesdames Tantes, the jealousy of Madame and the Comtesse d'Artois, and the covert enmity of Monsieur, the Queen possessed the frivolous liking of a twenty-year-old rope-dancer.

In the ensuing years Marie Antoinette was constantly at Trianon. Almost every day she went to inspect the works in the grounds, and was apparently resolved to make them interminable. Presently she passed whole days there, and the King would join her on his return from hunting. It became a custom for them to dine or sup at the little château. The princesses came through the two parks, on foot, and without escort. Sometimes a person not belonging to the private circle was invited, by special favour. The beautiful Duchesse de Gramont-Caderousse, having appeared in the costume of a peasant woman of Provence, and without powder, at a supper given by the Duc de Laval, and made a great success, the Queen invited her to Trianon one afternoon, that she might see her wear the dress. But, as a rule, the entrée was rigidly restricted to "the society" only, and the porters had orders to close the gates to all the rest of the Court.

This "country-house" life naturally led to an increase of familiarity and freedom. The Queen of France held less place in it than Madame de Montesson or the Maréchale de Luxembourg held in their Parisian circle. She was simply an unpretending "lady of the house," who willingly allowed her guests to group themselves around another woman, Madame de Polignac for instance, while she devoted herself solely to the cares of hospitality and the providing of amusements and pleasant surprises. Her only desire was to please these guests, all of whom were her friends; friends chosen by her trusting heart, and who loved her, as she believed.

"The Queen," writes an eye-witness, "sometimes resided for a whole month together at Little Trianon, and had established all the customs of country-house life there; on her coming into her salon the ladies did not rise from their embroidery-frames or the piano-forte, nor did the men pause in their games of billiards or trick-track. Madame Elisabeth accompanied the Queen, but the ladies-of-honour were not established at Little Trianon. Persons invited came over from Versailles for the dinner hour. The King and the princes came regularly to supper. A print gown, a gauze fichu, and a straw hat formed the sole adornment of the princesses." Mercy writes, in 1780, that Marie Antoinette passed all the morning "en famille" until one o'clock, which was the dinner hour. "Only the strictly necessary servants were in attendance," he says, "not any of the Court officials. In the afternoon things assumed quite a different aspect; the princesses and princes of the royal family, Mesdames Tantes, the most distinguished members of their suite, the ladies of the Palace and some of the most favoured outsiders repaired to Trianon and passed the remainder of the day and the evening there. The charming gardens of that pleasure-house afforded pleasant and varied walks, and the game of Commerce filled up the intervals before and after supper."

Among the diversions of Trianon, mention must be made of the game of "the Rings," which had been set up by the Queen's directions on the lawn, sheltered by a Chinese pavilion, also billiards and loto; these Louis XVI. particularly liked. But everybody's chief pleasure was walking in that well-cared-for, widely-varied garden, whose beauties were analysed by Prince de Ligne with the skill of a connoisseur, and which suggested the poetic descriptions of the Chevalier Bertin in the *Almanach des Muses*. The number of exotic trees, the "surprises" in landscape effects to be met at every turn, the refinement of this contest with nature made foreigners who were admitted to see it understand the young Queen's love for her little domain, which she had so greatly embellished.

Baroness Oberkirch gives us her recollections of Trianon in the month of May: "What a delightful walk! How delicious were those groves perfumed with lilacs and peopled with nightingales! The air was full of scented vapours; butterflies spread their golden wings in the sunshine of the spring. Never in my life have I passed moments more enchanting than the three hours of my visit to that retreat. The Queen stayed there the greater part of the summer, and I perfectly understand it." Even now, although time has destroyed many of the wooded dells and altered more than one prospect, the grounds of Little Trianon have retained some of their olden charm; and the visitor, whose purpose it is to recall the emotions of history only, involuntarily slackens his pace in the deserted paths, and yields to the enchantment of the eyes.

Marie Antoinette delighted in going out at late hours. To this Monsieur de Mercy objected for various reasons, and especially because it gave rise to some malicious gossip; but the Queen did not listen to him. She revelled in evenings passed under the great trees, and in the calm air of the summer

nights. The "society" of Trianon gave the Queen an entertainment one night in June, 1779; Grimm describes it as follows: "All the trenches surrounding the garden were strewn with burning faggots; their light, mingled with that of several lanterns carefully hidden in the foliage of the thickest groves shed a soft radiance like moonshine or the first ray of daybreak. Her Majesty's attention having been called to the singular effect of this novel dawn, she immediately desired to go down into her gardens There, she was surprised by sounds of celestial harmony, and following the melodious strains she descried in a corner of the bosquet a shepherd playing a flute; this shepherd was the Duc de Guines; farther on, two fauns, Begozzi and Ponte, first executed a duet with horn and hautbois; and afterwards uniting with the flute, formed a charming trio. Verses sung by other sylvan divinities terminated this pretty impromptu; but those verses have not come forth from the sanctuary for which they were composed. At the beginning of the century, almost in the same place, similar nocturnal walks and concerts had been the "great passion" of the Duchesse de Bourgogne.

Now and then, on festive occasions, numerous invitations to Trianon were issued. The fête given on the 3rd of September, 1777, for the inauguration of the new garden was one of the most original. A fair, in which the Court ladies were vendors, was represented. A market-place was set up on the lawn in an enclosure of boards, lath partitions dividing the stalls where the baker, the confectioner, and the purveyor of "charcuterie" dispensed their wares (gratis), and even the cook's shop was busy in the open air. All these stalls were connected by garlands of roses. The Queen kept a rural tavern (*guinguette*), surmounted by twenty-one trellised arbours, each bearing the name of a royal House upon a signboard.

There were shows of all sorts. The most amusing was a bird-seller's shop; Carlin, of the Comédie-Italienne, and Dugazon, of the Comédie-Française, were concealed in basket-work shapes representing a magpie and a turkey-cock. Actors from the two "Houses" gave several performances on an improvised stage. The "Jeu de bagues" near the house was the centre of a Chinese fête, arranged in accordance with the "Anglo-Chinese" style of the garden (*), and the musicians of the Gardes Françaises, disguised as Mandarins, played in the pavilion. The avenues leading to Trianon were lined with the booths of Paris shopkeepers who had been engaged to come, their expenses being paid.

Although this fête went off to the satisfaction of the spectators, the outside effect of it injured Marie Antoinette. This was the period of Necker's first Ministry, and the word "economy" was on the lips of all, with only too good reason. People who were already displeased by the creation of the park, spread the report that the Queen's fête had cost four hundred thousand livres. This figure was, as usual, greatly exaggerated, but where a grievance is concerned, it is not the reality, but the impression made on the mind of the public that counts.

When a great foreign personage was to be received, there was more show of justification for the profuse expenditure of the Queen, and thus Marie Antoinette associated Trianon with the honours done to Joseph II. by the Court of France. The fête given to the Comte and Comtesse du Nord may convey an idea of these receptions. It began with a play in the new garden theatre. The Queen herself guided her imperial guests through a canvas corridor lighted by lamps, which connected the château with the theatre. The Russian gentlemen and the Court followed, in full dress. Baroness Oberkirch, with her little water bottles and her fresh flowers in her hair, was a centre of attraction as a friend of the Grand Duchess. The company being seated in the little theatre, books of the play, specially printed for the evening, were distributed, according to a pretty custom; twelve copies were bound in morocco, with the arms of the Queen and the "Grand-Dukes," as the imperial couple were called. There was, as usual, a varied performance; a comic opera, *Zémir et Azor*, by Marmontel and Grétry, acted by the Comédie-Française, and *La Jeune Française au Sérail* "an

(*) See Appendix, Note 7.

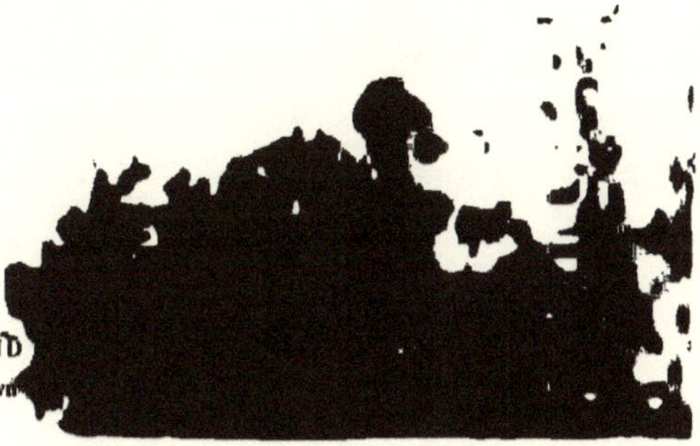

SECOND

Drawn

acted ballet by Gardel the elder, ballet-master to the Queen," with new scenery.

Three hundred guests were invited to the royal supper at the château. Madame Oberkirch was placed by the side of Madame Elisabeth, with whom she felt quite at ease, and who had the tact to talk to her at some length about a Lorraine family whom they both knew. The Queen caught a few words of their conversation in the midst of the noise, and joined in it several times with her unfailing grace. The remembrance of so much honour was enough for the baroness, she has not noted any other particulars of the banquet. Yet she might have recorded many; for instance, what quantity of "hatreaux de lapreaux (young rabbits) en hatelets" or "ailes de campines (a fine kind of pullet), à la d'Armagnac," was eaten; but the enumeration of the tables will give a better idea of the importance of the feast. The Queen's table and the three tables "of honour" were served in the four first rooms. In the ground-floor rooms and in the offices, those for the "seigneurs Russiens," the Intendant of the Menus—the French and Italian actors supped with him—the Guards' musicians, one hundred covers for the Opera and the King's own band, and lastly a small table "served to four ladies on the part of the Queen," and another to Madame de Polignac. Provisions were also supplied to the waiting-women, the women attached to the service of the Queen and of the Grand Duchess, the Guards, the officers of the King's table, the footmen, the men employed in the stables and the chair porters, the sempstresses, the under-cooks, and "an infinite number of workmen whose number it is impossible to fix." We have an official note of the dishes. At the Queen's table there was served, in meat only, four sorts of removes, twenty-four entrées, and eight dishes of different roast meats: and more than twelve hundred persons sat at table that evening in the Queen's little château.

After this gala supper, persons belonging to the Court, but who had not been invited, arrived. The company resorted to the gardens to listen to the bands of the French and Swiss Guards. The night fête began with an illumination described as follows by a contemporary. "The art with which the English garden was not illuminated, but suffused with light, produced a charming effect; wicks floating in oil in earthenware, pots hidden by boards painted green, lighted all the flower-beds and the shrubberies, and brought out the different tints in a varied and agreeable manner; some hundreds of faggots burning in the trench behind the Temple of Love, kept up a great light which made it the most brilliant point of the garden."

One of the prints by the Chevalier de Lespinasse represents this corner of the fête. In the groves out of the glare we can picture a contrast which must have been pleasing to behold; the Comtesse de Sabran says of similar evening fêtes at Montreuil and Bellevue, that the "discreet lighting of the groves made the shadows of objects so faint that water, trees and persons all alike seemed aerial."

These were the great days of Trianon, when the crowd invaded it for a few hours; but it quickly resumed its charm of stillness and privacy.

Let us now enter the house; let us visit the uninhabited rooms, from whence the sound of laughter and the echo of the harpsicord have fled, and briefly recall the recollections that cling to them.

We cross the threshold and are transported into another age. Everything evokes an idea of life and art different from our own. The walls of the deserted entrance hall are white and bare, the staircase is of wrought iron, and amid the reiterated designs of lyre and caduceus, the gilded cipher of the Queen appears. It was placed there after date, for the work is of the time of Louis XV. But it was truly the period of Louis XVI. that hung the lantern of chased bronze and blue enamel from the ceiling, a beautiful slight thing, supremely expressive of that refined delicacy, too frail perhaps, which was the supreme grace of the old régime.

On the first floor we come to the apartments. Here the great panels of carved wood still bear the shell and the baskets of flowers of the Oppenord period; but the side panels, where garlands of fruit are tied up with ribbons, are treated with a different sentiment. It is seen at a glance that two styles in juxtaposition have contributed to the decoration of the

THE STAIRCASE AT LITTLE TRIANON

From a photograph.

[illegible]
[illegible] ported [illegible]
[illegible]t from [illegible]
[illegible], the [illegible]
[illegible] and [illegible]

house, a charming and instructive contradiction which we find at Trianon even on the cases of the door locks. The frieze panels of the antechamber were painted for Madame de Pompadour, they are signed by Natoire, and Telemachus in the Island of Calypso wears the features of Louis the Well-Beloved under his heroic and gallant costume.

The dining-room is not of the time of Marie Antoinette. It belongs to the former style of decoration, and Gabriel made the drawings for Madame Du Barry. But the error is easy to explain; that the architect, whose best work had been done for Louis XV., had two styles would easily lead to similar mistakes. The wood-carvings are, besides, ingeniously conceived for the place. At the top of each panel is a two-fold garland; from this hangs a sash sustaining the classic trophy of Love; two crossed quivers beneath a wreath of roses. Could we be more plainly told that we are in the abode of a queen of beauty? The special purpose for which the room is intended is revealed lower down; a pyramid of pears, apples, pomegranates, grapes, pines and currants rises from a dish surmounted by boughs of the orange tree bearing both fruit and flowers. Again, upon the frieze of the mantel-piece, which is supported by two goats' heads, there are fruits; medlars, filberts, cherries, and lemon boughs, mingled with half-open pomegranates. Ornamentation of the same order is employed in the spandrels of the doors, where two chimeras crouching among vine-branches lay their paws on a carved cup. The ornament in the ceiling from which the lustre is suspended is equally symbolic; around a group of cornucopiæ are entwined vine and olive branches, oil and wine.

The adjoining salon, which had been used as a small dining-room in the time of Louis XV., was converted into a billiard-room by Marie Antoinette. The decoration has not the same unity of purpose; flowers and fruits are accompanied by theatrical and rural objects, masks, shepherd's pipes and crooks. The pictures are like those in the antechamber; mythology again, made pretty and insipid by the brush of a Lépicié and a Natoire.

A few handsome pieces of furniture of the Queen's time are collected in this room. But the only one which beyond all doubt she actually used, is the large jewel-chest made under the direction of Bonnefoy du Plan, the head of her private "garde-meuble;" this had figured in her Versailles cabinets. The date is fixed by the paintings, signed J. De Grault, 1787. Under the Restoration, the jewel-chest was placed at Saint-Cloud, from whence it was afterwards removed to Trianon. This chest is the most sumptuous piece of furniture ever made for the Queen, and also the least pleasing, for she unfortunately succeeded in inducing the artists to adopt her ideas respecting it. "The Marie Antoinette style" is a term generally applied to the exquisite Louis Seize decoration, which surrounded the châtelaine of Trianon everywhere, but was not of her invention; that posthumous flattery is plainly contradicted by the jewel-chest; in that instance the personal taste of the Queen in her maturity was opposed to the current until then taken by French art.

Bronze is predominant. The large oblong coffer of solid mahogany is supported by eight clusters of spears forming columns with eagle heads for capitals, and is divided into panels by figures of the seasons. In the middle, a medallion in high relief represents the Genius of France crowning the Arts, and the group at the top exhibits Minerva between Simplicity and Adornment. Small ornaments are used in profusion; mother-of-pearl, marble, and biscuit trying to break the monotony of bronze. A score of ivory medallions, painted black or red, contain antique, rural, or allegorical designs in white. The chief of these is worthy of the elegance of the age, it represents France summoning the Arts and the Sciences to embellish her dwelling: on the threshold of a temple adorned with garlands by Cupids, Renown draws the nine Muses, encircled by a chain of flowers, to the feet of a woman in royal costume, who resembles Marie Antoinette.

We are now in the large salon. In the cornice-angles are infantile scenes, and garlands formed of the simplest flowers of the fields are carved upon the wood of the panels, with, for contrast, the tall upstanding stems of lilies surrounded with laurels. Again we find the royal flower in half-blown clusters upon the frieze of the mantel-piece. All the woodwork, now white, was of a pale sea-green, the carvings stood out in white, enriched with gold; this must not be forgotten, if we would realize the aspect of the salon in the Queen's time. The present furniture also is of a later date; the Queen's was in crimson silk, striped with gold. Trianon has been inhabited since then; other women have lived there; first, the Princess Borghese (Pauline Bonaparte), whose beauty Canova has immortalized; afterwards the Duchesse d'Orléans, daughter-in-law of Louis Philippe and mother of the late Comte de Paris. The furnishing of the château has therefore undergone several alterations since the period which we are endeavouring to retrace.

It may be that those personages by Pater, who display their arch and lively graces above the doors, are the only survivals of the old time. They have seen Marie Antoinette seat herself at her harpsichord. It was here that she gave her Trianon concerts. She placed the music of Mozart and Grétry on a gilded stand by her side, and Monsieur de Polastron took his place at it while he accompanied her with his violin, or Monsieur de Guines did the same with his flute; a true diplomatist's flute, for it charmed the friends of Maria Theresa's daughter after it had played duets with the great Friedrich at Berlin.

The rooms that come after, boudoir, bed-chamber and dressing-room, are less important, the ceiling becomes abruptly lower; we feel that we have reached the homely corner of the house. In the time of Louis XV. the bed-chamber was the King's cabinet, and the little boudoir which precedes it included the staircase leading to the entresol, where the library was situated. Marie Antoinette, who did not read, abolished this communication, and the room that replaced it was called the "Cabinet of moving mirrors." It contained a mechanical contrivance by which mirrors were slid up from the floor, and concealed the windows. The apparatus was destroyed and the fragments were sold during the Revolution; but the white marble mantel-piece has been preserved, and also the panels which were carved for the Queen. These, with the panels of the Versailles cabinets, are the most perfect remaining from her reign. The price of them is known; they cost fifteen hundred livres. The narrowest are encircled by rose blooms on their branches; on the others, the shield, bearing fleurs-de-lys, supported by ribbons, appears among lightly-smoking cressets, doves, wreaths and quivers: above these pretty emblems is a lyre, and here and there the Queen's gilded cipher shines in the midst of the roses, between two torches, symbolical of the flame of love. Flowers, as we see, play a large part, suggested by its gardens, in the decoration of Little Trianon. One flower above all has supreme charm for the artist, and on leaving this boudoir, which might be called the rose cabinet, we shall find it, mingled with jasmine and narcissus, in the adjoining room.

On entering the Queen's bed-chamber, a closed sanctuary, securely her own, we must beware of believing, as we would dearly like to believe, that everything in it has been respectfully preserved in its former condition. A few articles of furniture only are of royal origin: that marquetry table with the interlaced initials of Louis XVI. and Marie Antoinette; that chest of drawers adorned with bronze transformed into ivy and vine branches by Gouthières; lastly, those light moveable chairs with the letters M. A. between two arrows bedecked with ribbons on the back. The bed is of the Louis Seize style; that is all we can say for it; but the flowers on the quilt were undoubtedly embroidered for one of the Queen's beds, for her cipher and the King's form part of the design. That the hangings in her time were muslin, embroidered in coloured silks, we know from one of the Queen's pages.

Several articles upon the mantel-piece look as though they were authentic. Marie Antoinette was fond of nick-nacks, the trifles of art. In the salon there are two vases of petrified wood, mounted in bronze, the design being hop-leaves, with the inscription: *Jos. Worth fecit Viennæ,* 1780. This work by a Viennese artist probably figured in the bed-chamber, where the Queen had collected all the memorials of her country, out of the reach of malevolent curiosity. The time-piece recalls the arms of Austria: two eagles support the dial, surrounded by roses and foliage; beneath the heraldic birds, the emblems of Florian's shepherds are grouped on the pedestal; at the sides are carnations in vases; never has bronze been carved with greater grace, or finer feeling for nature; all the art of Trianon seems to be summed up in this work.

Now we must visit the second floor. Two flights of stairs lead to it: one is the continuation, behind a door, of the great vestibule staircase, the other is placed beyond a bath-room which communicates with the Queen's bed-chamber. The Queen assigned this part of the château to her friends when they visited her. In 1780, we should have found it occupied by Madame de Polignac, Madame de Guiche, and the Comtesse de Châlons. Madame Elisabeth and the royal children had also lived in it. The rooms are small and numerous. "Although the château is not large," says Baroness Oberkirch, "it is admirably laid out. and can contain a great many people." We cannot endorse her opinion on visiting the rooms, for nothing could be farther from our modern notion of convenience. We find a labyrinth of intersecting passages, dim anterooms, dark cabinets, and partition walls. The only articles of furniture are a few armchairs which were left there and forgotten by the Empire. Footsteps sound sad in the silence. We are arrested once, by some beautiful carving in very low relief, over a door-top: a shepherd's hat, a beribboned crook, a bagpipe and a birdcage. Here and there a marble mantel-piece or the brass of a door-lock distantly recalls the marvels of the first floor. Everywhere else we might suppose ourselves to be in an ordinary apartment, long since abandoned, which has the odour of a deserted dwelling.

Leaving the château, on the French garden side, we observe an ordinary sort of edifice, but rather lofty, which looks at first like a farm-building, half hidden by the thickets on the little hill. It is without ornament, except over the door, where a little sprite holding a lyre floats in the air amid the classic emblems of Comedy and Tragedy.

This is the Queen's theatre. It has suffered by time, but more severely at the hands of men who have not respected the associations that ought to have protected it.

From 1776, Marie Antoinette habitually summoned the best actors from Paris to Trianon. Each of the little fêtes given by her included a play, and one day the play was *Le Barbier de Séville*. The accommodation for the company and the stage in the Orangerie was very insufficient and uncomfortable. Why should not there be a real theatre, with a proper stage, and appliances for scenery and decoration ? The Queen's wish was immediately gratified, and she herself decided upon the plans, selected the ornamentation, and arranged with the property-men. But this theatre, which was her own creation, was her craze as well. It involved expenditure which might fairly be called superfluous, because the plays given at Versailles amply sufficed for the Court. Entire companies who came at the cost of the Queen, were royally entertained at the château, and received liberal gratuities as well. Nothing was spared in scenery and properties. Of course it was easy for the malice of the newsmongers to pervert the facts and distort the details of these entertainments. We know the use that was made of the alleged "decoration in diamonds," which was a scene painted by Mazières, in which pillars studded with coloured glass were introduced. Thus everything concerning Marie Antoinette's Trianon was perverted and distorted.

In May, 1780, the works were finished, the plaster was dry, and the Queen had witnessed the first play. It had a symbolic prologue: Mademoiselle Raucourt as "Tragedy" and Despréaux as "Opéra," contended with each other, in indifferent verse, for the honour of inaugurating the theatre ; and the "Opéra-Comique," arriving just in time, made peace between these two powers ; and a parody of *Castor et Pollux* in five acts was played.

What a pretty theatre that was ; in its fresh, bright daintiness, like an eighteenth century ball-dress ! It was blue and gold. The back and the sides were hung with blue mohair, and the seats and supports of

)UR DE MARLBOROUGH" AT THE TRIANON "HAMEAU."

From a photograph.

[illegible] seemed to some [illegible] more severely [illegible] associations that ought [illegible].

[illegible] commanded the best actors from [illegible] had been given by her included a play, [illegible] The accommodation [illegible] was very insufficient [illegible] stand one times be a real theatre, with a [illegible] scenery and decoration!" The Queen's [illegible] granted, and she herself decided upon the plans, [illegible] and arranged with the property-men. But [illegible] as well. It [illegible] because [illegible] the Court. Entire com- [illegible] were royally entertained at [illegible] spared [illegible] and [illegible] for the malice of [illegible] scandalmongers to [illegible] the details of these [illegible]ertainments. We have the [illegible] of the alleged "decoration in diamonds" [illegible] which [illegible] with [illegible] glass were [illegible]. Thus everything [illegible] Trianon was [illegible].

[illegible] 1780 the [illegible] were finished, the [illegible] dry, and the [illegible] first play. [illegible] "Tragedy" and [illegible] "[illegible]" [illegible]ended [illegible] the [illegible] and the [illegible] in five [illegible].

[illegible] bright [illegible], like [illegible] blue and gold. The [illegible] and [illegible] supports of

the boxes and galleries were covered with velvet of the same colour; the splay of the stage was painted to imitate veined white marble. All the rest, mouldings, figures and ornaments in relief, were in the pleasant tones of yellow or green gold.

The statuary work was lavish; it was only in pasteboard, to be sure, but although the material was common the elegance of the execution was remarkable. The supports of the second gallery were lions' faces with the skin attached, forming the well-known design called "the spoils of Hercules," the frieze above these was composed of interlacing wreaths, and still higher, in the coving, which admitted of twelve oval apertures serving as boxes, nude children twisted in a long garland of fruits and flowers were at play. Above the stage were other children grouped about lyres; two reclining nymphs guarded the initials of the Queen. On the right and left of the orchestra two female figures formed a group supporting a candelabrum, and from either side of the blue curtain the torso of another figure projecting from a terminal held up the blue silk hangings, gold-fringed and looped with golden cords, which fell from the frieze. On the ceiling, the god of Music and his train were depicted in a cloud.

This theatre, now almost a ruin, was then worthy of a queen's appearance on its little stage. Here Marie Antoinette gave those amateur performances in which she and all her circle chiefly delighted. Her early education had developed a taste for the drama in her. It was formed by all the music, dancing and singing masters provided for her by Maria Theresa. She had "come out" in scenic entertainments at ten years old, and a picture, placed by her at Trianon, represents the mythological ballet which she danced with her brothers at Schœnbrunn, at the marriage fêtes of Joseph II. (*) As Dauphine she had also acted in plays in the entresols of the château de Versailles, but only with her sisters-in-law, and somewhat on the sly. The freedom of her life at Trianon suggested to her the idea of beginning again upon the stage of her garden play-

(*) See Appendix, Note H.

house. A few weeks after the inauguration of the theatre by the King's comedians, in the summer of 1780, she realized her project. The cast was composed of herself, her personal friends, and the Comte d'Artois, and she decided that the only spectators should be the King, Monsieur, and the princesses. She would not consent to receive the Court, not even Madame de Lamballe, who claimed, as Superintendent of the Queen's Household, an exception which was not granted to her as a friend. In order, however, that the boxes might be filled, and the actors stimulated by the presence of an audience, certain persons of no account were admitted; the readers, the Queen's waiting-women with their sisters and daughters, and, a little later, the officers of the Body-Guards and the King's equerries, also those of the princes.

Nobody was displeased by the Queen's imitating Madame de Pompadour, who, thirty years before, had organized theatrical performances which gained a lasting renown in the King's cabinets. Amateur acting by ladies was quite usual in France at this time. Numbers of people had a stage with its properties for the entertainment of their company either in Paris or in the country. Monsieur de Vaudreuil possessed the most ably managed of these theatres at Gennevilliers, where a select "pit" applauded the beauty of Madame Lebrun by the side of the talent of Madame Dugazon, and "Proverbs," a dramatic novelty, came into existence.

It is useless, in truth, to seek excuses for the Queen, who took her share of all the pleasures and the modes of her time. She might be justified, were it necessary, by the consent of the King, who was frequently present at the Trianon rehearsals and performances, and encouraged the applause.

We have abundant information concerning the Queen's theatre. The date of the performances, the cast of the pieces, the accounts of expenditure for costumes and scenery are all preserved. In contemporary memoirs, and even in the literary correspondence of Grimm it is more than once mentioned. Let us take Mercy in preference. "For a month past," he writes in September, 1780, "all the Queen's occupations and all her amusements are concentrated in the one and only object of two little plays acted in the Trianon theatre. The time required for learning the parts, the time that had to be employed in frequent rehearsals, added to other accessory details, has been more than sufficient to make up the day. The King has given proof of his liking for this kind of diversion by assiduously assisting at all these preparations. He has not been able to make time for cards, or even for his evening walks. I learn through the people in attendance, all of the lower ranks, for only such have entered the theatre, that the plays are agreeably acted, with grace and spirit, and that the King manifests his satisfaction by continual applause, particularly when the Queen executes some of the pieces in her part. The plays, which last until nine o'clock, are followed by a supper confined to the royal family and the actors and actresses. On rising from the table the Court retires, and there is no later entertainment."

Mercy himself was admitted to one of these performances. This was not only an act of friendly favour on the Queen's part; she apparently wished him to see for himself that none of the objections that might be raised by her mother really existed. He was privately conducted to the theatre, and took his place in a railed box without being remarked. "I saw," he says, "the two little comic operas, *Rose et Colas* and *Le Devin de Village*. The Comte d'Artois, the Duc de Guiche, the Comte d'Adhémar, the Duchesse de Polignac and the Duchesse de Guiche played in the first piece. The Queen took the part of Colette in the second; the Comte de Vaudreuil sang the part of the fortune-teller, and the Comte d'Adhémar that of Colin. The Queen's voice is agreeable and in perfect tune, her manner of acting is noble and full of grace; as a whole the performance was as good as private theatricals can be. I observed that the King entered into it with attention and pleasure which showed in his countenance; between the acts, he stepped up on the stage and went to the Queen's dressing-room."

Nevertheless, the correspondent of Maria Theresa was not without anxiety for the future. The favour that he had received was extended to some other persons. The Queen yielded to the desire of being seen and applauded, and to the entreaties which were made to her on every side. But, as the royal representations were still kept to a certain exclusiveness, those who solicited admittance in vain resented the affront, and raised a clamour. Already the little Duc de Fronsac, First Gentleman "in reversion," had regarded it as an offence that he was excluded from the Queen's pleasures, although, by right, his post gave him the direction of them. All were convinced that it was their right to be admitted; they affected not to understand why it should be easier to be presented at Court than to enter a theatre. Slander dealt freely with the rôles of the Queen and her friends. A rumour that the King found fault with her, and hissed "the company of seigneurs," was set afloat. The documents of the period are full of silly anecdotes on this subject.

The animosity openly shown towards her favourite amusement induced Marie Antoinette to renounce it by degrees. As a matter of fact, with the exception of a few isolated instances, only three consecutive series of plays had been acted, in the summer of 1780, 1782 and 1783 respectively. In 1784 no performances took place, and in 1785 one single representation, that of *Le Barbier de Séville*, put an end to the acting at Trianon.

It is curious to compare the Queen's theatre, so private and unpretending, with that of Madame de Pompadour. The Marquise did not hesitate to attack the great repertory of the seventeenth century, Quinault and Molière; and indeed she once had a tragedy by Voltaire acted. Her numerous and well-taught associates formed two distinct companies, one for drama, the other for opera. They were supported by an orchestra, a corps de ballet, and choruses. There was nothing like this at Trianon; plays with or without music were acted there; most frequently one of each kind figured on the same programme. Only plays of the second order, or comic operas not too difficult, were attempted; such for instance as those by Sedaine and Monsigny, with simple ariettas which anybody might sing without much study.

As they sought only their own pleasure, the Queen's friends were reciprocally indulgent. There was only one really trained singer among them, the Comte d'Adhémar. He always had the lovers' rôles assigned to him, although he was no longer young, and his voice was tremulous. In the part of Colin, in *Le Devin de Village*, his age made the shepherd's dress rather ridiculous, and the Queen, who played Colette, asked laughingly whether she was likely to be reproached for *that* admirer.

With the exception of a few well-selected pieces, we observe, to our surprise, that the musical repertory of the royal company of players was less than second rate, and worthy of the platitude of the librettos. The company was wise in not venturing upon any of the works of Gluck, but it is vexatious to find that *Le Sabot Perdu* of Piis and Barré was one of its greatest feats, and that the Queen enthusiastically admired those two sorry authors who then passed for great men. She made them come to Trianon, it appears, in order to act before them and establish their fame. The fame of Piis and Barré! The comedies were generally better than the comic operas. *La Gageure imprévue*, *Le Sage étourdi*, *Les Fausses infidélités*, and lastly *Le Barbier de Séville*, ought to induce us to forgive the noble actors for such stuff as *Isabelle et Gertrude*, and *Le Tonnelier*, an opera which had been hissed at the theatre of La Foire before it failed once more on the Trianon stage.

The performance of *Le Barbier* is especially famous. It had a certain success, if we may believe Grimm, who tells us that the Comte d'Artois played Figaro; the Duc de Guiche, Bartolo; Monsieur de Crussol, Basile; and that Monsieur de Vaudreuil, as Almaviva, gave the cues to a Rosine who was the Queen. Grimm continues: "The small number of spectators admitted to this performance found an evenness and harmony in the acting very rare in pieces played by amateurs in society; it was particularly remarked that the Queen threw such grace and truth into the scene in the fourth act as could not fail to win transports of applause for even the most obscure actress. We have these details from a severe and fastidious judge whom no Court prejudice could ever blind on any point." These compliments are too skilfully distributed to be altogether sincere; but we may also regard them as a tribute to the efforts made by amateurs to perfect themselves in their art.

That performance was curious also for another reason. The author, a much-discussed person just then, and whose character was not above reproach, was none the less admitted to the entertainment. The vanity of Beaumarchais must have been flattered by finding himself interpreted by a Queen, and he must have experienced keen and subtle pleasure in listening to his own most daring tirades uttered by a Prince of the Blood. When the Trianon audience lavished the same applause on his play as the plebeian Paris pit, Beaumarchais must have thought these great people, who were so much amused by a declaration of war on their own privileges, singularly blind.

Precisely at this time the necklace affair occurred, proving too clearly how far respect for royal persons had declined in France. Four days prior to the performance of *Le Barbier*, Cardinal de Rohan had been arrested at Versailles. There was an end thenceforth to the merry rehearsals and the acting of plays.

Marie Antoinette in her unhappiness became still more attached to Trianon. Her children attracted her thither; a playing-place had been arranged for them, and she liked to join in their games. She inspired them with her tastes, and got up children's plays for them; she selected the little actors from the families of her friends, and after the play she served supper to them herself. At the same time she made her small domain the centre of the summer amusements of the Court. An elegant tent had been put up in front of the château, and there dancing went on in the open air all through the fine evenings, and the Queen now invited a great many people, in order to extenuate the effect of her former exclusiveness. On Sunday afternoon the gates were opened; all decently-dressed persons were free to enter, and the people of the neighbourhood came to walk in the grounds. Marie Antoinette looked on at the dancing, mixed with the various groups, and made acquaintance with the children. She was manifestly endeavouring to undo by Trianon the harm that Trianon had done to her, and to recover her short-lived popularity.

The time when these efforts might have availed her was past; but she found, on each recurrence of her new troubles, that the solitude and the greenery of her modest "home" exerted a soothing influence upon her; and one last creation, the Hameau, gave her recreation and forgetfulness for a while.

The Queen's hamlet has a greater number of visitors than the other side of Trianon. But neglect has altered, and ruin has touched it. Those who wish to visit that little village of a dozen houses, the fragile fancy of a woman, which is at the same time the memorial of the taste of a period, while it is still standing, have no time to lose.

The Hameau and the English garden had a common origin, the new birth of the love of nature. That sentiment became complicated in a few years. In addition to material nature, rocks, woods, and streams, the French mind was fain to love the manners and the ways of the dwellers in the fields; it was moved by the simple and frugal lives of the tillers of the soil. Greuze, in his village pictures, fairly represents the time when interest in the peasant had its beginning. The Trianon Hameau, at once real and ideal, might have been constructed as a background for pictures by the painter of *L'Accordée de Village*. The Queen's, however, was not the only creation of this kind, others existed in several places; for instance, "Monsieur le Prince" had one at Chantilly, and La Borde, the financier, at Méréville. Books took up the matter; farms and wind-mills replaced the hitherto fashionable mock ruins in the scheme of landscape gardens.

The Chantilly hamlet probably suggested the idea of her own to the

Queen, but she had it very differently carried out. The little rustic houses which were then erected in pleasure grounds, did not serve as dwellings; they were merely stage scenes; the humble portal being pushed open, the interior, richly ornamented or forming a deceptive painting of still-life, presented many a surprise; now an elegant salon, again the counterfeit of a grotto or a tent. In the Trianon buildings there was nothing of this kind; the houses were real village habitations, and most of them were utilized for the domain. One house, larger and handsomer than the others was reserved for the visits of the King and Queen. They liked to come and dine there; the rooms were well furnished, and the "billiard-house" which was joined to it by an outside gallery, provided pastime for afternoon leisure which had very little of the rural about it. There was also a boudoir with a thatched roof wreathed with foliage, and a "belvédère" called La Tour de Marlborough. But all the other houses, prettily grouped around the pond, were adapted to the purposes of rural industry. Let us glance at these. Here is the mill, its wheel turning and humming under the current of a little river; it does real grinding; a miniature by Van Blarenberghe depicts a miller with his ass conveying a sack of corn to the mill. Here is the dairy; the tables are of white marble, and the walls are lined with the same; but it is none the less a real dairy, furnished with milk-pans, cups and butter-dishes; the Queen and her friends amuse themselves by making butter and cheese there with their own hands, under the direction of the farmer's wife. The cows are not far off, and close to the meadows where they are grazing, we perceive the buildings of a very complete farm. Still nearer are the gardener's house, the barn and the fowl-house, all indispensable buildings, although they seem to be placed there merely to charm the eye. Accounts of the Hameau have been given which have no foundation whatever; in fact, it is one of those legendary places into which authentic history does not penetrate, and tradition prefers gravely to record many an absurdity respecting it. According to some compilers, Marie Antoinette had twelve dwelling-

THE QUEEN'S HOUSE AT THE TRIANON "HAMEAU"

From a photograph.

[illegible] of the king and
[illegible] and formed
[illegible] gallery
[illegible] of the nave
[illegible] with
[illegible] But all
[illegible] adapted to the
[illegible] in the wall
[illegible]; it does
[illegible] with
[illegible], the
[illegible]
[illegible] and
[illegible] by making
[illegible] of the
[illegible]
[illegible] a very [illegible]
[illegible] and the [illegible]
[illegible] to be placed
[illegible] have been
[illegible] of those
[illegible], and

houses built at Trianon; there she placed twelve families, taking upon herself the entire charge of their maintenance; she loved to visit these humble villagers, to live in the midst of them with her children, and she installed an old hermit in the presbytery to instruct them in the virtues. This statement is false in every particular; three households were lodged in the Hameau: the farmers, the care-takers, and the gardeners, not one more; the hermit with the white beard did not exist, and the little house which is still called "the presbytery," never housed anything but poultry.

A no less ridiculous fable represents the royal family playing shepherds and shepherdesses seriously, and sojourning at the Hameau in pastoral costume. In one version of the story the King is the "seigneur" of the village, in another he is the miller. Marie Antoinette is the farmer's wife; the Comte d'Artois is game-keeper, Monsieur is schoolmaster, the Duc de Polignac is bailiff, and Cardinal de Rohan, as Curé of the place, naturally inhabits the famous presbytery. We need consider the assertion respecting the Cardinal only. Always detested by the Queen, it is well known that he was not admitted to Trianon; he never entered the château but once, and then he got in uninvited and by bribing a porter, to see the evening fête in honour of the Comtesse du Nord: in addition to this fact, at the moment when the Hameau was completed, in August, 1785, Rohan was starting for the Bastille. Facts and dates all unite here to give the lie to the baseless tradition concerning him, and to prove how worthless is the authority for the rest. Is not the reality more affecting than that distribution of masquerade characters? A fair queen, weary of her Court, seeking repose in nature, sharing the taste of her time for rural life, allowing herself the pleasure of realizing that life to some extent, even trying her hand, for pastime, at dairy and farm work: this, I think, is a sufficiently touching and pleasing spectacle to interest very deeply those who visit the Hameau of Marie Antoinette.

At Trianon we successfully evoke the image of the Queen in her simplicity and feminine grace, either with her children, as Wertmüller depicted her—her brow already overcast by anxiety for the future—or leaning on the arm of a friend, while she confides the troubles of the hour to her, and solicits her affection. We see her "gliding" alone along the paths, a cane in her hand, to the edge of the narrow river meandering through the turf; she is going to visit her estate, to inspect the embellishments, to ascertain whether anybody in her service stands in need of her bounty. She wears a crossed scarf and hood of lace, and a plain gown of white lawn, "à l'enfant," which adds to her loveliness.

Everybody at Trianon dresses after the Queen, beginning with Madame Elisabeth, to whom simple attire is becoming. "She has all the charm of a pretty shepherdess," says Madame Lebrun.

During that one month in each year which Marie Antoinette devotes to the "home" that is her very own, a rarely beautiful spectacle is presented by those princesses and great ladies who lay aside the luxury, the pomp, and the pride of official state, shake off the trammels of etiquette, and enjoy a simple life in the delightful retreat which one of them has made for all.

It is the afternoon of the 5th of October, 1789. Marie Antoinette has walked across the park to Trianon, according to her custom, with only a footman to attend her. She has visited the Hameau, where the festoons of Virginia creepers along the walls are already turning red; she has watered her favourite plants in their white china vases bearing her initials; she has amused herself by milking a cow, and given the gardener orders for the winter. No friend is coming to join her there to-day, and the King is shooting at Meudon.

Her walk is ended, she has come to the grotto to rest, and she seats herself on the moss. She thinks of the son whom she has recently lost, the gentle Dauphin, whom she has often led by the hand to this very spot. She recalls the recent public events, each one is a blow aimed at

MARIE ANTOINETTE AS "LA BELLE FERMIÈRE.

Drawn by Césarine F., engraved by Buotte.

[illegible] with her children, to Westmuller [illegible] by anxiety for the future—or [illegible] the confides the troubles of the [illegible] We see her "gliding" alone [illegible] to the edge of the narrow river [illegible] going to visit her estate, to [illegible] whether anybody in her service [illegible] she wears a crimson scarf and hood [illegible] town, "A l'enfant," which adds to

[illegible] after the Queen, beginning with Madame [illegible] becoming. She has all the charm [illegible] Madame Lebrun

[illegible] year when Marie Antoinette devotes [illegible] time, a rarely beautiful spectacle is pre- [illegible] great ladies who lay aside the luxury, [illegible] official state, shake off the trammels of [illegible] in the delightful retreat which one of

[illegible] of October, 1789 Marie Antoinette [illegible], according to [illegible] has visited the Hameau, where the [illegible] The walls are already [illegible] in their white china vases hanging [illegible] milking a cow, and given the [illegible] is coming to join her there [illegible]

[illegible] grotto to rest, and she seats [illegible] whom she has recently lost, [illegible] by the hand to this very [illegible] is a blow aimed at

herself; the States General transformed against her will, the Monarchy disarmed, the King wavering, the Third Estate in revolt, the Bastille destroyed, and those who pass for her friends denounced to the public or fleeing for their lives; and her own dignity, both as woman and queen, insulted every day. She puts the question to herself as to what fate is reserved by the revolution which has begun, for the son who remains to her, for the heir of the Bourbons. These thoughts pursue her everywhere, even into this quiet spot, so full of happy associations. The sky is in harmony with her mind; it is overcast, and a few drops of rain are falling.

Meanwhile, through the mouth of the grotto which opens upon the meadows, and allows anyone approaching to be seen, she recognizes one of her pages; in his hand is a folded paper, and he seems to be seeking her in all haste. She advances to meet him and takes the note. It is a line from the Minister of the King's Household, who sends her grave tidings; the people of Paris are marching in arms on Versailles; the Assembly is bewildered, the Château without orders; already the vanguard of pikes is at the end of the Avenue de Paris, and in an hour the mob will be thundering at the gates. The Queen departs immediately; she is fully aware that a tragic moment has come and that the great trial of her courage is at hand. Perhaps she pauses and turns in the avenue, once more to gaze down there beyond the poplars at the home of her happy days. Does she mean that long look to be her last farewell? Does she foreknow that never more will she come back to Trianon?...

* * *

THE DAYS OF OCTOBER.

The 5th of October is the last day of Royalty at Versailles: it is also the last day of the reign, which belongs henceforth to the Revolution.

The uproar raised around the Château by hunger and hatred lasts throughout the evening. The squares and the avenues swarm with ragged women and armed men, who demand bread and seem to desire blood. Rain falls, the night grows dark; the few street lamps give but little light, and the shops in the streets are shut. The people from Paris knock at the doors, seeking food. From time to time one of the body-guards is recognized, jeered at, pelted with mud, followed and fired at.

One part of the crowd occupies the barracks of the French Guards on the Place d'Armes; another has invaded the hall of the National Assembly and passes the night there, mixed up with the deputies in session. In order to avoid irritating the people, the regiment of Guards has been ordered to fall back, by way of the gardens, upon Trianon, then on Rambouillet. Will the King's Household be sufficient to guard the Château in case of an attack to-night?

The situation is still threatening. Ill-looking fellows are going about sword in hand, and distributing pass-words. It is well known that the spite of the mob is against the Queen, and conversations overheard in the groups make the intentions of the ringleaders plain. Besides, Mirabeau, speaking from the tribune, has just demanded inviolability for the King alone! What is this but an excuse by anticipation for the crimes that may be committed? Marie Antoinette was entreated to leave Versailles, and the carriages were brought to the park gates. She refused: "Since there is danger," she said, "my place is with the King."

At midnight, Monsieur de la Fayette arrives with the National Guards from Paris. He goes at once to the King. His face is scrutinized; does he come as a friend or as an enemy? Yes, it is peace that he brings; he assures Louis XVI. that with his twenty thousand men he can answer for order in Versailles. He goes on then to the Assembly to say the same thing there, and breaks up the sitting. It is three o'clock in the morning. The King goes to bed, the Queen retires and seeks rest also. The General passes the rest of the night at the Hôtel de Noailles; his patrols are on duty in the streets, the town is quiet.

At half-past five Marie Antoinette is suddenly awakened. There is a great noise under her windows. Women have got into the gardens through the ill-guarded railings, and are trying to get into the Château. They are shrieking "Death to the Austrian! Where is the wretch, that we may twist her neck?" "What is the matter, again?" asks the Queen in alarm. A waiting-woman opens the inner window-shutters and looks out; "It is the women from Paris," she says, "they have not found beds in the town and are walking about till morning." The Queen accepts the reply and says no more.

A few minutes elapse, and then comes the sound of the rush of a great crowd in the direction of the marble staircase, with shouts and pistol-shots. All this tumult reaches the royal chamber confusedly; it is caused by the invasion of the staircase and the foremost rooms; the body-guards are killed, and presently two bleeding heads will be paraded in the courtyards. The Queen's waiting-woman goes to the door of the guards'-room; Monsieur de Miomandre, one of them, half opens it for an instant and has just time to cry: "Save the Queen!" Almost instantly the room is filled with an armed mob; Miomandre is struck on the head by the butt end of a musket and falls senseless across the door.

It is evident that the crowd is in search of the Queen's apartments; but it passes on before the entrance, and ranges from room to room hap-hazard: if it be true, as it is said, that there are emissaries of the Duc d'Orléans among these furious people, they are very ill-acquainted with the Château. This uncertainty is the salvation of the Queen. Her women have barricaded the door, they make her rise, they put on her stockings and a petticoat, and wrap a small cloak about her shoulders. She flees by way of her cabinets, gets the Œil-de-bœuf opened to her, and reaches the King's chamber.

During this time the King, also awakened by the noise, has witnessed the invasion from his window, and has seen the people rush towards the staircase which leads to the Queen's apartments. In great alarm, he hurries through the secret passage leading from his room to hers. He finds the Queen's chamber empty, the body-guards who have taken refuge in the apartment tell him that she has gone to his. He rejoins her instantly, and they both go down by the inner stairs to the ground floor, to seek Madame Royale. Madame de Tourzel has brought the Dauphin, Madame Elisabeth comes in, and also Monsieur and Madame: the royal family is assembled.

The morning is advancing. The King, who is quite calm, has summoned his Ministers and is holding a council. The passages are occupied by the body-guards and the Flanders regiment. A portion of the Château is at the mercy of the armed bands who are smashing the doors, pillaging, and flinging the furniture out of the windows. The National Guards of Paris and Versailles are mustered by degrees and come on the scene at a run; the rioters are driven out and overflow into the Cour de Marbre. In an instant the vast courtyard is filled with pikes, sticks, muskets, and a deafening tumult of oaths and threats. The women especially are savage in their hatred of the Queen; they howl their resolve to "take her head back to Paris, and to make ribbons of her entrails."

Marie Antoinette is standing at a window in the King's room. The crowd does not see her, but she hears the crowd, and looks on; her eyes are fixed, reddened with unshed tears. Monsieur and Madame are seated at the end of the room, in silent consternation. Madame Elisabeth and Madame Royale are close to the Queen; the little Dauphin has climbed on a chair in front of her, and is playing with his sister's curls. The child is fretful and complains. "Have patience, my son," the mother answers, "all this will soon be over." But the Dauphin softly repeats: "Mamma, I am hungry."

Monsieur de La Fayette enters the room: "Madame, the people are calling for you—on the balcony." The Queen falters; she hears the cries which summon her, she sees musket-barrels levelled at the balcony. The General insists, respectfully : "It must be done to quiet them." "So be it," answers Marie Antoinette. "Should this be death, I go to it." She takes the children by the hand, and steps out on the balcony of the King's room. A cry of "No children!" is raised in the crowd. By one movement she pushes them behind her; she is alone now, her hand on the rail. . . . The cries cease, the gun-barrels drop. Marie Antoinette has learned never more to fear death.

The royal family sets out for Paris, brought back in triumph by the people. It is a singular concourse which throngs that once royal road; women on horseback or perched on gun-carriages, laughing and singing, wear the hats and the bandoleers of the body-guards; grenadiers, carrying poplar branches, escort waggon-loads of flour: then come the Court coaches, occupied by ladies, Ministers and deputies. The deputation from the Assembly and some of the disarmed guards, exhausted by hunger and fatigue, and hooted all the way, follow the King's coach. In that carriage no one speaks. The Queen, quite impassive, seems resigned. She starts only at the sound of gun-shots, fired in the air, as though she feared a second massacre for "her own." For six mortal hours they travel thus at a walking-pace. (*) Occasionally, Marie Antoinette bends forward to see whereabouts she is on this interminable road. Her eyes gaze towards Paris, her thoughts go farther still; they plunge into that future which is already so terrifying, but even her agonized apprehensions do not forecast its reality.

At the end of the road that was travelled on the 6th of October, there is the Revolution. There is the first prison, the Tuileries; there is the return from Varennes, amid the mocking silence of the town (**), then surveillance, denunciations, a jail installed in the heart of the palace of the Kings of France, insults in the gardens, the foul writings of the Père Duchêne flung into the windows of the princesses' rooms. There is the 20th of June, the Tuileries invaded, the doors hacked to

(*) See Appendix, Note 9. (**) See Appendix, Note 10.

pieces, the furniture smashed, the march-past with weapons and revilings in front of the King and Queen, and the red cap on the head of the Dauphin. There is that day, the most cruel of all the "days," the 10th of August, when the Queen is fain to die with her faithful servants, and when the King, even now King no longer, prefers to live. There is the tower in the Temple, the daily life under the eyes of municipal guards, and on a third day of September, a bloody head is paraded under the prisoners' windows, the last salutation of the Princesse de Lamballe. Then the separation, the weeping family, the father's farewell, the dole of the widow's weeds made to the Queen by the Convention, and the child torn from his mother to go and learn, he too, to calumniate her. . . . After these, the trial without documents, without witnesses, without defence. . . . then, the waking on the 16th of October in the condemned cell of the Conciergerie.

Marie Antoinette is to have her last interview with the people to-day. Never has she been rendered so much honour. The whole of Paris, aroused at dawn by the drums of the sections, is afoot to see her pass. There are thirty thousand men under arms; the National Guards line the way from the Palais de Justice to the Place de la Révolution. The open spaces are packed with sightseers; the roofs are crowded, every window is full. The cart jogs, slowly, along the Rue St. Honoré.

The Queen is seated on a board, her hands are bound by a cord which the executioner holds. A lawn cap covers her hair, grown grey of late; she cut it short this morning. (*) She wears a white quilted bedgown, a black skirt, and a muslin kerchief about her neck. This last toilet, these poor prison garments, render her more majestic than she was at Versailles. And yet, she is quite aged, worn out by the fatigue of those last days, and very pale; her eyes are bloodshot. She seems neither to see nor to hear, but to be given up

(*) See Appendix, Note II.

to inward prayer, to remembrance of the [illegible] same journey, of the children whom she [illegible] of a far, far away past, when the people [illegible] loud acclamation. . . Behind the cart, a [illegible] obscenity.

It is noon. The terrace of the Tuileries [illegible] The Place de la Révolution bristles with [illegible] ment. The Queen ascends the wooden [illegible] executioner stoops and does his work. An [illegible] head; the eyelids are fluttering. A shout is [illegible] But the great crowd remains silent. The [illegible] what the Republic has gained by killing this [illegible]

[illegible] with weapons and [illegible] the [illegible] cap on [illegible] cruel of [illegible] the Queen [illegible] fain to [illegible] King [illegible] Temple, [illegible] third [illegible] the prisoners' [illegible] Then [illegible] the dole of [illegible] Convention, and the [illegible] to calumniate [illegible] without witnesses, [illegible] October in the con- [illegible]

[illegible] with the people to- [illegible] rendered [illegible] honour. The whole [illegible] by the [illegible] sections, is afoot to [illegible] thirty thousand [illegible] under arms; the National Guards [illegible] the Palais de Justice to the Place de la [illegible] are packed with [illegible]; the roofs are [illegible] full. The cart [illegible] slowly, along the line [illegible]

[illegible] board, her hands [illegible] cord [illegible] A lawn cap [illegible] grown [illegible] this morning [illegible] a white [illegible] and a muslin [illegible] about her neck. [illegible] more majestic [illegible] aged, worn out by the [illegible] are blood-shot. She [illegible] given up

(1) See Appendix, Note H.

to inward prayer, to remembrance of the husband who has made the same journey, of the children whom she has not seen again, and also of a far, far away past, when the people saluted a young queen with loud acclamation. . . . Behind the cart, a tumult of drunken cries and obscenity.

It is noon. The terrace of the Tuileries is crowded with spectators. The Place de la Révolution bristles with bayonets and thrills with excitement. The Queen ascends the wooden stair with a steady step. The executioner stoops and does his work. An assistant holds up the dissevered head; the eyelids are fluttering. A shout is raised: "Vive la République!" But the great crowd remains silent. The people are already wondering what the Republic has gained by killing this woman.

AUTHORITIES DIRECTLY CONSULTED.

THE FIRST CHAPTER.

Correspondance Secrète of Mercy-Argenteau with Maria Theresa, published by MM. d'Arneth and Geffroy (1874), and with Joseph II. and Prince Kaunitz, published by MM. d'Arneth and Flammermont (1889-1891); *Gazette de France, Mémoires secrets de la République des Lettres, Correspondance de Métra*, correspondence edited by M. de Lescure; Swedish documents, quoted in "Gustave III.," by M. Geffroy; papers belonging to Bernis utilized in "Le Cardinal de Bernis," by M. Frédéric Masson; the proceedings in the "Affair of the Necklace," examined and assorted by M. Campardon; Memoirs of the Lamottes (husband and wife); *Letters of Baron de Staël-Holstein, Letters of Madame de Sabran, Memoirs of Besenval, Belleval, Beugnot, Mesdames de Genlis and Campan, La Marck, Lévis, Montbarey, Ségur, Soulavie*, etc.

Manuscripts.—Archives du département de Seine-et-Oise: *Recueil de chansons satiriques, Correspondance de Xavier de Schomberg*.—Bibliothèque Nationale: *Journal de Hardy*.

Private Archives.—*Mémoires véridiques pour servir à l'Histoire de la vie de Louis XVI*, by Davy de Chavigné.

THE SECOND CHAPTER.

Printed Works.—A portion of the preceding works; Memoirs of Papillon de la Ferté, of Mesdames Oberkirch and Vigée-Lebrun, of Lage de Volude and the Comte d'Hézecques; the works of Prince de Ligne; *Walpole's Letters*, translated by M. de Baillon; the record by the Abbé de Pichon, of the "Sacre" of Louis XVI.; *Modes et Usages*, by M. de Reiset; *Versailles au temps de Marie Antoinette*, by M. de Nolhac; Lord Ronald Gower's *Iconography*.

Manuscripts.—Musée du Louvre: Unpublished drawings made by Bocquet for the "Sacre" of Louis XVI., costumes and decorations. Bibliothèque Nationale: *Journal de Hardy*.

THE THIRD CHAPTER.

PRINTED WORKS.—A portion of the preceding works; Letters or Memoirs of the Chevalier de L'Isle, the Duc de Saxe-Teschen, Tilly, Fersen, Lauzun, Grimm, d'Allonville, des Cars, Vaudreuil, Mesdames de Gontaut, de Tourzel, Diane de Polignac; the "Instruction" to Madame de Tourzel, published by MM. de Goncourt; the Letters of Madame Elisabeth, published by M. de Beauchesne; M. de Molmenti's *Vie privée à Venise*; the Alvimare and Garat articles in the "Dictionnaire" by Jal; the Feuillet de Conches (with the distrust inculcated by so many fabricated or doubtful pieces.)

MANUSCRIPTS.—Archives du Musée et du Palais de Versailles: *Etats des logements de la Cour sous Louis XVI.; Registres des Magasins; Plans anciens des cabinets de la Reine*, etc.—Archives de Seine-et-Oise: *Correspondance de Schomberg.*—Bibliothèque Nationale: *Dépenses de la chambre aux deniers de la Reine: Travaux d'ébénisterie et autres exécutés au garde-meuble en 1786: Journal de Hardy.*—Bibliothèque de Clermont-Ferrand: *Mémoires du Comte d'Espinchal.*

THE FOURTH CHAPTER.

PRINTED WORKS.—To the definitive work by M. Desjardins on Little Trianon, one printed document only has been added: the *Prologue for the Opening of the Trianon Theatre*, by Despréaux. The days of October are related according to the *Abrégé de la procédure du Châtelet.*

MANUSCRIPTS.—Archives de Seine-et-Oise: *Souper offert au Comte et à la Comtesse du Nord.*—Private Archives: *Notice sur la Duchesse de Gramont-Caderousse.*

Various art documents, painted portraits, drawings and prints are mentioned in the course of the narrative.

APPENDIX.

NOTES BY THE TRANSLATOR.

Note 1 : Chapter I., page 2.

As M. de Nolhac does not adopt it, we fear the often-told and touching story of the first movement of the Dauphin and Dauphine on learning that Louis XV. was dead and they had come to their kingdom, must be rejected. It was to the effect that the young sovereigns, "a king of twenty, a queen of eighteen," clasped hands, and knelt down, by a common impulse, while the young man exclaimed : "Mon Dieu! Nous sommes trop jeunes pour régner," and the girl wept. In connection with the remarks of M. de Nolhac upon their youth, their good intentions, and the early promise of the reign, it is interesting to recall the testimony of Mr. Burke, in his famous "Letter to a Member of the National Assembly" (January, 1791) which followed his "Reflections on the Revolution in France" (1790). (Of the latter, one of his biographers writes : "No political work was ever read with such avidity on its appearance.") Mr. Burke, protesting against the conduct of the National Assembly, describes Louis XVI. as a "virtuous monarch who, after an intermission of one hundred and seventy-five years, had called together the states of his kingdom to reform abuses, to establish a free government, and to strengthen his throne; a monarch who, at *very outset*, without force, even without solicitation, had given to his people such a Magna Charta of privileges as never was given by any king to any subjects." It may also be interesting to recall, in connection with this passage, that Mr. Burke, from a very early stage of the Revolution, expected the murder of the king. In the same letter he writes, refuting the notion that any utterance of his might hasten the designs of the revolutionists : "They will assassinate the king when his name will be no longer necessary to their designs, but not a moment sooner. They will probably first assassinate the queen, whenever the renewed menace of such an assassination loses its effect upon the anxious mind of an affectionate husband. At present, the advantage which they derive from the daily threats against her life is her only security for preserving it." This was the sole instance in which Mr. Burke's forecast was not verified. In 1793, the war between England and France, which he had predicted for some years, broke out, and during the four succeeding years which closed his life, his previsions were fulfilled to the letter.

Three years later, after the death of the King, Mr. Burke again rendered a calm and reasoned tribute to his excellence, in the following passage :—

"The unhappy Louis XVI. was a man of the best intentions that probably ever reigned. He was by no means deficient in talents. He had a most laudable desire to supply by general reading, and even by the acquisition of elemental knowledge, an education in all points originally defective; but nobody told him (and it was no wonder he should not himself divine it), that the world of which he read, and the world in which he lived, were no longer the same. Desirous of doing everything for the best, fearful of cabal, distrusting his own judgment, he sought his ministers of all kinds upon public testimony. But as Courts are the field for caballers, the public is the theatre for mountebanks and impostors. The cure for both these evils is in the discernment of the prince. But an accurate and penetrating discernment is what in a young prince could not be looked for.

"His conduct in its principle was not unwise; but like most other of his well-meant designs it failed in his hands. It failed partly from mere ill-fortune, to which speculators are rarely pleased to assign that very large share to which she is justly entitled in human affairs."

In October, 1775, Walpole wrote from Paris, to the Countess of Ossory: "Messieurs de Turgot and Malesherbes are every day framing plans for mitigating monarchy and relieving the people; and the king not only listens to but encourages them."

Note 2 : Chapter I., page 3.

Ceinture de la Reine : a tax imposed, under the old régime, for the benefit of the Queen on an accession, upon merchandise brought to Paris by the Seine.

Note 3 : Chapter I., page 5.

The following are the letters of Marie Antoinette to her mother and the reply of the Empress Maria Theresa. These letters are more interesting in the original than translation can render them. The Queen's rather clumsy French, and the homely, unhappily-prophetic pathos of the response of the Empress, lose by transfer to another language.

1. The letter of the Queen to the Empress :—

"Quoique Dieu m'ait fait naitre dans le rang que j'occupe aujourd'hui, je ne puis m'empêcher d'admirer l'arrangement de la Providence qui m'a choisie, moi la dernière de vos enfants, pour le plus beau royaume de l'Europe. Je sens plus que jamais ce que je dois à la tendresse de mon auguste mère, qui s'est donné tant de soins et de travail pour me procurer ce bel établissement. Je n'ai jamais tant désiré de pouvoir me mettre à ses pieds, l'embrasser, lui montrer mon âme tout entière et lui faire voir combien elle est pénétrée de respect, de tendresse et de reconnaissance."

2. The letter of the Empress :—

"Vous êtes tous deux bien jeunes, mes chers enfants ; le fardeau est grand, j'en suis en peine et bien en peine....."

Note 4 : Chapter I., page 29.

We find in *A Friend of the Queen* (Heinemann), the English version of M. Paul Gaulot's well-known work *Un Ami de la Reine*, the following passage in reference to the "benefits forgot" that were heaped upon the Polignac family, and which Kaunitz tersely described as "pillage."

"By what chance Marie Antoinette first saw 'the angelic face' of Madame de Polignac, and became infatuated with the woman to the point of summoning her to Court, heaping benefits upon her, her husband, her lover and her sister-in-law, and appointing her to the great position of 'Governess of the Children of France' is not known, but only too surely that chance was fatal."

To this the translator has appended the following note : "Madame de Polignac was true to her base nature in all vicissitudes. Madame de Rémusat, in her celebrated *Memoirs* (Sampson Low) gives some interesting details of the Polignacs' falsehood and ingratitude to the restored royal family and to the writer herself." M. de Nolhac makes it clear that the Queen's delusion was not lasting, although the evil it had wrought was beyond remedy before she was cured of it.

Note 5 : Chapter II., page 57.

"*L'évêque du dehors*," a phrase which profoundly puzzled the translator, and which may not be generally intelligible, has been explained by Mr. Edmund Bishop as follows : "The King was so styled because he stood in the relation of advocatus, avoué, temporal protector of the Church, and as executor civilly of its sentences on recalcitrant members. As advocatus he would be expected to defend the civil rights, temporal possessions, etc., of ecclesiastical persons who were supposed to be incompetent on account of their state to enter into conflict in self-defence. All this, as I understand, is implied by the expression "évêque du dehors."

"Officers of the Election" : The Election was a tribunal established for the settlement of differences concerning the taxes, the excise, and the salt duties. It also signified the whole extent of country which was under the authority of that tribunal. When the entire administration of a province was governed by the Intendant, and that it had established "Elections," the province was called "*Pays d'élection*" as opposed to the "*Pays d'états.*"

Note 6 : Chapter III., page 106.

The Queen's Needlework. Marie Antoinette and her sisters were taught needlework from their early childhood, by their mother, the Empress Maria Theresa, and were, like her, proficients in the art, in both its plain and fancy branches. This useful and elegant accomplishment was kept up by the descendants of the Empress. Her grand-daughters, Marie Adelaïde, wife of King Louis Philippe and daughter of Marie Caroline, Queen of Naples, and Madame Royale, Duchesse d'Angoulême, were experts in needlework. The latter was carefully taught by her mother, who had also instructed her beloved young sister-in-law, Madame Elisabeth. In the celebrated picture of the royal family of France in the Temple, by the late E. M. Ward, R.A., the Queen is represented as mending the King's coat, while he sleeps.

Note 7 : Chapter IV., page 160.

Walpole, in a very amusing letter to the Rev. William Mason, dated Paris, September 6th, 1775, relates "the conversion of the French to English gardening." He describes his visit of inspection to M. Watelet's Isle, called "*Le Moulin Joli,*" and in "Chap. II." of his letter (so divided by himself), written on the 10th, relates how he went to see the English garden at Auteuil, belonging to the Comtesse de Boufflers, and found it strictly English, the work of an English gardener. After a fine description of the splendid landscape which the garden commands, including all Paris and the surrounding country, until it is closed in by Meudon and the forests on higher hills, he concludes : "In this sumptuous prospect, nothing is wanting but verdure and water, of which you do not see a drop. In short, they can never have as beautiful landscapes as ours, till they have as bad a climate They call the Anglo-Franco gardens, by the bye, Anglo-

Chinois, as they say that by the help of Sir William Chambers's lunettes they have detected us for having stolen our gardens from the Chinese."

Note 8 : Chapter IV., page 169.

The picture referred to has been reproduced, and forms one of the illustrations in "Marie Antoinette, the Dauphine," the English version of a preceding work by M. de Nolhac.

Note 9 : Chapter IV, page 183.

The drive from the Château of Versailles to the Palace of the Tuileries, which was the first stage of the Queen's journey to the Place de la Révolution, is one of the salient points of her history most impressively dealt with by historians of all shades of opinion and also writers of historical romance, whether sympathetic or otherwise; but it was not marked by one of the most intolerable incidents of the ignominious return from Varennes. In M. Paul Gaulot's story of Count Fersen, the frustrated attempt of the King and Queen to escape, naturally occupies a place of foremost importance, and the tale is told in "A Friend of the Queen" (Heinemann) with dramatic effect. The author gives some extracts from that unparalleled document, Pétion's account of the return of the royal captives (first published by M. Mortimer-Ternaux in his *Histoire de la Terreur*) which make the reader thrill with indignation and disgust at the distance of a century and seven years.

In connection with this supremely interesting portion of M. de Nolhac's work, it seems appropriate also to give an extract from Mr. Burke's famous recapitulation of the journey from Versailles to the Tuileries, in his "Reflections on the Revolution in France," written in 1790:—

"On the morning of the 6th of October, 1789, the King and Queen of France, after a day of confusion, alarm, dismay, and slaughter, lay down, under the pledged security of public faith, to indulge nature in a few hours of respite, and troubled, melancholy repose. From this sleep the Queen was first startled by the voice of the sentinel at her door, who cried out to her to save herself by flight—that this was the last proof of fidelity he could give—that they were upon him, and he was dead. Instantly he was cut down. A band of cruel ruffians and assassins, reeking with his blood, rushed into the chamber of the Queen, and pierced with a hundred strokes of bayonets and poniards the bed, from whence this persecuted woman had but just time to fly almost naked, and, through ways unknown to the murderers, had escaped to seek refuge at the feet of a King and husband, not secure of his own life for a moment. This King (to say no more of him) and this Queen, and their infant children (who once would have been the pride and hope of a great and generous people), were then forced to abandon the sanctuary of the most splendid palace in the world, which they left swimming in blood, polluted by massacre, and strewed with scattered limbs and mutilated carcases. Thence they were conducted into the capital of their kingdom. Two had been selected from the unprovoked, unresisted, promiscuous slaughter, which was made of the gentlemen of birth and family who composed the king's body-guard. These two gentlemen, with all the parade of an execution of justice, were cruelly and publicly dragged to the block, and beheaded in the great court of the palace. Their heads were stuck upon spears, and led the procession; whilst the royal captives who followed in the train were slowly moved along, amidst the horrid yells, and shrilling screams, and frantic dances, and infamous contumelies, and all the unutterable abominations of the furies of hell, in the abused shape of the vilest of women. After they had been made to taste, drop by drop, more than the bitterness of death, in the slow torture of a journey of twelve miles, protracted to six hours, they were, under a guard composed of those very soldiers who had thus conducted them through this famous triumph, lodged in one of the old palaces of Paris, now converted into a Bastile for kings."

Note 10 : Chapter IV., page 183.

Says M. Gaulot : "Thousands of posters, put up by unknown hands, and reflecting the general feeling, prescribed the aspect which the people were to assume on the return of their sovereign : 'Any one who applauds the king shall be beaten. Any one who insults him shall be hanged.'"

Note 11 : Chapter IV., page 184.

In the portrait of the Queen taken at the Conciergerie, which exactly realises the description given by M. de Nolhac, of her appearance as she went to the scaffold, her hair is cut short, not only to evade the toilette of Samson, but for another purpose also. Marie Antoinette cut off the long thick tresses which we see in the famous portrait of her by M. Delaroche, as she leaves the scene of her mock trial, and placed them with her last letter addressed to Madame Elisabeth, on the morning of her execution. It is said that the precious deposit was duly handed over to Fouquier-Tinville, but what became of it is, I believe, not known. The one thing certain is that it never reached the hands of the prisoners of the Temple, who knew nothing of the fate of the Queen until the one went to her death and the other long after was released.

The following is an entry in the journal of Count Fersen, who was handed, at Brussels, a letter which had been written from Paris, and contained this atrocious sentence : "This morning Marie Antoinette is to appear at the National Window." The words form an affecting record of a pure and lofty friendship which slander never assailed successfully : "Although I was prepared for it, and, since she was removed to the Conciergerie, have been expecting it, the certainty overcame me ; *I had not strength to feel anything*. I went out to speak of this misfortune with my friends Madame de Fitz James and Baron de Breteuil, whom I did not find. The Gazette of the 17th speaks of it. It was on the 16th, at half-past eleven, that this execrable crime was committed, and the Divine vengeance has not yet fallen upon the monsters! *Monday, 21st*—I can think only of my loss. It is dreadful not to have any positive details. That she should have been alone in her last moments, without any one to speak to, to hear her last wishes. That is the horror!"

LIST OF ILLUSTRATIONS.

CONTENTS.

www.ingramcontent.com/pod-product-compliance
Lightning Source LLC
Chambersburg PA
CBHW020945030726
47496CB00005B/1363
9783337322212